Four Two One

Four Two One

...

Craig Zecher

ISBN: 1530257824
ISBN 13: 9781530257829
Library of Congress Control Number: 2016903530
CreateSpace Independent Publishing Platform
North Charleston, South Carolina

Four Two One
Craig Zecher

For Abigail, Aurora, and Jessi
For being unmistakable symbols of love

"Your mistakes do not define you now. They tell you who you're not."

Prologue

• • •

CASE'S HEART RACED AS HE stared blankly at his own pale face in the rear-view mirror. He couldn't quite remember how he got there. Along the side of a familiar backroad in Jefferson, Maryland, sat his Mustang; The remaining tires settled amongst the rarely treaded bits of gray and blue gravel.

The lights were so bright they were blinding his vision for a second at a time. Blue. Red. Blue. Red. Blue. Red.

Case blinked quickly several times as though a photographer had caught him off guard. He looked down at himself again, only to have his attention drawn to figures moving alongside both sides of the vehicle. At the sight of the movement his fingers went to the window controls of the car without reservation or hesitation.

"Sir, do you know why I pulled you over?" the officer said.

"N-No, sir," Case said. "What can I do for you, sir?"

"Well, your tire appears to be flat back ay'r," the officer said. He spoke deeply and condescendingly in what seemed to be a Southern drawl that required practice and was not at all genuine. "Have you had anything to drink tonight, son?"

Case paused to think for what could have been 30 seconds. 'What do I say?' he thought. 'Do I tell him I have been drinking? What could happen?'—What—"Yes, sir. I had two drinks some time ago," Case's subconscious said to him. Case realized that his last thought had registered not only in his mind, but also through his lips.

"Well, couldjee please hand me yer license and registration and take a step outside the vehicle? I think you should take a look at what me and Offsir Upton saw that caused us to stop you here this mornin'."

It was an uncommonly warm winter for the area. A chilly breeze that normally would accompany a late-September high school football game blew across the Park & Ride directly adjacent to where the three stood. The night was darker in some places than others. The full moon shot rays of the sun from the other side of the world down onto the pavement. No street lamps were present, but the road was lit by more than the fluorescent lights of the patrol vehicle. The earth stood still while still rotating like a quiet audience waiting for the curtains to open.

Case tried to hide his initial reaction to the shredded tire. "I didn't realize it was that bad, officer, I ran off the road texting my brother a couple miles back, it felt a little rocky, but nowhere near as bad as it looks."

"I see. Where were you headed, son?"

"I only live a couple miles further, it's late, and I just wanted to get home."

"Do you realize the dangers in driving a vehicle with the tire almost off the rim? To yourself and to others. We can't have this type of behavior on the road. It's unacceptable."

"I understand, sir. I shouldn't ha—"Case was cut off.

"Now you advised me and Officer Upton you have had a couple of drinks tonight," the officer said followed by a long but brief pause.

Case knew now that the accent was fake. He also knew he hadn't just had a few drinks. He had indulged in an amount closer to the equivalent of his name. He had been at 'The Hollar' for a few hours prior to being stopped. The Hollar was a local sports bar nicknamed for the golf club it accompanied: Hollow Creek Golf Club in the neighboring town of Middletown. His heart raced to the point where it no longer felt like a pulsating sensation, but as if each beat blended into one.

"Yes, sir. I did," Case said in response. "Well, Upton and I are gonna halfta putcha through the field suh-bright-e then," the officer said confidently, the accent thickening once again. "Please proceed to the front of the vehicle with Officer Upton and he'll ad-minster the test."

Case quickly learned how fast one can fail a sobriety test, and the bright lights atop the police car still shined brightly into the night as Office Upton escorted him toward it. His eyes no longer were bothered by their indecisiveness to choose a color. The wind howled across the open field to the left of the road, but seemingly avoided him. He only felt cold steel pressed firmly against his wrists as he sat down in the passenger side of the patrol vehicle.

The officer's face was much clearer inside of the car as he sounded off a 10 code to a female voice on the radio. He was short with a flat top and ears that were pinned to his head like a frightened dog. His general presence was that of someone who yearned for approval from his subordinates; as if he wanted constant reassurance from others that he indeed was 'The Law.'

Case stared into the night as he heard the officer reciting some lines from the paperwork in front of him. He knew he was in for a long night and disappointment had begun to set in.

"Yes, sir, I understand. I agree to the blood alcohol test," Case stated with more than a hint of remorse in his voice.

As the car pulled into a double-sided garage at the state police barracks, Case tried to remember how he had gotten there. The last thing that he could remember was sitting at an almost empty bar talking to middle-aged woman, or maybe there were two. His mind wandered back further to the context of his thoughts while at 'The Hollar.' He couldn't remember names, or what they had been talking about, but he knew deep down that any conversation was a temporary relief from where his mind never seemed to leave: his latest failed attempt at a relationship. His reminiscence of earlier was halted by the slam of the driver's door and shortly followed by a buzzing sound similar to the end of a basketball game.

"Right through this door, Mr. Metzger," sounded the officer. Case's only signal that he heard the request was that of his movement from the seat of the vehicle to the three steps that led to the door.

Once inside the building, he was sitting in a stiff chair that was big enough for more than one person, but not nearly large enough for two. The room resembled a miniature version of a doctor's office, with a counter running from wall to wall, a machine he had never seen before, and stacks of paperwork neatly stacked against the backsplash.

By this time, the night had begun its evolution to morning. Case's eyes wandered to the clock in between blowing into the device, to see that it was now just after 2:00 AM. The results of the test came back with more confidence than his earlier statement: Twice the legal limit.

The officer spoke almost the entire ride back to the local station where they would hold Case until a ride would arrive for him. His Southern accent was merely background noise to the thoughts racing through Case's mind like an AM station that was just out of reach, but not unclear enough to change the tuner. Case's disappointment in himself loomed throughout the car, and the officer could sense the regret radiating from him.

As Case's thought-process flipped back and forth from *"What will my parents think?"* to *"How am I going to fix my car?"* to *"My brother was with me earlier, I hope he didn't make the same mistake"* to *"Nobody knows where I am… they must be worried sick"*, something the officer said chimed in clearly.

"I'd say you have four to one odds of just getting probation before judgment, bud. Most the time if it's your first time, they'll take it easy on ye'."

"What did you say, sir?" Case said as if awakening from a trance. "I said four to one odds says you will learn from this and they'll—"

"I thought that's what you said…" muttered Case. "Four to one."

Four. Two. One.

Numbers that had told the story of his life to this point suddenly appeared again. The numbers that he was convinced were meant for him. The numbers that he saw when nobody else did. The numbers that resembled Lacey Sewell.

CHAPTER 1
Two Years Earlier

• • •

CASE STOOD STILL OUTSIDE OF the convenience store, leaning up against the brick wall next to what appeared to be a broken phone booth like a cowboy from an old Marlboro advertisement. He was a tall kid, if you wanted to consider him that. Standing at six foot one with dirty blond hair, he was far from a tower, yet was never picked on growing up for being short. At 21, he was much stouter than he was in high school, yet smaller. He developed a love for the endless lines at Chinese food buffets and Golden Corral as a child. Not to mention the Nintendo's impediment on his outdoor activities. By this point in his life he resembled more of a linebacker than the offensive line position he had held in college just months earlier. He had certainly gotten much more attractive with his age, and still had the only feature he had ever had confidence in: his eyes.

Being a larger body in his teenage years, he would make it a point to always look his conversation counterpoint directly in the eyes, in hopes they would notice them.

They were blue, with an almost frosty look to them, and once they were locked in a woman's gaze, they didn't leave until her eyes gave him permission. He had been taught to be a great listener by his grandmother from a young age and rarely would prepare his thought before it was his turn to speak.

It was what Cheyenne loved about him the most. "He listens to me," she would tell her friends. Cheyenne was much younger than Case, about to graduate from high school from a town nearby. She was athletic and outgoing with straight, shiny, brunette hair that looked like it should be photographed for a box of hair color. He thought that she resembled a few famous actresses, and he was elated when she had changed her mind about him almost a year prior. His elation was from the unknown wonder of something new and something real. He had longed for a female in his life who wanted to spend time with him and enjoy his company. The facts that Cheyenne knew his family from church and she was a beautiful, exciting, and extremely intelligent young woman, were just an added bonus.

They fell into young love quickly. Cheyenne and Case shared the same passion for sports and a highly competitive nature. In the months throughout what had become a more than casual relationship, Case found the times that he would feel the most alive were when they were spent in her company. What once was friendship had become so much more. He didn't care that she was four years younger than him, or that the guys would rattle him around about it.

"What time is the middle school dance?" Scott would ask while letting out an eruption of laughter immediately afterward.

"Yeah—he's gotta take her to buy school supplies for the New Year. He, he, he's gotta buy her a smock for art class!" Ben would stutter. Even his younger brother, Cage, would chime in. "You know it's bad when Case is hanging up pictures in his room with glitter and macaroni noodles glued on them!" Scott and Ben would laugh hysterically almost to the point of tears. Yet, somehow it didn't bother Case. He had convinced himself that his ideas of what love was supposed to be were backwards, and that God had brought Cheyenne to him to show him that.

Case was born a Christian to Lorrie and Brett Metzger in the same town they had always been from. He was the oldest of three boys, all named to a single syllable and from the same country mold. Cage was brought along three years after Case, and Case always knew that his brother's footsteps weren't long behind him. Cage was a humorous and bright boy from the start, and where Case would go, Cage was sure to follow. Case was always reluctant to have his brother be his shadow, but as he matured he realized more and more that his brother wanted to be like him, and that he was someone who shared the same outlook on just about everything.

Their voices were almost identical, and dependent upon the amount of sunlight reflecting off their faces, you could see the same amount of Lorrie's round eyes, that would wrinkle along the sides of her face when she smiles, as you could see the distinguished Metzger nose that cascaded out from the tan face of their father, Brett. They appeared to be a poster board for evolution, and that in three years one would resemble the other as an exact replica of the one who preceded him.

Call was the youngest, significantly younger than his two siblings. He was born just prior to adolescence for Case, and he and Cage had developed a passion for protecting him like none other.

Call was born to several complications, including being diagnosed with Down Syndrome and a heart defect that required surgery before he could ever breathe in the air within the Metzger home, which sat alongside a field-surrounded backroad eight miles from the West Virginia line. Call's special needs brought the brothers together in an unspoken pact that they would always put each other before themselves.

Case learned that his youngest brother would never have the life that Case aspired to, at least not without constant supervision and inordinate amounts of aid from others. Since the day Call was born, even though he was only in 5th grade, Case had always used his brothers as motivation for all that he did, and their approval of a friend, especially girls, was held in the highest regard.

Case used the weight of his back to push off the multicolored bricks outside of the store. He had found that his leg was almost asleep from the way he had it propped against the extended foundation of the property. He straightened his leg out and rolled his ankle in a clockwise fashion a few times to assist circulation, noticing that the hairs of his legs seemed almost non-existent in the light of the Maryland sun that day. He wrenched his hands together to crack his knuckles as he heard the bell to the door ring as an older couple walked in.

'*What is taking her so long?*' he thought. Cheyenne had run inside the store for a drink over ten minutes earlier. "She must be reading one of those magazines she never puts down," Case said to Lincoln as he pulled up.

"What?" expressed Lincoln, stepping out of his Jeep.

Lincoln was a brother to Case, too. His family had split up before he and Case had met. When his father left a couple years earlier, Lincoln moved in with Case and his family. He was a regular 'ladies' man' and gym rat, and Case had found himself astonished on rare occasions when a girl would utter the words "he's not that hot." Case referred to his brother Lincoln as "P" for short, since his last name was Picks, and he always seemed to be the first pick for everything. He stood at about 5½ feet tall, with dark skin and even darker hair, when he had any. Lincoln would buzz his head down to the scalp, and take care of the rest with a straight razor. He was also very particular about who he shared his presence with. He served as Case's sounding board on almost weekly occasions, and always seemed to understand the situation placed in front of him. He was quiet and reserved, and for good reason.

"Cheyenne," he said. "She's been in there like an hour."

"Oh," said Lincoln, "was wondering why you're standing out here trying to look all tough."

"Yeah, were headed back to the house now, or whenever she gets the hell out here," Case muttered as Lincoln headed toward the door, which was now being held for him by the older couple who had gone in before.

"Well, I'll see you out there later on," responded Lincoln, "I'm getting a Mountain Dew and then hitting the gym."

"Alright, brother," said Case as the door shut behind him, swinging in free release from the old man's hands, who now had made his way to a rusty LeBaron where he opened yet another door for his wife.

The bell to the door rung again, as the store clerk came out holding a pack of cigarettes between three fingers. He stopped and held the door with his back as if a patron was about to follow him out. He looked back inside the store and then looked at Case.

"Is that your girl in there, man?" he said, straightening his palm to hit his pack of cigarettes against it.

"Cheyenne? I mean... the brunette?" Case said as he took a couple steps along the pavement past the broken phone booth.

"Yeah, Cheyenne," the clerk said. "She's in there crying."

A puzzled Case responded. "How do you know her? Wait, you said she's crying?" The clerk pushed back against the door with his arm and his head joined his back in leaning against the glass as he tried to avoid Case's stout figure shooting past him into the store. The door swung shut as the clerk peered into the reflection of the smudged glass while lighting his cigarette.

"Glad that's not me," he said to himself. "Good luck with that one, buddy."

The ride to her house to drop her off was silent, with the exception of the occasional sniffle from her and a deep breath from him. He had been so struck by the idea of being with somebody and the opportunity to feel bliss he never had with such a sense of realism, he hadn't fathomed the possibility that it could ever end. But it had. She had made up both of their minds for weeks now and something inside her broke down while at the store. She couldn't face him anymore. She couldn't break his heart. It wasn't an unfamiliar feeling as she had been with another older boy before Case. She remembered the feeling of helplessness that accompanied her feelings being placed into words before, and couldn't imagine doing it again.

Cheyenne was the first reality Case had experience with. His heart had always been for someone else behind lock and key. Before Cheyenne, he could never convince himself that he could fall for someone else. All the signs in his life had pointed toward one person before that point, and he truly believed that one day they would be together. Cheyenne's personality resembled Lacey's, and he bought into the fact that waiting for Lacey to randomly profess her love would cause him to miss out on a lot. He let his guard down, and opened his heart like the gates of a Southern dam. Cheyenne's birthday was December 4th, One Two Four, and he saw it as a sign. The numbers that constantly emerged in his life were simply backwards. Since he couldn't run from four, two, and one, he figured maybe the numbers themselves were the true sign and not their order.

"I was wrong, God. I saw what I wanted to see," Case stuttered to himself as he watched Cheyenne walk through the moonlight into her family's home for the last time. He closed his eyes and a single tear escaped, barreling over his red-tinted 5 o'clock shadow onto his now tightened lips. He moved the gear shift to reverse and backed into the dirt turnaround. He had taken it well, all things considered. As he moved to first gear and the car's momentum changed, so did gravity's resistance to his eyelids and the buckets of tears they stored inside.

CHAPTER 2

Fourtwonate One

• • •

He couldn't remember when they started; all he knew was that he saw them everywhere. He knew he saw them sometimes because he was looking for them, but that never felt the same. When he would force himself to see them, just to make himself feel better about the day, or where his life was headed, the numbers didn't have the same effect. He knew they were fake; Similar to how one feels at the end of a movie they've seen before. When they know what is coming and the rush of blood and adrenaline throughout the body doesn't create that distinct feeling of uncertainty conjoined with opportunity.

Case's friends consoled him when the news got to them. "She'll come back around, man, Give her time to spread her wings a bit. She'll be back," said Scott. It felt good to Case to have his best friend confident in her return. Scott was always willing to give advice, and despite his joking nature, supported Case in every way.

The text from Scott had interrupted a conversation between Case and his father on Interstate 70.

"Who was that?" he said.

"Just Scott, Pop," said Case. "Checking up on me."

Case leaned his head back against the headrest of the passenger seat and closed his eyes while exhaling deeply. "Everybody's gotta check up on me, and it's like nobody really knows what this feels like. They understand but they don't, you know?"

"I get it," said Case's father.

A rarity in Case's thought-process; his response had been prepared to his father's words even prior to him saying them.

"Why me, Dad? I never saw it coming."

Case knew his father didn't have the answer to that question, but he knew that his response, rhetorical in nature or not, would help him feel better about everything. Even if it only was for the duration of his father's dialogue.

The two had become great friends, father and son, and Case held his mentor relationship with his father above all others. It hadn't always been that way, nor would he have dared consider his father a best friend growing up. Being the oldest son, and mirroring the image of the man of the house, Case landed himself in the middle of many household arguments. Growing up as the most rebellious force in the house against his parents, Brett Metzger in particular, it took Case years to realize his true connections with him. Brett was an understanding and kind man, but also a fair and demanding man, as made evident through so many who admired him. Brett had led a construction crew for upwards of 20 years, and not a single member lacked respect for him.

Their arguments never seemed to lack an audience. Case's friends Scott, Alan, and Keith had expressed to him in more than one instance that they wished their fathers would care enough to have the arguments and the conversations that Brett had with his sons. It took Case over 17 years to realize that when his father would end a yelling match with the words, "I wouldn't say anything if I didn't love you boys so damn much," it was the truth. Of course, those words were normally accompanied by the flat, calloused palm of Brett Metzger slamming onto the table top before he would walk away from the room. The echoes of the boom it would create carried on long enough to act as a prelude to the distinct, heavy footsteps of his work boots on the hardwood as he would exit the room, subliminally gaining his son's respect with the same rhythm.

"You didn't have to see it coming, Case, you weren't supposed to."

"But Dad—" Case tried to interject.

"I know you're hurtin', son, I been there, but it gets better." There was a surprisingly un-awkward silence that filled the vehicle, only to be interrupted by Call's laughter in the back seat of the SUV.

Call didn't speak. He knew sign language to an extent but had become lazy when it came to it. He had his own way of communication through different noises and pointing at things when he wanted them. He was a star swimmer in the Special Olympics and by his own path was following the family legacy of being a leader. Case knew that having Call's outlook on life was true happiness, and he loved that his youngest sibling would smile in the darkest of situations. Call seemed to have a particularly high emotional intelligence, as most Down Syndrome children do, that told him something was wrong.

While Brett continued to explain to his oldest son that destiny was something that humans have no control over, Case felt a hand slide onto his left shoulder with a firm grip. As he turned to look back at Call, he felt the small hand squeeze his shirt into a fist.

Call's smile was new. It held hope and shined empathy. His mouth was covered in the remnants of a few unlucky Oreo cookies, but Case felt touched all the same. Before Case could grab his brother's hand to express a silent thank you, Call's hand loosened itself from the fabric of his shirt and proceeded with a gentle pat to his shoulder. What started as an intentional silent thank you had become a loss for words. The pats to his shoulder were a symbol of "You'll be OK, big brother." They only continued for a few short seconds, but the thought of what they resembled played in Case's head like a metronome.

"It's amazing how he knows when you need a boost, isn't it?" his dad said, taking a sip of coffee with a smirk. Case just nodded in agreement, still not able to shake the overwhelming feeling of being lost and being grateful together as one.

"There it is again!" Brett exclaimed, pointing at the dashboard clock. "I swear those must be my lucky numbers, I should play the lottery with 5:24… Sometimes I'll happen to glance at the clock both times in a day."

Case knew the feeling, except it wasn't only the clock.

"You know, I've seen that time on the clock for years now, and I have always thought they must mean something." Case still didn't speak: he didn't want to think about the signs that he had always thought meant something.

"I just know one day those numbers are going to lead me to something truly amazing, like the day I met your mother, or when you boys were born, something life-changing."

It was all too familiar to Case. He had engaged in a conversation with his dad a few years earlier about how they each had times on the clock that they always saw, it seemed, independent of the circumstance.

Case never went into the detail his imagination would venture to each time he saw the numbers with his dad. It was merely a coincidence to him that his father had a similar situation occur. The thing that he took most from the conversation was reassurance in his own thoughts: the numbers meant something. Well, they meant one thing, that he was on a crash course with the woman of his dreams.

The conversation dwindled in the car as they pulled into the garage and headed into the house. The smell of fresh cut grass and motor oil filled the air, and the evening dew had begun to present itself on the windshield of the Explorer Case had noticed as he glanced back at the vehicle before walking inside.

He caught a glimpse of his reflection in the mirror outside of the hallway on his trek to the restroom after the long drive back. His cheeks were no longer puffy and swollen as they had been the night before, but it was as if the tears that occupied his face previously had left a trail behind. They were not clear-cut lines like a fingerprint along a dusty piece of metal, but much more subtle. His eyes remained red and had a dry appearance about them. The normally radiant glow from his baby blues was distraught by the concurrent effort they had put in to produce tears for the last 24 hours.

He closed the door to the bathroom and stared into the mirror and began to speak aloud to himself. "Don't buy into those numbers," he said in a mild whisper as he shook his head at the appearance across from him. He set both of his hands onto the counter of the bathroom sink, looking down at them to each side before slowly raising his head to continue his personal conversation. "You see where they got you, you see how you feel," he muttered and looked down again, this time shaking his head in a downward motion as if in disapproval of his actions that had led him to this moment.

Despite his attempts to the contrary, his mind began to lead him on a journey as to why he had believed the numbers meant anything in the first place.

Case's belief in signs had come to him while at a church raffle in his youth. He had convinced his mother to buy him a one-dollar ticket for the fundraiser, and if his ticket was pulled from the box, he would win two tickets to a Maryland football game. He was eight years old and extremely naïve to the fact that just about every member of the church had bought a ticket, or several tickets for that matter. The possibility that his ticket would find its way to the pastor's hand later that day was less likely than finding a needle in a haystack.

Nonetheless, he walked to the children's church area by himself, bowed his head and prayed that he would get to go to a football game with his dad. He held no reservations and no grudges, as children don't. He was a kid of wants, and having the change to go was excitement enough for him in itself.

As Case remembered the jubilation that filled his soul at such a young age, and the furthest memory back of optimism that became reality, his mind drifted from sitting in Byrd Stadium with his father to the day of Call's heart surgery. Case and Cage were under the supervision of their father's older sister on that day.

Case squeezed his eyes into a tight squint to hold back the tears of a distant memory: He and Cage had requested that their aunt take them for Chinese food while awaiting the news of their younger brother's fate. As children often are, they were both easily distracted, but not that day. The absolution of uncertainty was understood by them if only for the day.

Case opened his eyes and looked up at himself once again. Tears had been rolling out of his face at the utter thought of what that day could have resulted in. He took his forearm from the shiny linoleum countertop and wiped the tears from his face in almost one fell swoop. He squinted tightly once again as if to squeeze the remaining tears from his eyelids like water from a sponge.

He had seen signs that meant good things to come from an early age and once again had quickly convinced himself that the numbers meant something. All signs from God meant something and that if he thought he could know what they meant beforehand, he was crazy. He chuckled to himself very discreetly as if not to break his own focus as he remembered the line from an old Van Zant song—"If you wanna hear God laugh, tell him your plans."

Case walked down the hallway quickly, fearing embarrassment if his dad would see that he was crying again, even though this time the tears consisted of hope and optimism. He wanted to get to bed and actually sleep, unlike the night before. He crept slowly down the steps toward his basement bedroom. The optimism had taken over, but he feared that his thoughts could soon turn. He slid into his bed and turned on the lamp atop his desk when he noticed the closed Bible next to a glass of water. It was good luck, according to his grandmother, to have an open Bible in every room, but he had not opened it for some time.

A chill ran through his spine that caused a subtle shiver within the backs of his arms through the tips of his bare feet as he suddenly noticed what had been placed in the Bible as a bookmark.

The childhood memory that had surfaced just moments ago had come with a reason. As he opened the book to a small sliver of paper that had been placed there several years before, he noticed five evenly spaced numbers and a Kenji word for "brother" in red text that had faded slightly, and they pierced into his still sensitive eyes. He held the Bible in one hand and the bookmark in the other, and flipped the fortune over to confirm the sign sent to him that uncertain day.

"God not only hears your prayers, but he will answer them."

CHAPTER 3

4:21AM

• • •

HE AWOKE IN A COLD sweat, like he had been swimming in a nearby pond and fAlan asleep on the bank as the sun set. Beads of sweat grouped along his brow, but were quickly removed as his left hand ironed out his eyes similar to the way a baker stretched pie dough with the flat part of his thumb. His clothes were still on, damp with condensation that had seeped through his pores. He blinked several times rapidly and wiped his eyes again, this time with the right hand.

It took him a few more seconds to come to the reality that he no longer had a girlfriend and he was alone again. They never lived together, as he was in college and she in high school, so his routine was not discombobulated immediately until the ton of bricks would hit again. He took a long breath and his mid-section rose as he held the air in. His reality was back and he gathered the previous day's thoughts into one extended moment. He let the air out slowly through a tiny separation of his lips which he still held together. If one had seen his breathing pattern at the moment, they probably would have thought he was about to shoot a free throw or kick a penalty shot. He continued the slow breaths, holding each one longer than the last, sifting through the madness and chaos in his mind that didn't make its way to an action. The last deep breath he cut off from releasing on and off, and it made his lips pulsate in and out subtly, making the air sound more like a vacuum when you put your hand on and off the hose.

As Case sat up in bed and unbuttoned the shorts he had worn the day before, he suddenly felt as if he had not been asleep long. The room had no windows, and had provided a great place to nap during the day through-out his life. His friends often expressed their jealousy that the sunlight would not get to his room which sat in the corner of the basement. The room made for deep and uninterrupted sleep, which Case needed no help with. He slept like the dead, but would wake up in the middle of the night often.

As he took off his shorts he stood up off the bed and yawned when he noticed the clock.

4:21.

He picked up his phone from the deck and pulled it off the charger. Scrolling down through the conversations in the text messages he stopped at one that was entitled 'Cheyenne.' He used his thumb to eliminate the message group from the phone forever and make a low, audible explosion sound with his lips as if to signify the abrupt end of something that had gone on too long. He tracked down through the conversations further until he found the last time he had talked to *her*; it was 4:21 after all. He opened the message that had last been active over a week before.

Case thought briefly to himself as he sat down on the bed. He typed out a message that read: "Hey, was just thinking of you… when can we talk?"

He stared down at the brightened screen until it dimmed to black. He flipped the phone over as he held it tightly in his palm, and rested the screen against the bare skin of his leg, taking his other hand and touching his eyebrows with his thumb and finger on either side. He brought his fingers together to the bridge of his nose with another deep breath. He shook his head at himself out of disappointment as he deleted the message a letter at a time instead of hitting send. He laid the phone down next to himself on the bed, where he was back to sleep within seconds.

Case never knew if the fours, twos, and ones came before or after her, but he remembered the day he met her like it had just happened yesterday.

She had curly blonde and brown hair, and the most amazing hazel eyes. He could remember the day he walked into the computer lab in middle school and saw her for the first time: although it was years ago, he could always envision her shorter frame and the blue flannel shirt she wore that day. He had known of her existence and that she was friends with some people he knew, but had never taken enough notice to ever see her around the halls. But this day, there she stood. Loud and clear. With her smooth, not pale, but not tan skin of her arms wedged behind her as she leaned against the chair in front of her computer, talking to the teacher as if she knew him already from some out-of-school activity.

Their friendship wouldn't start that day, but the paralyzing sensation that shot through his body each time she smiled would. She had nearly perfect teeth, and thin lips that, even when focused and serious, you could always tell were patiently waiting to light the world again.

She was born and raised across town, but they had gone to different schools for elementary. She was the captain of the cheerleading squad for both basketball and football throughout all of high school, and she was the most understanding person Case had ever exchanged words with.

Her family was tight-knit and had extended family dinner gatherings on Thursday of every week. She was feisty and cute, and a tomboy at heart; she also played softball and was the star pitcher in the county, a country boy's dream. Her figure was distinct, but in a good way, and Case was by far not the only person who thought so, but he would be the very last to tell her.

He had gotten comfortable with her by graduation, with regular conversations on a weekly basis to check up on her and vice versa. She was leaving to go to college in Georgia, and to be a cheerleader for their football team. She had chosen a school down south and further away, as she was interested in clothing design, and that was the small school's specialty.

He missed her while she was gone and when he was at school, but they still talked often. Even more often than they did while in the same state, she would call to see how he was on a regular basis like a doctor on a follow-up. Case would imagine the different reactions he would get from her, if he ever could muster the courage to tell her how he felt about her, but the result was always the same. Fear always triumphed. Fear of losing her as a friend. Fear of awkwardness, the fear of absolution. He took great optimism out of the small probability that he had that she would someday share the same feelings as him, as he did with the church raffle as a child. He didn't want to imagine having the beam of light that barely seemed to make it through the crack of the door, cast with darkness by the door slamming shut.

"I'd rather think that I still have the lowest shot in the world, than to know I have none at all," Case would tell Keith, his college roommate and fellow football companion. Keith was not fond of her, due to a failed attempt at the very same goal of Case's, but would always tolerate the dialogue that Case would offer when speaking of her.

Case's thought-process had been the same since college had begun. He would tell her how he felt after school was in the past, when they both moved home. He stood a better chance in his mind if it wasn't long distance, and it would take away the chance that her reasoning for denial was that they would never see each other. He thought through every scenario possible over those four years, sometimes with more emphasis than others. His mind would wander to a new female intrigue, but always found its way back to where it came from.

He didn't let it bother him too much when they would talk about her relationships, and he always felt awkward giving her advice about something he had no experience with himself. He was flattered that she sought his counsel, and often pictured himself as her basis for comparison. He thought that if he continued to be himself, and what she needed him to be, that his role would one day change and she would realize that everything he advised her to look for in a man was on the other end of the line.

Every song was her. Every kiss on television was him and her in the future. Every couple in town holding hands was them in his eyes. He was just waiting for it to happen. "It will happen when it happens, and it will be worth the wait," he would think.

He had chances to dive into love head first, but could never shake the idea of what he would lose in opportunity cost if she came around to the thought of him and her while he was with another girl. He knew it was a long shot, but it would be just his luck that it would go that way. He would never let the bobber sit in the water too long in one place, for the fear the wrong fish would take the bait, and leave him lonely with the tackle box.

It was no surprise when Case's world was shaken when he had let his guard down for Cheyenne. He had taken his thought-process and won his own emotions over with the idea that the signs and numbers he saw were simply backward. They did mean something, and he knew it all along, but his curiosity in the possibility that they meant something different than he had always imagined was enough for him. Cheyenne was fun and enjoyable to talk to, and had even entertained a few late-night conversations on his feelings about *her* before they started dating. "One thing always leads to another, and everything that happens in one's life is preparing them for something to come" was engrained into Case's very being.

Case had made himself believe that Cheyenne was the reason for the signs, and that seeing 4 2 1 everywhere wasn't showing him what was meant for him, but was allowing him a preview for what his life would decipher on its own. He had it all figured out up top: he felt and did the things that he did to lead him to the day he and Cheyenne came together. They paved the way for the rest of his life with her and had prepared him to be the best man that her life had ever seen. Case had it all figured out like an equation. The same equation with a different variable leading to a familiar calculation: Happiness.

He was awake again, but his eyes remained closed. He heard footsteps moving quickly above his head and the roar of the television that had been going for some time but not broken his sleep. He stretched his arms out from underneath the covers and spread his legs in a parallel direction, extending his toes as far as they could go. His outlook on the day was gloomy, for he knew questions of what happened and how he was doing were sure to follow. He scratched the middle of his chest between the tattoos on either side of his pectorals briefly and a raspy noise accompanied the movement of his fingers along the short hairs of his skin.

"Here we go again," he muttered in a whisper to himself as he sat up and shrugged his shoulders. He made his way toward the door to use the restroom and brush his teeth when he was stopped cold in his tracks by the echo of a song playing loudly. He about-faced and walked back toward his phone lying face-down on the bed. His eyes lit up and suddenly were no longer asleep when he saw the text of the screen. The music abruptly stopped as he opened the phone to find that he had not answered in time.

CHAPTER 4

21 years in the making

. . .

A MONTH OR TWO HAD passed and Case had realized that he was back on the right track. He worked at a local warehouse and spent a lot of time there that he normally wouldn't have. He began to focus on finding a job in his field of study and had scheduled interviews with a few local firms and a country-wide firm that had a local servicing center in the area. His degree was in business management and he wanted to eventually own his own company, but he was never sure what type of business he wanted to run. He had thought about restaurants, home improvement, grocery stores, other types of retail, and all kinds of ideas that came to him. He had a vivid imagination and constantly envisioned different ways that he could bring a smile to a customer or a stranger's face like a child when they get their ice cream cone on a hot summer day.

Case's passion was just that. He loved to help people in any way that he could. He got a personal high off of making things easier for someone, or helping them grow as individuals, helping them achieve things they never thought possible otherwise.

It was the heart of summer, and Case found himself having more and more conversations with her. She had come home for a short break from Georgia and was single: they were both single for the first time in a long time.

"Maybe she won't see it as a friend date," said Lincoln as he pulled down a box from the truck at the warehouse.

"Yeah, man, that would be nice, but I'm not that lucky," Case replied, taking the box from him and placing it onto the pallet at his feet. "She's everything I've ever wanted, and I can't even tell her that. I'm stuck going to dinner with her to talk about all these other guys who just eventually don't treat her right."

Lincoln paused as he lifted another box and stared at Case and shook his head. "You never give yourself a shot, so you're right. Why would she?"

The words didn't even affect Case anymore. He had heard them over and over and not just from Lincoln, from anyone he talked to about her. "Yeah, but P', she's not into guys like me, she wants a guy like you, somebody that fits that Abercrombie mold," he said with a breathy laugh.

"She tell you that? That she wants an Abercrombie model guy? I find that hard to believe. That's your assessment."

"I've seen who she goes out with, who she's been in relationships with, and not one of them resembles anything close to half of me. Literally and meta-phorically. It's ok, P', I'll eventually just be happy that she is in my life at all."

"Keep tellin' yourself that," Lincoln muttered and once again shook his head as he closed the door to the back of the 18-wheeler they had just un-loaded. "But there's a reason she confides in you and trusts you: if she don't see you that way it's because she's convincing herself not to."

Case chuckled. "I appreciate the confidence boost, man, but it ain't get-ting me anywhere! I'm gonna move these pallets over to Floor C, then I'm out of here. Picking her up at 7."

"Alright, man, I'll see you tomorrow then," Lincoln said back without pausing in his work or even turning to look. "Go get her."

Dinner was going just as Case had expected: they spoke about her continu-ing school to get her master's degree and Case's attempts and prospects of a 'real' job. She was even more beautiful than he had ever remembered. Her curly blonde hair lay along the sides of her face like a frame of a magnificent painting, and her eyes were brought out by the Georgia tan that seemed to make her face glow as if she was smiling even when she wasn't. Case had al-ways found her extremely attractive, but absence had multiplied the thought a thousand times over. She didn't need to wear make-up or even anything special at all to stick out to him. She was just as gorgeous in sweatpants and a T-shirt as she ever was in her Sunday best.

"I can't get over how good you look: you look fantastic," Case said. "Not to imply you haven't always, but that Georgia sun sure has been kissing you, hasn't it?

"Thanks, yeah, we've been outside a lot lately with practice and everything since I am coaching now," she said. "You look really good, too, taking care of yourself, I see."

Case was stricken. 'She thinks I look good? She's never said that before,' he thought to himself quickly. "Oh, well you know I do what I can," he responded as they laughed in unison.

The laughter drifted off and Case followed up with another compliment, being careful not to hint too much that he had always loved her more than a friend. "How did you convince all of those Georgia boys not to follow you up here? I know they still have to be lining up outside your door."

"There's a few, but they are so immature. I can't even hold conversations with most of them anymore, it hurts my head," she said as she rolled her eyes and played with her spaghetti with her fork back and forth across the plate.

Case's thought-process registered the fact that she was inferring she could have an intellectual conversation with him, in addition to the comment about him looking good. Maybe she had begun to think of him the same way he had of her for so long. But maybe not.

Probably not. Case was optimistic in almost all parts of his life except when it came to her; she couldn't possibly be interested in the slightest, as Lincoln had tried to convince him earlier. It would be too good to be true.

"Look at you playing with your food, when did you turn into a five-year-old again?" Case said as he laughed and smiled at her across the table.

"I don't know." She paused. "Guess I'm just nervous."

"Nervous about what?" he replied. What would she be nervous about? he thought to himself. I don't make people nervous. Especially her. Case quickly decided to discount what she had just said, and not look into it any further, because it would just lead him to thoughts that would end up empty. "Nervous, huh?" he said. "Not nervous like I will be later at karaoke."

"Karaoke?" she answered with a puzzled look on her face. "You're going tonight?"

"Yeah. Alan asked me to come out around like 10 or 11. I'm pretty sure that Scott and Marie are going along, too. And Cage might come, too, if he can get in."

"Well, I want to come, too!" she exclaimed. "Unless I'm not invited." She immediately followed this with a fake frown as she stuck out her bottom lip like a disappointed kid on Christmas morning if their list wasn't fulfilled.

"Yeah, of course. I was going to see if you wanted to go anyway. Just forgot to mention it until now."

Her face went from one of intrigue to one of happy anticipation in an instant, and Case's followed suit. "We can actually go watch TV or something at my house until then. I wasn't sure if you had other plans."

"No, we can do that, but I have to use the little girls' room first," she said as she excused herself from the table.

As Case paid the bill in her absence, an overwhelming sense of shock coursed through his system. He knew that her coming over meant nothing, and neither did her comments about him minutes earlier, but something about this night suddenly felt different than any other time with her before. The tiny bit of hope he had always given himself seemed to have some merit, but he didn't want to see something that really wasn't there.

But there it was. 'Store #421' printed in bold numbers at the top of his copy of the receipt.

'This is outrageous,' he thought. 'It can't be a coincidence, just can't be.' His heart had begun to have a silent conversation with God. 'You're sending me all the signs that tell me this could be the start of something I've always dreamed of.'

His heart's conversation was placed on hold as she returned to the table and he stood up. "Did you pay already?" she asked.

"Yeah, I did. I think you got it last time you were home." Case immediately thought about smacking himself in the head like one of The Three Stooges. 'Way to go, Case. You want this to be more than a friendship, but you are treating it like it is just that.'

"Oh, well thank you, I'll get it next time then," she said.

Case's heart fell into his stomach. 'Smooth move,' he thought to himself again. 'Oh well—that's typical Case.'

"What do you want to watch?" he said to her as she made herself at home in his room by crawling onto his bed and bending the pillow behind her head with one arm.

"I don't care, you know I never really get to watch many movies or anything," she said as she shrugged her shoulders in approval of just about anything. She had always made herself comfortable in his house on her visits, so having her lie in his bed was little cause for alarm with him. They had many conversations with her in his bed and he sat in the chair next to her in the past, but the chair was no longer there.

Case's eyes got big and scanned the wall in front of him as he faced the other direction to choose a DVD, realizing for the first time that he would need to join her on top of the blankets unless he planned to stand next to the bed awkwardly.

"I'll put Dane Cook in. You like him, don't you?" he said as he glanced over his shoulder at her for approval.

"Yeah, he is good, I think," she said with a subtle nod of her head.

Case contemplated his next course of action as he removed the disc from the shelf. 'Is she going to think I'm weird if I go find a chair?' he thought. 'Or will she be ok with lying next to me in the bed? I mean, it is MY bed.' Before he could finish his battle with the dilemma he found himself lying next to her in conversation about the comic that played back on the television across from them. It felt no different than a normal conversation they would have had on the phone while being miles apart. Except she was right there. Where he slept. He wasn't sure what was too close or too far away. As she spoke, his mind wandered to what would happen if he were to plant a kiss on her like the Georgia sun had done such a good job of. 'If she is into me, then this could be the start of forever!' he thought. 'If I'm reading into this and it isn't, how do I react from there? How do I explain myself when she says, "Case, what are you doing? I thought we were just friends?"'

He was never more unsure of what to do in a situation ever before in his life, and the repercussions of a misfire began to weigh in on him and the mood of his dialogue. He began to laugh at parts of the show that he didn't even find funny, and started repeating lines the comic would say like an awkward echo.

"So how is the family?" she asked as he turned his head without moving his body toward her. He could feel a million sets of eyes on him. He felt like the blue comforter on which they lay was rolling its eyes and laughing at him.

"They're good. Call won another medal at the Special Olympics in Towson last month, he's getting really good," he said. What Case felt was a hyperbole of what the scene really exhibited. She couldn't sense an ounce of his being uncomfortable, even though he felt beads of sweat forming on his skin like the first few minutes of an afternoon jog.

"That's good to hear. Where are they all at tonight? I haven't seen them in forever, either?" she questioned him.

"Well, Mah and Pop are at a 20/20 dinner and Call went to his teacher's house for a birthday party. I think he's staying there tonight." Case paused and portrayed deep thought with his eyebrows and icy blues for a moment and continued. "I'm not sure where Cage is. I think he might be working, but he said he was probably gonna come out later."

"Oh, ok," she responded. "That's good: I'd like to get to see him while I'm home. What's he been doing with himself? Nothing but trouble like his older brother?!" she said while laughing mildly and pushing his shoulder playfully.

If it was a non-verbal cue, it flew right over Case's head like a firefly that had come to the neighborhood from a nearby field. She was always "touchy-feely" since he or anyone else could remember. She made people feel at home, feel like they had known her forever even if they had just met seconds ago, so Case didn't pay any mind to the gentle push she gave him. He was too focused on the idea in his mind that he should try to kiss her. Something in him had solidified somehow. He had a newfound level of confidence and he didn't need a gentle push or a '2x4' to the forehead to realize that this was his chance. He was waiting for his moment. His mind was made up.

"Yeah, you know us, nothing but trouble," he responded in a sarcastic tone.

"Trouble's not always a bad thing," she said as he sat up on the bed on his elbows and rolled his broad shoulders forward to stretch. He let out a raspy exhaling breath as if he had just taken a thirst-quenching first sip of water after a workout as he lay back down simultaneously answering, "It sure isn't."

A few minutes went by as Dane Cook continued to rattle off ridiculous stories in the background, both of them pausing from conversation to pay attention to the screen for a few seconds at a time.

"I think this is the first time I've ever been in your house and nobody else is here," she said. "There is usually your entire family and a few extras hanging around."

"Yeah, it isn't too often that the house is empty, but it's nice when it is."

This was it. His perfect set-up. It wasn't obvious but it was the right part of the conversation to throw in one more line and lay one on her. As he scanned through his repertoire of quips and lines that he had developed over his lifetime, he couldn't think of the perfect response right away. Not a pick-up line, or something cheesy from a movie, but a quick thought for her to register in the time it took him to connect his lips to hers.

"I agree. I like having company but it's nice to have some quiet time every once in a while. Get away from all of the commotion," she said, interrupting his thought. But it hadn't really interrupted anything.

"Yeah, but quiet time with the right company is better than anything" was what Case had begun to say. But the word "yes" was all that had the chance to leave his mouth when his phone began to ring.

"You comin'?!" Alan said before Case could even say hello.

"Yeah, man, I'm about to leave soon," Case said back to him.

"Me, Scott, and Marie are out here waiting on you in the driveway. Let's go!"

"Oh. Alright, well, two minutes then," he said.

"Lacey's coming, too."

CHAPTER 5

February 1

• • •

LACEY HAD LEFT TO GO back to Georgia weeks ago, but Case found it difficult to erase the night from his memory. How it was there one moment and gone just as fast. He tried to convince himself it wasn't the moment he had previously decided that it was, but his mind wouldn't allow it to sink in. He held no vendetta against Alan for calling at the worst possible time, but instead chalked it up to bad luck. Case's luck.

It wasn't all bad luck, though. The large firm he interviewed with had decided to bring him on in an entry-level position, and he focused all of his attention that wasn't spent on his missed opportunity with Lacey on his new job. He moved up through the initial ranks quickly, using his brains as opposed to his brawn for the first time toward being successful in the workplace. He was a bright young adult and, when he applied himself to his studies, had been a straight-A student, but at times his mind wouldn't be in the right place.

Within six months he had been promoted: A step closer toward his goal of managing and coaching others. He helped others at the firm whenever he could, leveraging his strengths and knowledge picked up along the way. He became a "go-to guy" for his department, but something was still missing. He was sure it was Lacey, and their talks had become less and less frequent. But nonetheless they had an ongoing conversation that would sometimes have breaks a week or two long in the wavelengths.

He had become friends with several co-workers, but none closer than with a woman named Kylie. She was a good listener and always seemed to give good advice. She had been in a serious relationship for several years, and was blindsided by her ex-boyfriend right about the time that she and Case met in their initial training class. Case adored the strength and courage she displayed when she would talk about how her fiancé left her for someone else. She was a cute and bright individual. Case found her shoulder-length, black hair and medium-sized frame attractive, along with her dark green eyes and great smile. But she had a big sister-like aura that he had picked up from her on day one. Case's mind explored the possibility that maybe he and Kylie could be an item: they certainly got along well enough, but the thoughts never extended longer than a thought or two. He enjoyed their talks and he had mentioned his previous relationship with Cheyenne and how he had a secret crush on his best friend. Kylie thought it was cute that he found himself among the butterflies whenever he would speak of Lacey. She felt like she had met her already from hearing all of the stories and signs that Case would convey repeatedly.

If there was one thing about Kylie that bothered Case it was that she always had the answer. No matter what he would say to her, no matter the predicament that he had created in his mind, she had a rebuttal, most of the time the one that Case didn't want to hear. She had made it clear that, unless Case would ever break down and confess his ongoing love, he wouldn't end up with Lacey. Kylie knew from her short time being acquainted with Case that he would never do so: She saw that he valued Lacey's friendship and her being so important to him and couldn't possibly imagine Case rocking the boat, for the fear of falling into the water. And she was right.

"Okay, Ky. Since you know everything, then exactly who am I going to get married to? Huh? What's her name going to be and how many kids are we going to have?" Case said in a condescending tone as he held the door open for her as they were leaving work on a Friday afternoon.

"Man, it is f-f-freezing out here," she said as she pulled up the hood of her winter jacket and tucked her hair into the inside of it. She walked past Case into the parking lot as Case continued to hold the door for a few others who had been walking out the same door.

, it is cold, but answer me, Miss Know It All!" Case said loudly to her from behind as he walked quickly through the brisk February wind.

"Oh, your wife? Kylie paused. "Her name is going to be…"

"Let's hear it, Ky', you've got all the answers, don't you?!"

"Lara," she said. "Her name is Lara and you're going to have three kids, mark my words."

"Ah-ha," Case exclaimed. "Well, see, you're wrong because I want to have four."

Kylie rolled her eyes as she reached deep for another answer. "Well, the fourth is going to be adopted, Case, and I don't think you get to just flat out decide how many you have, you'd have to be really lucky."

"Well, that's great news, and a guy can dream, can't he?" Case said with a laugh back at her.

"I mean you are usually pretty lucky, I'm friends with you for some reason," Kylie said as she rolled her eyes again and then followed it with her teeth chattering loudly as she opened the door to her car.

"I suppose I am, but when you find this Lara chick, you make sure she makes her way to me, ok?!" he yelled sarcastically over the truck and van parked between their cars.

"Yeah, you know I will. I'll see you later tonight," said Kylie as she sat down in her car and closed the door.

Case squinted as though smoke from a fire had entered them due to the wind and yelled once again, "UFC at The Hollar! Can't wait!" Even if it had been a still day where the lake beside their building was not frozen and there were no ripples in the water, his words could not have been deciphered through the closed door of Kylie's vehicle. She backed up the car and honked the horn twice quickly as she drove away through the lot.

He started the Mustang and opened his phone to call and confirm Friday night's plans with Alan and Scott, calling Scott first for he knew it would probably take a few attempts before he would answer. Scott was engaged to be married to Marie and they had been together since Case had known him. They graduated high school together and Scott was Case's best friend, or at least held the title. Case had a special place in his heart and his life for all of his friends, but Scott taught him lessons without ever intending to do so. He had been friends with Alan from birth, and Scott from middle school, but neither friendship had an expiration date. Nor did the length of time Case knew someone play a part in his devotion and loyalty to a friend.

Scott was a social butterfly and his appearance resembled the actor Ben Savage from the 90s show 'Boy Meets World.' He came from a difficult background, moving back and forth from living with his dad in Virginia, to living with his mom in Jefferson. He was the greatest storyteller that Case had ever met, and the only arguments that he and Case would ever have were about Scott's inability to commit. To commit to anything but Marie, that is.

It had only gotten worse since high school, at an exponential rate. On several occasions Case would become angry with Scott because he wouldn't want to do anything with anyone without checking with Marie first. What bothered Case even more was that it was self-induced. Marie was as easygoing as they came. She didn't mind when Scott would do things with Case, Alan, Cage, or anyone for that matter, and she certainly didn't have any problem scheduling outings for herself that didn't include them. She wanted him to do his own thing, but Scott would double- and triple-check with her before saying that he was definitely going to take part in any event, unless of course she would be coming along, too.

Case had become more comfortable with Marie over the years, and ultimately accepted the fact that she was number one in Scott's eyes and that his feelings of bitterness and annoyance with Scott stemmed from jealousy that he didn't have someone of his own to live for. Marie was a former cheerleader as well, and she lived up to the reputation that all redheads before her had set as a precedent. She was short and bubbly, Case would describe her. She wasn't the poster child for common sense, but was bright as the North Star when it came to books and studies. She and Scott were the perfect couple, and Case couldn't imagine a better-suited partner for his best friend, even if he hadn't always felt that way.

He was alarmed when he heard Scott answer the phone after only one ring.

"What's up, man?" Scott said quickly, in his normal smooth but fast-talking voice.

"Nothing, just leaving work. What time are you all coming out tonight?"

"Well, we have to stop by her parents' house for a bit, but we will be out before 10 probably."

Alan's call would never have to be made, as Case heard the beep of call waiting come in as he made the final right before merging onto the highway to head home.

"What's goin' on?" Case said as he switched over to the new call.

"Not gonna make it tonight, gotta help Dad at the lake house so I have a two-hour drive up to Deep Creek." Alan's words played out.

"Well, that sucks. Won't be the same without you, man. I've got Scott on the other line still. I'll see if he wants to scoop me up later since you aren't coming."

"Alright. Yeah, my bad. I'll talk to you tomorrow or something," Alan said as Case bid his farewell and switched back to his prior conversation.

"Yeah, he's not coming now: guess he's doing his best impression of you. Bailing out last minute," Case said without even providing notice that he had resumed the call. By this point, Scott was immune to Case's smart remarks and he had developed a block in his mind which allowed him to not be fazed by the frequent stabs at his way of life. Case eventually agreed with Scott that he would be the designated driver for the evening's festivities, and he reached out to Kylie and offered a ride to her as well. Kylie had met Scott and Marie a few times previously, and she fit right in with the group, being a similar age of 22.

By the time Case's driving service arrived at The Hollar it was almost 10:30PM. The Hollar was a typical sports bar that served as a diner and clubhouse to the golf course that neighbored the tall, mansion-like building. It was a fairly new establishment, having just opened along with the golf course a couple years before. Vine plants outlined the corners of the white aluminum siding that wrapped along the building, and forest-green shutters provided a Southern plantation feel to it. On the north side of the structure was an outside fire pit feet away from the bar placed on an elaborate patio which served as a typical mid-twenties hangout during the summer months. The stones that were lined beneath several palm trees and assorted flowers and other greenery were all unique in size and color, and provided an astonishing view of craftsmanship both before and after the sunset over the 18th hole that approached the building.

"There better be seats inside because the patio is bumpin'!" said Scott loudly to the others as they exited the Mustang one at a time.

"I'm sure there is," said Case in a normal tone of voice. "It's too nice out for the inside to be as packed as that," he continued sarcastically as he nodded toward the patio which was playing a large projector screen of the undercard fights of the Ultimate Fighting Championship pay-per-view the group had set out to witness.

"Is that Drew?!" Kylie exclaimed. "Oh my God, I haven't seen him in forever." Case and the couple looked at each other as if to confirm as a team they had no idea who Kylie was talking about. "I'll catch up with you guys in there," Kylie said as she sped in front of them toward two girls standing right outside of the patio entrance.

Case and Scott's hypothesis of the interior of the bar was confirmed and they began talking amongst themselves as they waited to be carded at the entrance. "That makes no sense, everybody outside in the freezing cold watching these fights," said Scott. "I'm half-inclined to run over to James Gang Pizza and see if they will order it."

"Yeah, really surprising to me, too, that there are open tables in here," Case responded as they both followed Marie to an open table in the corner near one of many flat-screen televisions mounted to the wall. "And James Gang has like one television, so I hope you're joking."

"Yeah, I know," laughed Scott. "Even with how busy this is, can you imagine going into downtown tonight? Bushwaller's, Firestone's, and Brewer's Alley probably have no room to walk."

Through the loud music and the high decibel level of the surrounding TVs, the three continued in conversation as they sat down in anticipation of the main event. Case merely followed Scott's lead as he didn't know the name of many of the UFC participants or even who was fighting later that evening. Case saw it as an opportunity to be social with his friends and to keep his mind off of the previous workweek. So the watching of a fight on a big screen was an added bonus.

The conversation continued and transitioned to the subject of Kylie being missing in action. "I'll go see if I can find her. You all want something to drink? I'm gonna get some water while I'm up," said Case.

"Yeah, man I'll take a beer, you know what kind," said Scott. Which Case did. He knew that all Scott drank was Coors Light and nothing but. "I'll take one of those pink thingies you and Alan got me last time—Thanks, Casey!" Marie followed in her quick and stereotypical cheerleader voice.

"Ok, Marie-e," Case said as he pushed in his chair and began toward the bar adjacent to their table. He hated being called Casey, but for some reason it didn't bother him when Marie would do it. Nonetheless, he treated his response to her addition to his name as he always did, by adding an "e" to the end of the other person's name in a sarcastic voice. His given name was Case and that's the way he liked it. He didn't want to be confused with anyone else and wanted it to be clear that his name was NOT Casey.

As he continued toward the bar, Case noticed Kylie talking just inside the patio exit door to a tall, dark, and handsome man wearing a black leather jacket and a knit beanie.

'Good for her,' he thought simultaneously while acknowledging he no longer needed to find her location. He rarely saw or heard of Kylie flirting with guys since he had met her, and he always accounted that to the emotional scars her ex had left behind. "Maybe she will finally bring the walls down," he said audibly to himself very low as he continued to wait in line to order the table's drinks.

"Here's your drinks, Case," said Glen, the bartender who now knew him by name. Case retrieved and paid for the drinks and proceeded to walk back toward the table, holding a glass in each hand and gripping the neck of Scott's beer between his left ring and middle fingers when he heard his name called from behind.

"Case!" he heard again as he 180'ed slowly to ensure the drinks wouldn't spill. It took his eyes a second to focus in and match up the distance from which the noise had come from. "Over here!" he heard as he recognized finally the voice and its place of origin. His eyes enlarged and his eyebrows slid up toward the top of his head in excitement as he saw it was his old friend Tess from high school, sitting with a table of other girls who appeared to be his age. Tess had gone to Linganore high school on the other side of the county, and it had been a while since they had last seen each other. It had been at her wedding to a mutual friend who played high school football with Case a couple years earlier. Case lifted his left hand which held both his water and Scott's beer and somehow managed to extend his index finger to signify the words 'be back in a second' toward Tess. He turned and continued to finish his deed as the fetcher of beverages and sat the drinks down on the table.

"Thanks, man," said Scott. "Thank you, Caseyyy," followed Marie as she immediately took her lemonade-looking drink from beside Case's right hand. Case continued to stand as he relayed the message he was supposed to return with as well.

"Kylie's by the patio talking to some guy. I'm sure she will be over soon," he said with a pause. "And Tess Smith is over there, I told her I'd come back and talk to her, so I'll be back in a bit."

"Oh ok, man," Scott replied as he was cut off by his fiancée—"Have fun, Caseyyy, seeyousoon!" Marie had only begun to sip her drink but had begun to act and speak as if it was her fourth of the night.

"I will, Marie-e," responded Case half-heartedly as he looked at Scott and shook his head slightly and began to walk back toward the table where he saw Tess sitting moments earlier.

"So how have you been?!" exclaimed Tess as she hugged Case when he sat down at one of two open chairs on her side of the table.

"I've been good. Just working, ya know? How about you? Where's the hubby tonight?"

"He's working on the Jeep as usual: he never wants to come out," Jess said in response as her facial expression went from bitterness back to one of happiness instantaneously. "But Dakota and Michelle invited me out! So I'm here!" she exclaimed, looking at the two girls across the table. Case vaguely recognized the other two girls sitting at the table, but he didn't know where from. They appeared to be sisters but they were not, looking eerily similar to one another with the only exception being one had blonde hair and the other brunette. Before he could introduce himself to them, the blonde one stood up and yelled, "There she is! Birthday girlll!" loudly followed by a disturbing scream that would normally be heard in a movie theatre on the opening night of a teenage Disney movie.

A medium-height, petite girl with highlighted brown hair down just past her shoulder wearing a black shirt and tight dark blue jeans returned to the table with a loud "Yeah, drinks for the birthday girl! That's meee!"

The new addition to the table wore a "Birthday Girl" plastic crown covered in glitter and a matching sash over her shirt.

"I take it you're the birthday girl?" Case said sarcastically toward the girl in the crown across the table. "What gave you that idea?" the girl responded, noticing Case had joined the table for the first time. At the same moment Case's sarcastic demeanor went serious. As she looked him in the eyes with a smirk as if to say, "You're an idiot," he noticed what appeared to be a reciprocation of his own eyes.

Her eyes were bright blue with the same sheet of ice that christened his own and they grabbed his attention immediately. The shape of the corners of her eyes was like something from a magazine, and the skin where her cheeks met them wrinkled as she smiled. These eyes were mesmerizing and for the first time at The Hollar Case heard and felt nothing as he stared blankly back into them.

"Who's the hottie?" he heard the girl say to the blonde as all three girls on the opposite side of the table turned together and looked at him.

"Who, me?" Case said, pointing at himself in the chest with his right hand and thumb. A few seconds passed and Case continued. "I'm Case, and I know these two are Dakota and Michelle, so that makes you Ms. Birthday, then."

"What'd you say your name was? Casey?" said the crowned girl.

"No, not Casey," he said, sure that she still would assume he was saying Casey.

"Ok, well, if it's not Casey, then what did you say? I don't tell my name to strangers," she said over the noise of the bar.

"It's Case. Casey without the Y."

"Case? Like a CD case?" she said while chuckling to herself and the two beside her to her left.

"Yeah. Like a CD case. And you must be Mildred, then. You look like a Mildred."

"Mildred?!" the crowned girl said loudly, continuing her laughter. "What kind of name is that?"

"Yours tonight," he replied as he shot a mischievous smile at her and took a drink of water.

"Well, if I'm Mildred, then I'll just have to come up with a name for you, too," said the crowned girl as she stood up and walked around the table as if playing musical chairs to take the last vacant seat of the 6-top next to Case.

"Cedric," she said as she sat down.

"So I'm Cedric now?" he said flirtatiously as he watched her look him up and down. "Yes, Cedric, and I like your tattoos, Cedric."

"Oh really?" said Case as he rolled both of his shirt sleeves up a bit further to reveal the words 'Metzger' on one arm and 'Case' on the other with identical Old English lettering in front of a smoky backdrop on either bicep.

"Yeah, but that shouldn't say Case. It should say Cedric," she said, touching his right arm with her hand gently. "Any what's the other one, your last name?"

"Yeah."

"Well, I absolutely love tattoos. And you smell amazing," said the crowned girl with a wink and a tipsy smile. Case knew she was drinking, and felt odd about flirting with her while being completely sober himself, but continued the conversation. He wasn't the type to hook up with a random girl, but was all for flirty conversation.

"Thanks, Mildred—Keen sense of smell you have there," he said with a laugh. "So is today your birthday? Or it was this week?"

"Yes, sir, February first!" she said as she leaned over into him looking away for a moment at the Main event fight that had already began.

"And how old are we?" Case followed up.

"We are 22. How old are you?"

"36," said Case with a straight face as she leaned back into her own seat.

"You are not! You can't be more than 25 or 26!"

"Well, if you won't tell me your real name, you don't get my real age," he said with a smile again, this time leaning his head against his hand with his elbow propped on the table in front of him. The crowned girl sighed and returned the smile. "I guess fair is fair," she said. "Tell me how old you are and I promise I'll tell you my real name, Mr. Cedric."

"Ha you think I'm gonna fall for that?" Case laughed as he glanced up at the screens and then back toward Scott and Marie's table where he could see Kylie had returned and was talking amongst them.

"No, but it was worth a shot," said the crowned girl as Case's attention reverted back toward her as she continued.

Case's eyes flipped back toward Kylie as a chilling sensation coursed through every vein in his body and the background noise went silent to him once again. The words the crowned girl spoke echoed through his ear canal like a shout in an empty auditorium.

"I'm Lara."

CHAPTER 6

Dinner Four Two, Date 1

• • •

CASE WAS EXTREMELY EXCITED THAT Lara seemed really interested in him, even if she was having birthday drinks the night they had met. He had gotten her number for what he said was to help her possibly get a job at his firm, which was only partly true. He had spoken with her a few times over the next week. When he conveyed the good news to Scott and Alan, who didn't meet her at The Hollar that night, they both were thrilled for him.

"I'm tellin' you, man," said Case over the phone. "Scott… Man, I have a feeling about this girl. She's going to be my date to your wedding in May. Mark my words."

"I hope so, dude," replied Scott. "I just want to see you happy."

Case switched the phone to his left hand and propped it between his shoulder and neck with his head bent to the side as he opened the car door. "I'm going to meet her right now."

"Oh yeah? Where you guys going?—It's Case, baby," Scott said as Case heard Marie rattling off twenty questions in the background.

"Tell her it's your other fiancé," Case said with a laugh, inviting himself to the conversation taking place on the other end of the line. "Anyway, she said she loves Texas Roadhouse so we're going there and then maybe to a movie."

"Uh-oh," said Scott. "Dinner and a movie must be pretty serious, huh?"

"Ha yeah, I mean most meaningful relationships start off with a unique first date. So I figured I would go with something out of the ordinary."

Scott recognized the sarcasm and began to play along. "Yeah, I wish I had your imagination when it came to impressing females: Case-a-nova."

"You only wish, sir, you only wish."

Case backed the car out of the driveway and switched the phone to speaker while sitting it in the cup holder at his side. Scott's laughter trailed off as you could hear him wildly over the phone. The Mustang sped over the hill and Case began to register in his mind what the night could bring. As he ended the call he thought about how amazing Lara had seemed in their prior conversations leading up to this night. How she enjoyed music and movies at the same level he did. And most of all, that she seemed to be just as interested in him as he was in her. The possibilities that reeled through his mind at a speed faster than his wheels on the cold, damp pavement seemed endless. As he reached the stop sign, the numbers crossed through his mind in a way that he hadn't encountered yet.

They had met on her birthday, which he knew was February 1st, but the numbers didn't click until that fork in the road. He didn't need to see them this time to create a new equation for what they could mean. Maybe all of this time he had been waiting for 2/1. Four Two One. Maybe his life was headed in the direction where he and Lara would become very serious in the future. Maybe every stop sign and roadblock in his life was guiding him toward tonight. Maybe he would one day live his life for her as opposed to himself. Living for 2/1. Four Two One.

He smiled to himself at the very thought that had just been formed and shook his head, realizing once again that God sends messages to all people in mysterious ways. Nothing was for certain, of course. He knew that. They hadn't even gone on their first date yet, and it hadn't even started, for that matter. However, the way he was able to manipulate the numbers that he knew were leading him somewhere to intrigue himself further with his newest female acquaintance was enough for him at the moment. A higher power had led them together that night, whether it meant for him to learn something from a few conversations, or to one day walk down the aisle together. Or somewhere in between.

He pulled into the parking lot at the steakhouse 20 minutes before they were to meet. He did not want to be late for their first encounter, and actually had to stop himself several times from leaving the house even earlier than what he did. He was so excited at the opportunity which lay in front of him and was focused on not messing it up. He wanted to be himself and only himself, and prayed that the date would go well sporadically throughout the day which got him there. He nervously batted his fingers up and down on the steering wheel as he waited.

She arrived right on time, and parked adjacent to him unknowingly. They had spoken about what vehicles each other drove, but Case was unsure what a Chevrolet Cobalt really looked like. He wasn't into cars enough to know about what each model looked like – just the ones he really admired – like his midnight blue Mustang.

All he knew to look for was a silver car with the Chevy symbol on the front of it. He didn't recognize the silver car to his left when she pulled in, but her face was burnt into his eyelids when he blinked like he had been staring at an artificial light too long. He noticed her right away when he looked up to scan the lot for the eighth or ninth time.

"Good to see you again, Mildred," he said with his hands in his pockets as he approached her car and she stood up out of the vehicle.

She smiled and laughed as she quipped back, "Same to you, Cedric. How long have I had you waiting?"

'Almost 22 years,' he thought. 'Nope, not saying that: that'll sound like I am a psycho.'

"Not long, I knew I was early anyway—you look gorgeous this evening," he said, noticing the dark brown shirt and tight black dress pants she wore. "Put me to shame."

"I wouldn't say that, I think you look nice," Lara said and they hugged each other as if they were long-lost friends.

As they both released their embrace from one another, they began to walk toward the restaurant and Case's phone made a loud beeping noise from the pocket of his favorite jeans. He reached down as if nothing had happened and switched the volume button on the side of the phone from on to off without removing it to see who had sent him a message. He held the door for her to walk in and proceeded in after her to a dimly lit setting crowded with patrons.

"So you were saying that you're about to finish college?" Case said as he took a drink of water.

"Yeah, I've been taking classes online and in Hagerstown. After this semester I'll have my associates degree."

"That's awesome, what field?"

"Accounting."

"Oh, ok, I think I told you that mine was in Business Management, but I took a bunch of accounting classes. Hated them," he said, chuckling.

"Yeah, I have always liked numbers and anything is better than working part-time at a grocery store like I am right now."

They thanked their waiter as he set down a loaf of bread and a cup of butter on their table.

"Thank you," Case said in his politest tone and reverted back to their conversation. "Yeah, I get that for sure: I worked at a warehouse back here all throughout college. Even when I was playing ball, I couldn't get out of there soon enough, so makes sense you asked me that first night if my firm was hiring."

"Well, that will be nice if they are, but I really was just trying to entice you to ask for my number. You sure didn't seem like you were going to otherwise," she responded with a smile that looked as though she held back a sarcastic laugh.

"No, you said you love numbers. Well, so do I. Numbers are a passion of mine, so I definitely would have asked for yours."

"Ohhh, one with wordplay I see. Well, I'm glad you asked for it, anyway— even if I didn't have to trick you into it." She winked at him across the table.

Case's smile stretched from ear to ear as he looked up toward the light hanging above their table in embarrassment and what he had previously said.

"But in all seriousness, I do love numbers, too. I love math. I always like that in math there was one answer and you were either right or wrong. No talking your way out of a wrong answer."

"That's true, I always liked it for the same reasons kinda," she said. "But I also like that they can have so much meaning."

Case acted confused, even though he felt the same way for his own reasons. Curious as to what she meant, he asked, "What do you mean?"

Her face still looked at him across the table as her eyes wandered in deep thought. She repeated herself as if to buy time to explain. "Like how they have so much meaning?"

"Yeah."

She became focused on him once again as she had formulated a response that she was satisfied with. "Like, how they have so much more power than words sometimes… Like you can explain something for an hour. Or you can bring amounts or numbers into the explanation and get your point across in 30 seconds."

"I see." He took another swig of water and cleared his throat. "I agree, kind of like them not being able to be changed. They are what they are."

She nodded her head in approval. "Why? What did you think I meant?"

Case didn't want her to think that he was weird about how he found more meaning in numbers, a few in particular, and what they could represent at times, so he didn't voice that opinion. "Nothing, really. Just wasn't sure."

They continued their conversation over the meal, going back and forth with stories about bad first dates and they both agreed that they were having a good time with each other subliminally. As the waiter took away what remained on their plates, one of her stories made Case erupt in laughter.

"You left him at the restaurant!?" he bellowed.

"Well, I didn't say I was proud of it," she responded, scanning the room to see how many people's attention had been drawn to their table from the laughter.

"So, let me get this straight." Case paused. "You told him you were going to the bathroom, and then just ducked out and went home? Ok. You win. That's hilarious."

"Well, he was really creepy. He kept asking me to go back to his friends' house to look at paintings or something. I couldn't take it another minute. He was relentless." They both smiled at each other and shared another laugh or two before enduring further into discussion.

"So do you still want to go to the theatre or do you need to use the restroom?"

Lara smiled brightly and spoke through her grin. "No, I still want to go. I am having fun and you aren't *that* creepy."

"Ha—good. Me, too."

"But I do seriously need to go before we leave."

"Should I wait by your car or do you have a getaway driver waiting?"

"I texted and told them I wouldn't need them."

"Alright, ha, well I will just take my chances here at the table, then."

"I can actually drive us both over and bring you back to your car if you want," he said, walking toward his car, grabbing his keys from the right side of his jacket.

"Works for me. What time will we be back, do you think? I have to work at 8 tomorrow."

"I think it is only like an hour and a half, but we are still kinda early, though. Doesn't start until 10."

"Oh, late night for me, then. I am usually in bed by then. I will probably be exhausted tomorrow."

"Well, I'm sure that we can find some way to spend the time before-hand," Case replied as they both sat down into the Mustang. Case hadn't realized how bad what he had just said sounded until it had already escaped his mouth. He didn't even want to look at her when he started the car and began to move toward the stop light across the parking lot. She discarded his previous statement and carried on.

"I didn't realize your car was a stick, it is really nice."

"Yeah, I like it. A to B, ya know?"

"I'm sure. Most people who drive Mustangs just have them because they were the only thing available," she responded sarcastically.

"Ha-ha. Well, I'm really not a big 'car' guy. I just like the way it looks. And it sounds nice, too. But don't ask me anything about under the hood. I'll have to make something up to sound manlier."

"When you told me you drove one, I thought that was so hot. I love these cars."

"Well, I guess it is good for that, too," Case said, turning on the three-lane strip of highway shifting into third gear.

"So when do I get to drive it? I'd love to drive a Mustang."

Case's eyebrows lifted and he looked over toward her for a moment. "I don't think I've ever let anyone else drive it." He paused for a split second. "We'll have to see."

They pulled into the parking lot behind Regal Cinemas, forty-five minutes prior to the start of the show. For a Friday night, the lot seemed deserted, but the lamps that lit the nearly vacant lot provided a surprisingly romantic glow as the car came to a halt.

"I'm sure they aren't even seating it yet. Sorry I didn't time this better," said Case, pulling the keys from the ignition.

"It's ok, it is nice to sit and talk, I suppose."

"Or."

"Or what?"

Case took the keys rested on his lap and held them in front of her with one finger, dangling from them like a porch chime. They swung back and forth on his hand, light-sounding like loose change in an old man's pocket.

"Really?!"

Case exhaled deeply. "I guess… not gonna hurt anything in the parking lot. At least I would hope not. You can drive a manual right?"

"Yeah, I learned how to drive on one!" Lara exclaimed with excitement as she exited the passenger side mid-sentence, the keys jangling in her hands, walking around the back of the vehicle. He noticed her smile glowed into the night in anticipation, slowly removing himself from the car, one leg at a time.

He felt his legs begin to shake back and forth in a nervous twitch as the start turned over and the engine rumbled. "I seriously don't let people do this," he winked at her as she adjusted the mirrors as if preparing to leave on a long road trip. He looked out his window and turned to look behind in an obvious way. "Good thing you adjusted the mirrors, don't want any blind spots in this high traffic…"

Her smile seemed to be permanent. She seemed even smaller in the seat next to him, and he uncomfortably sat still in the passenger seat. As nervous as he was, he seemed to be more intrigued by the alternate view from this side of his car, for he had never sat in this seat while the car was moving, only while cleaning it or getting something from the glovebox. He was nervous, but not about her driving his car. His nerves stemmed from how well the night was going. He thought he had said all of the right things for once, at least more than normal, and he couldn't shake the expression on her face when he had offered her the keys. Like he had just handed her a briefcase full of money or a winning lottery ticket. Case didn't allow himself to show any emotion as she rounded the front of the promenade for a second lap. She appeared to be so content, and he didn't want to take that from her.

"So, do you like it?" he said.

"I love it, I could get used to this. Although I would like to open it up," she smirked.

"Baby steps," he chuckled. "Maybe date number 3 or 4."

"You mean I gotta go out with you at least two more times? Ugh," she remarked with a grin to ensure he knew she was kidding. She pulled the car into the same spot from which it first rested and let the car run. "Are we switching back?"

"No need. I'm starting to like it over here anyway." Case looked at the clock on the dashboard to confirm how much time before their movie started. "Still got a half-hour," he said, turning the power to the radio on and hitting the button marked 'CD.'

"Is this John Mayer?" she said in response to the tune.

"Yeah, I like this version better than the original," Case said, mimicking the words as they played through the speakers.

'She's a good girl. Loves her mama. Loves Jesus, and America, too. She's a good girl, crazy 'bout Elvis', loves horses, and her boyfriend too-yeah, yeah'

The song played on like a soundtrack to their lives that had joined together for a night as she stared into his eyes. He had been leaning closer and closer toward the center console since turning on the music.

"This is a good song. I like this one, too," she said softly as his body moved closer.

"Well, I like you," he whispered as he leaned into her and put his left arm on the headrest of her seat and right hand on her face gently. Her lips met his as they both closed their eyes and entered into a state of euphoria. The bristles of his face were rough but felt smooth against her cheeks. Both of them stopped breathing for what felt like minutes. Case pulled away slightly while lightly biting her lower lip. An overwhelming sensation of warmth scaled Case's entire body as he pulled away once again, this time long enough for them both to open their eyes.

"Wow," she whispered toward him, his face still just inches away.

"Sorry, couldn't help myself," he said softly back at her, moving his body slowly back to a seated position on the passenger side.

"Don't be. That was—"

"Amazing? Yes."

"Was it just me, or did that not feel like a first kiss? It felt… right. Like we had done that before."

She looked at him in awe, like having been struck by lightning, the both of them slow-dancing with one another's eyes to the strums of John Mayer.

"We should probably get our tickets." Case broke the trance they had shared.

"Yeah." She shook her head up and down slightly, eyes wide open underneath the moonlight that spotlighted the lone vehicle remaining in a row of empty spaces. Case held her hand in his as they walked toward the box office, and was surprised when he found himself more nervous than before they had shared a moment of intimacy. 'Now what?' he thought. 'I just gave her the end of a great first date right in the middle.'

The movie played on as he tried to carry on low conversation with her, his arm around her shoulder. He was his own worst enemy, and for as good as the night had gone leading up to this moment, he felt it had begun its descent to mediocrity. Her body language was not reassuring, and he could tell that she did not like that he was talking during the movie.

He began to overcompensate, trying to save the enjoyment they had been sharing, by removing his arm from her side. She sensed that he was nervous, and when the movie ended, she tried to reconcile the unspoken messages her body had sent to him. Lara grabbed Case's hand from his side, walking under an archway toward the lot where the car rested. The silence between them was broken by his apology.

"Sorry I talked so much. Movies probably aren't the best choice for a first date. Wasn't trying to ruin it for you."

"I didn't leave you to go to the bathroom," she joked to lighten the mood. "Even though I couldn't because you had the keys."

"I wouldn't have blamed you: should have just told me to shut up."

"Ok, shut up," she said abruptly. "I had a good time, even if I couldn't pay attention to the movie; let's just not let it happen again."

"Won't be a problem, I learn from being a moron most of the time," Case replied, the two of them sharing a brief smile before entering the car.

Conversation was in low demand on the ride back to her car, but Case felt better about being awkward after talking about it with her, and she found it cute that he was stumbling to finish the night. Her mind traveled back to how well the night had gone, despite the constant interruptions to her focus while in the theatre.

The chill of the winter night grasped them both as they stood outside of her car back at the restaurant. "Thank you for dinner. This was a great night." Her words echoed toward him while she bundled up into her drive seat.

"My pleasure, I'm glad you had a good time. So did I."

"I need to get home so I'm not a zombie at work in the morning, but text me tomorrow sometime."

"I'll do that. Be careful on the way home. Let me know when you get there," Case responded as he leaned in and kissed her on the cheek and closed her door with the swipe of one arm. He waved at her, moving his fingers up and down like a fan with a steady palm. As she drove away, he noticed something that he hadn't before in the back seat of her car that suddenly froze his feet to the concrete. He had paid no mind to the juice box he saw on the cup holder moments earlier as he bid her farewell, but now he found himself trying to develop a photographic memory of what he had just seen. The vivid images of the car seat in the back of her vehicle entered his mind once again and he blinked several times quickly in confusion.

"She has a kid?"

CHAPTER 7

The crowned girl's princess

• • •

BAILEY WAS ONE OF THE cutest little girls that Case had ever seen. At 23 months, she stumbled through chopped-up sentences and phrases like most near two-year-olds do. Case hadn't had much direct contact with a toddler since his teenage years, but embraced the opportunity to spend time with the little one. He had always loved kids despite his limited experience with them. He was amazed at the amount of emulation Bailey showed and the level of accuracy at which it was performed.

She wasn't your typical toddler you would see in a stroller on the street with her parents. She resembled a miniature form of her mother with blondish-brown hair, and her innocent smile revealed a slight gap between her baby teeth. Her level of smarts had grown exponentially over the few months leading up to Case's introduction to her.

"She was barely talking at all at Christmas," said Lara.

"That's amazing. She sure is talking now. She is so smart."

"I was actually kind of worried that she was behind other kids her age. She didn't even start walking until 16 months."

"Well, I am pretty sure she is the cutest little girl I have ever seen. I don't have much experience, having come from a family of nothing but boys and my mom. She used to babysit my younger second cousins when I was in middle or high school—but I was always too busy to ever spend much time with them or play with them like this."

"Well, she really likes you," Lara said with a smile, talking about her daughter as if she wasn't sitting on the floor in Case's lap playing with her dolls.

"She is amazing. Like her mama," Case said as Lara leaned down from her chair and kissed him on the chops with a peck of her tightened lips.

Case never asked why she hadn't mentioned her daughter during their earliest conversations. He understood that having something like that is quite a bomb to drop on someone. He also imagined that Lara didn't want to introduce Bailey, or acknowledge her existence to just any random person. She was not only responsible for her own life, but also for a child's—even if Case hadn't pegged her as the motherly type before being privy to the fact she had a daughter.

He still didn't. It was hard to put together. Lara was extremely good with her, and he appreciated the strong sense of structure that he saw her instilling in Bailey. But she was still the crowned girl to him, having a worry-free night with her girlfriends that night in The Hollar. The woman who spoke of a career at the steakhouse, making no reference to raising a daughter.

Nonetheless, the honeymoon phase rolled on. Having a new female suddenly thrust into the picture was exciting to Case, and he was equally excited to continue to get to know her daughter as well. The two made their dating official later that month. Case had broken through the wall that Lara had built around her life in a very short period of time. The biggest hurdle for him was adjusting to the fact that she didn't have a close relationship with her parents, even though she lived with her mom and stepfather.

Her mother resembled an older, slightly heavier version of Lara. Yet Case could tell right away where the fire in her soul came from. Lara and her mother's relationship was one of necessity. She explained to Case many times early on how the only reason she was allowed to live under the same roof was due to her mom feeling bad about how she had treated her and her half-sister, Rachel, growing up. Without going into great lengths of detail, she would paint a picture of an evil soul that supposedly was submerged beneath the surface of her mother.

Case would always listen patiently, realizing that they were cut from completely different cloths. He appreciated their differences in background, and was always careful when choosing his words. He knew that anything he would say to try to help the situation would only complicate things. And having never been in her shoes personally, his outlook on her life was nothing but speculation. He was interested in hearing the entire story before judging a situation he had no familiarity with.

He quickly developed a fatherly relationship with Bailey. Within weeks of meeting her, she would run to the door in excitement when he would arrive to greet him with a two-year-old bear-hug. She would wrap her short arms around his bulky neck as if he was carrying a life supply of chocolate or ice cream with him at all times.

"You better be careful, son," boomed Brett Metzger across the table.

"What do you mean, Dad? Careful with what?"

"You're in a very precarious situation."

"In what way?"

"Well… you've suddenly got everything that you seek in life. Everything you've told me you want. Just fell into your lap. Almost overnight."

Case tapped his left hand on the kitchen table and took a moment to reflect on what his father was conveying to him. "So you're telling me it's a bad idea to date Lara because she has a kid. Is that what you're saying?"

"Absolutely not," his father said immediately. "All I'm saying is be careful."

"Do you not like her? I've only brought her here a couple of times. And when you meet Bailey you will see how cute and smart she is, Dad."

"I don't think you are hearing me, son. She seems like a real nice young lady, and I'm sure beyond a doubt that her little girl is as sweet as a buttermilk pie." The look in Brett Metzger's eyes could stop a burglar dead in his tracks, and at the same time was a look of reason. His view always came without prejudice, and Case understood where he was coming from, but had refused to see the situation with the same candor as his father. Across the table sat the icon of integrity that had been passed down as if it was hereditary.

"Just be careful," his dad continued slowly, reassuring Case with his facial expression that he wasn't trying to talk him out of anything, but to approach the situation like any other, with a level head. "I know you, son, I know your aspirations, and I don't blame you for feeling like you do right now. It's new.

It's exciting. Beautiful girl. Your own family. Your own path…Just appeared right in front of you. The temptation to move even faster than you already are is going to come at you like an addiction. I just want you to take your time. She ain't goin' anywhere, I can tell she sees who you are—and she's probably more ready for those things than anyone can see."

"Alright, Pop, I understand," Case snapped back quickly as he stood up from the table to refill his sweet tea from the pitcher on the counter. Brett closed his eyes for an extended blink, hoping that his words were not just noise, but that Case would be rational as he had always taught him to be.

Case put the tea up to his lips, finishing the entire glass without stopping to breathe, and grabbed his keys from the counter. "I'll be back around 11:30 or 12."

The drive across the county seemed longer this night. He had been awaiting her call to say she was done with class and that he could come and spend the rest of the late-evening hours together. Out of character, Case wound around the turns of several backroads without the sound of a mix CD or the radio, but only the repeated words of his father resounding in his mind.

'What's wrong with moving fast?' he thought. 'Like he said. I know what I want. And I'll figure out if this fits the bill quicker this way.' He continued to fight hard to justify his thoughts as he continued along the bridge, crossing the Monocacy River into Urbana and New Market. He had timed it perfectly. The red lights of the Cobalt's brakes lit up the dark blue-purple sky that surrounded the town house parking area. The sky seemed to drop from the stars and fill up the air around them as the Mustang came to a stop beside her car. The clicking sounds of a cooling engine played behind them as he greeted her with a kiss.

"How was class?"

"Boring. As always. I can't wait to be done with this crap so I can get a real job."

"Soon enough, babe." Case grabbed her book bag from the back seat and threw it over his white T-shirt, resting on his broad shoulder as the two walked toward the end unit where Bailey had already been put down for the night.

"I feel like it's been forever since I have seen Bailey. Sucks she is in bed already," Case whispered, setting down the book bag next to the stairwell leading to her bedroom as Lara exited from checking on her.

"She was not in a good mood today, I think she might be getting a cold."

"Well, that's a shame, little squirt doesn't deserve to not feel good. I hope she was just tired or something."

"I'm really nervous about leaving her this weekend. She's never been away from me that long, I hope she will be good for her dad."

Case tiptoed into the bedroom at the end of the hall behind her and quietly closed the door, speaking somewhat louder now that walls separated them from the others on the same floor. "I can't imagine what it feels like, but I'm sure she will be fine."

Lara lay down on her small, single-sized bed after changing into an old band's T-shirt and sweatpants, preparing to retire for the night. She turned on the television propped in the corner of the room as Case somehow found a way to squeeze in beside her on the inside of the bed that was flush with the wall. He wrapped his arm around her and squeezed the lower part of her shoulder and opposite arm with his hand. The two sat in silence from a few minutes before resuming a conversation he could sense she was avoiding.

"What did you want to do this weekend after we drop her off? Did you have any plans already?" Case said, looking at her smooth skin as the lights of the screen reflected off of her face, changing color with each new scene playing across from them.

"I haven't really thought about it much. I need to do our laundry and get schoolwork done, so it won't be much different. I am going to worry about her the whole time anyway."

"Well, Alan asked if we wanted to come up to his family's lake house near Deep Creek on Saturday and stay the night. Ben is going, he said, and I think Cage and his girlfriend are going to go if we do. I told them that I would talk to you and see."

"Ben, your cousin?"

"Yeah, the one you met last week at Scott and Marie's house."

Case could tell she was eager to say yes, but was afraid to. "We could leave right after Bailey gets dropped off and by the time we leave to come back on Sunday, it will be time to go get her." Case didn't want to push too hard, but he wanted her to meet Alan. Alan was a great judge of character and didn't filter his intuition toward any girl that Case ever introduced to him. The only female interest that Case ever had around that Alan approved of had been Lacey, but lying in the bed thinking back, he couldn't remember a single female friend that Alan had liked. He was hopeful that Alan would accept Lara into the group. He felt good about her chances, but still had an uneasy feeling deep in his stomach that Alan may not be as receptive of her as his other friends had to this point in the short relationship.

"I think it sounds fun, I just don't know if I will enjoy myself being away from her overnight," Lara exhaled heavily, turning her body in the bed to face away from the rapidly changing images of the television. Case sat idle and held her tighter in his arms for a few moments, watching the shadows the small screen created dance along the drywall.

"Listen, babe," Case whispered softly, briefly transforming his voice to one closer resembling the same tone his father had spoken in earlier in the evening. Flexing his bicep and shoulder muscles to move her body closer to his, he moved her on top of him in the bed. Brushing her hair behind her ear, he pulled her in for a gentle kiss, first to the lips and then to her cheek. Looking into her eyes profoundly, he continued to whisper lightly. "I know that it is early, but I want you to know one thing." Her tired eyes seemed to hold back a flood of tears, as they began to well up as she stared patiently back into his gaze. Pausing ever so slightly between them, Case continued his words of reassurance.

"I know this guy up in Heaven, and he made us all. He made me and he made you. He always seems to make everything ok. No matter the circumstance. No matter how bad you let yourself feel. And I trust him. I believe him. So when I look you in the eyes and I tell you everything is gonna be ok, you can believe me."

Case repeated his words once again, following them by sharing another tender kiss. "So, when I look you in the eyes and say everything is going to be ok, what does that mean?"

"That everything will be ok," she said softly, squeezing his body as a child does their teddy bear while resting her head on his chest. "I believe you."

"Goodnight, sweetheart," he said, rubbing her back up and down smoothly. He closed his eyes, fighting back tears of his own as she fell asleep in his grip.

Being careful not to wake her as he got up from the bed, he located the remote to the television and turned it off before kissing her on the forehead. If it weren't for the moonlight leaking through the blinds onto her silky skin, he would not have been able to see her peacefully sleeping face in the darkness, or find his way to the door. As he closed her bedroom door behind him, he stopped outside of Bailey's room before walking down the steps to the front door. Even though she was sound asleep behind the entryway, he whispered, "Sweet dreams, squirt" toward the door as if she could hear him. Like a trained assassin, he exited the house, locking the front door's handle as he shut it without a sound.

Realizing he had left his sweatshirt in Lara's bedroom at the foot of the bed, he put his hands into his pockets, taking in the cool, crisp air of the mid-March night. He had a deep feeling of serenity within himself as he walked toward his car. A feeling that he hadn't felt in some time. He felt a sense of inner pride in being able to comfort her during a new experience in her life that they both knew was inevitable.

Unlike his ride there previously, he sang along with John Mayer on the way home, thinking back to the look on her face the night they had first listened to the song together. *And I'm free. Free fallin'.*

CHAPTER 8

Lakeside Love

• • •

THE COBALT SAT IDLE OUTSIDE of the gas station as the three impatiently waited Bailey's dad's arrival. Case sat in the passenger seat, sweating from the heat blasting at his feet. The mugginess in the vehicle could have been coming from Lara's uneasiness as she nervously bit her fingernails and glanced in the back seat at her daughter. "Daddy will be here soon."

She looked over toward Case and spoke under her breath so that the words would not make their way to the back seat. "He better be." Case tried to reminisce back to the previous week when she had explained that Bailey's father wanted nothing to do with her until he had been court ordered to pay child support earlier that year. The very thought angered him of how someone who had done nothing to deserve a gorgeous baby girl could walk back into her life at the drop of a hat. He couldn't help but feel bitter about the whole situation. He knew that it was out of his control, and Grandma Metzger always preached to "not ever worry about things that were outside your control." Yet he found himself committing the sin of judgment. He didn't know Bailey's father from Adam, but saw the sad and enraged complexion of Lara's face when describing what had happened.

"I still can't believe some people," he said, full of resentment. "It's so dumb that he can just up and decide, 'Hey, Lara – I want to take responsibility now that my wallet's involved."

"Please don't talk about it in front of her."

"I'm sorry, I just don't want to see you hurt. Or her," replied Case, looking out the window into the tree line that framed the outskirts of a small town in Northern Virginia.

"Baby, I think I see Daddy." Lara turned her entire body in the seat and faced Bailey to see her innocent smile as she looked around the vehicle. Bailey had never met her father. She didn't know what a daddy was, other than a character outside the car that her mother brought to her attention.

Case tried to focus elsewhere as he heard the little girl crying, and looked away. In the side mirror he could see a shorter, mid-twenties man holding her as she screamed. He couldn't see Lara but he could hear her voice through the sharp noise. "Hold on, she needs her blanket." Case maneuvered his arm, extending it toward the blue-stitched blanket to his left that was just out of reach. As he pulled back to unhook his seat belt, the door opened. The sheer look of pain reflected clearly toward him when she retrieved the blanket was enough to make him weep. Holding back the strong emotions within, he tried to comfort her as she sat back down.

Her eyes didn't seem as heavy as he had thought they would be. And given the circumstances, she seemed to be doing quite well. Silence filled the air like after a bullrider is thrown to the ground and the audience awaits his destiny. The strong will she exhibited was short-lived, to say the least, and Case placed his hand on her leg as he saw the color of her face disappear. "She doesn't even know who he is," she cried, clearing her tears with her thumb and index fingers together beneath each eyelid. Case was at a rare loss for words and she grimaced as if in physical pain. Real pain.

His conscience begged him to speak, but the words were not there. Another part of him urged him to stay silent, but to make sure she knew his shoulder was there to cry on. The words attempting to escape her mouth were muffled, and he couldn't understand them, but he understood why. Over the next ten minutes he didn't utter a word outside of whispering "I know." For a moment, he thought about the situation he had placed himself in. He wasn't sure if he was helping or making things worse by being there. It was one of many times in Case's life he knew he would never forget. The smell of the air and the sound of each breath would travel with him forever. His sensical memory would bring him back to this moment several times. Not only the next few times he found himself realizing a familiar surrounding, but also for the rest of his life.

Case offered to drive back to Jefferson so that she could attempt to rest both her mind and body, but her sense of protection would not allow her to do so. Still, she appreciated the offer and sat quietly, staring out her window for most of the ride.

The closer they got to Case's house, the more her personality began to re-surface. Case decided that it was the right decision to let her handle this on her own without adding fuel to the fire. Any advice or words of empathy would have only made her day more gloomy, and he was proud that he held back and consoled her in other ways. Lara perked up as Cage and his girlfriend, Liz, came out of the house to join them when they pulled into the driveway.

"Hey, guys," said Lara.

"What's goin' on?" replied Cage. "Lara, this is Liz. I don't think you met her yet, did you?"

Lara, unbuckling her seat belt to move to Case's car with the others, faked a smile toward the young girl. "No, we haven't met. I'm Lara. It's nice to meet you."

"Hi" was all that they would hear from her throughout the entire ride, two and a half hours to Western Maryland. Liz and Cage had been togeth-er for some time but Case was not fond of her. He didn't even know why. Something about her made him feel uneasy, like she couldn't be trusted. Her silence around him didn't help his impression of her. Cage pleaded to his older brother that she was outgoing, but Case didn't see it. When she did speak around him, it was to ask Cage to do or get something for her. But he tolerated her. She made Cage happy, at least on the surface. The boundaries set up around the Metzger household were not difficult to cross, being very receptive of anyone to step through the door. All it took to be accepted as an acting member of the family was a pleasant greeting and being able to joke around with everyone.

Case was the exception. Unlike his parents and younger brothers, he need-ed to test everyone who stepped foot on the property. He needed reassurance from anyone new that they could take his sarcasm, and wouldn't take his jabs seriously. If he thought someone was a stiff, or they appeared to be condescending in any way, they knew it. Rarely would he allow a second chance to earn his respect, but that would come to change.

"Is this it?" Lara said, sitting up in the front seat.

"Yep, that's Alan right there," acknowledged Case, pointing toward a large, tall man wearing an orange backwards hat, cargo shorts, and button-up T-shirt. He stood on the front deck of the cabin with tongs in one hand and a beer in the other.

Stopping the car along the gravel driveway alongside the deck, Case yelled out the window at his friend by his last name. "Good to see your startin' early, Klein!"

"Yep. Ya'll get on over here 'n' eat. Been ready for a half-hour."

As the four joined Alan on the deck, Case suddenly became nervous about Alan meeting Lara for the first time, flipping through his mind like pages in a book for anything that his lifelong friend possibly wouldn't like about her.

"Allllannn," exclaimed Cage as he and Liz made their way inside with the clothes that stored their bags. Alan mocked Cage in an unusually high voice as he turned to grab another beer from the cooler. "Caaage." Alan reverted his attention toward Lara standing next to his buddy on the ground-level deck built of treated wood, opening the fresh beer in the process.

"So, I'm gonna take a shot in the dark and say you're Lara?"

"Yeah, sorry, dude, this is Lara." Case spoke up for her before she could respond. Alan looked her over before plopping down in a deckchair at his side and crossing his tree-like legs as he leaned back.

"Sweet, well, grab a brew, don't cost nothin'."

"No thanks, I don't really like beer," Lara uttered her first words toward Alan, standing awkwardly at Case's side.

"Well, I'm sure there's other stuff inside," Case interjected. "If not, we can run out and get you something else." He could feel Alan formulating a first impression of her without even looking in his direction. And he prayed for the best.

The subject matter of the dinner talk outside went from professional football to getting thoughts on what to do for the rest of the evening. Case and Alan jabbed at Cage with their words between bites of the steaks that had been prepared. Lara found the conversation hilarious and for short periods even let Bailey slip from her mind. She was surprised to be having a good time, despite feeling so low earlier.

"I'm down for just chilling tonight and turning the hot tub on," said Cage, ignoring the frequent jokes at his expense.

"Whatever, I have enough booze to occupy us for the night," said Alan, cracking open yet another beer, exerting a loud belch that bellowed through the woods that surrounded them.

Case grabbed the plastic containers of ketchup and other condiments and addressed the group, standing up from the picnic table. "I'm gonna start taking this stuff back inside."

Without a verbal response, Cage arose and grabbed extra plates and utensils to help out and Liz followed suit.

"Be right back, babe," Case said toward Lara, placing a hand on her shoulder before filling up both hands and walking inside. As he got to the door held open by his brother, he looked back toward the table, realizing that Lara and Alan were left there to talk alone.

Ben showed up shortly after dinner, carrying his own cooler of beer from his truck. Through the darkness, the group that had been drinking outside on the deck could hear his boots crunching along the gravel leading to them.

"Yeahhhhh!" shouted Ben loudly as he approached the crew. "Cage, what the hell are you doing!? Where is your beer?!"

"I'm drinking cranberry and vodka tonight, it's Liz's favorite."

"Wuss," Ben muttered, reaching into the red igloo cooler he held at his side, throwing one in the direction of Case.

With a free hand, Case caught the beer just before it would have struck Lara's face. Thankfully the beer didn't strike his new lover, Case tried continuing in conversation before being cut off by Lara.

"Wow, Ben. You're such an asshole," she said, referring to the close call. "You got water in my eye."

"My bad, Lara," Ben uttered, just loud enough for the group to hear. An awkward silence filled the air of the forest like how the wind suddenly stops before commencing in a storm. "I wasn't trying to hit you with it."

In the waiting seconds before her reply, not a breath or a cricket could be heard. The bubbling sounds from the warming hot tub in the distance seemingly came to an abrupt stop to make way for the uncomfortable situation that had been created.

"Well, you almost did. I–"

"Babe, he didn't mean to do it. He said he was sorry," Case interjected.

"Right. Never mind," remarked Lara quickly. "I am going to go inside to call and check on Bailey."

"Alright," said Case with a surprised look on his face.

Lara made her way into the cabin, gently slamming the door behind her. Loud enough to know that it wasn't normal, but not loud enough to signal that she was truly upset. Case watched her walk away, puzzled to say the least. For the first time, Liz fit in with the group as they all sat silently watching Lara's silhouette fade through the kitchen window into the living room of the cabin. Case's eyes appeared to be glued to the door that she had just entered. He wasn't quite sure how to react to what had just transpired in such a short amount of time. He was fearful to look toward Alan. He didn't know what the two had spoken about earlier for the duration he himself was inside. Although hopeful that Alan's impression was a good one, his fears were confirmed as he slowly turned his head toward him as he heard his large friend speak.

"Um." Alan paused, tightening his lips and turning them to the side while lowering his eyebrows down close to the bridge of his nose. "What was that all about...?"

"I'm not sure, man. I've never seen her get upset like that before. At least not from something like that," Case rebutted toward Alan, turning his attention toward Ben to see him shrug his shoulders, taking a long gulp of the beer gripped tightly in his hand.

"Wow, dude. Really?" Alan questioned rhetorically, finishing off what could have been his tenth beer since their arrival.

"She is probably just on edge, man. She's never spent a night away from her daughter before. She's trying to hold on loosely, ya know?"

Cage spoke up to join in on the dialogue he had been witness to for several minutes now. "Welllll, were gonna go around to the hot tub. Any of you all comin'?"

Alan shook his head side to side as Case spoke. "Yeah, I'll be over when Lara gets back." As Case's younger brother and his quiet partner faded off out of his peripheral vision, Case continued to the conversation.

"Give her a break, though, Klein, she really wants you guys to like her."

Ben leaned to the side of his chair, maneuvering his hand around the ice-filled water of his cooler as he spoke up. "Ha, I like her just fine. That was my bad. I mean I am an asshole... so," he said, cracking open another cold one and setting it on the arm of his chair.

The crackling sounds of a bug zapper filled the air along with the hoot of an owl off in the distance as Case awaited a similar response from Alan that would never come.

"So what took you so long to get here, Ben?" Alan changed the subject purposely.

Case felt that Alan had overreacted to the entire situation, and felt bitter thinking that he was already not giving her a chance. He knew it would be an uphill battle to clear the water that had just been muddied by such a simple mistake. Alan was a great friend, and always would provide his forthright opinion, regardless of the ramifications. Case admired that most about his great friend he had known basically from birth, and held himself to the same standard. But he still couldn't help believe that Alan's thoughts of his girlfriend were not currently in a positive light. He expected a more understanding approach from Alan when he had mentioned how she was spending her first night away from Bailey. For the first time since meeting Lara, a sense of uncertainty crept into Case. It scared him. So much, to the point that he arose from his deckchair to go check on her. She had been inside for the better part of a half-hour.

"I'll be back, fellas, I'm gonna go see if she is ready to get in the hot tub."

Alan nodded his head like a stereotypical high school jock toward another in the hallway between classes, and Ben raised his hand, pointing a finger at Case in acknowledgement, not breaking from his long-winded explanation of the traffic on his trip to the lake.

Case found Lara sitting on the bed of the spare bedroom in which he had previously dropped off their bags, having just got off the phone. "Hey," he whispered softly as she brought the phone down to her lap. "How's she doin'?"

"She's good. They said she played in the snow all day and didn't cry at all except for like a half-hour right when she got in the car," Lara said in low, disappointed tone. "It was so weird to talk to my own daughter on the phone."

"Ha, I'm sure that's a unique experience for you," replied Case jokingly in an attempt to lighten the mood of the room. "It's good she's having fun. And it's ok for you to, too." Lara looked up toward his body towering in front of her at the end of the bed for the first time since he walked in the room, revealing a look of disdain in her eyes. He couldn't tell if she was upset that her daughter was having a good day without being by her side, or if it stemmed from being away from her in general. "Let's go get in the hot tub. Have a couple drinks. You will feel better, I promise."

"Yeah, let's go outside with your cousin and your best friend who don't like me. That should be so much fun," she responded sarcastically.

Case quickly became serious. "What are you talking about? Why wouldn't they like you?"

"Apparently it was blasphemy to call Ben out on throwing a beer at my head."

"Babe, he was throwing it to me, he wasn't thinking."

"Well, I saw how Alan looked at me while we were sitting there," she remarked, "Don't act like you didn't see it, too."

"Larebear..."

"I'm sure they talked about how much of a bitch I am, when I came inside."

"Babe. Where is this coming from? I know it's been a really stressful day for you, but they don't even really know you yet. This is only like the second or third time you've met Ben. And you've known Alan for what? Three hours?"

"Well, you didn't even say anything to either of them. Why didn't you say something to Ben about it?"

"I didn't think it was necessary, he didn't do it on purpose. And he said he was sorry."

"Yeah, after I called him out on it."

"Well, I'm sorry. I just didn't want to cause a scene. And I know Ben. He can be cold-hearted at times, but I know he wouldn't deliberately throw something at you."

"It's fine. I will live," Lara said reluctantly. "But I can tell when someone doesn't like me."

"Who doesn't like you!?" Case raised his voice slightly. "They don't know you. So there is no way that either of them disapprove of you." Even though Case knew deep down that her emotional intelligence had given her a read like a professional poker player, he insisted that the evening's brief verbal scuffle had not been enough for a lasting first impression. "They know that you are going through some stuff right now with Bailey. They understand."

'But did they?' Ben seemed to let the entire thing roll off of his shoulder, while Alan had evidently provided his thoughts of the situation toward her with body language or facial expressions. Case struggled to find a way to calm her down and convince her that his friends outside waiting took her reaction with a grain of salt. But he needed to convince himself first.

Digging deep for the right words to bring what had become a production into perspective, Case sat down next to her on the bed, hearing Jason Aldean's 'Amarillo Sky' playing faintly through the window from the radio between the hot tub and horseshoe pit in the backyard. He grabbed her hand in his, pulling it up to his lips, and kissed it gently. Lara's mannerisms hadn't changed one bit since he planted his broad frame at her side. As he put their hands back to their waists he gripped hers firmly, interlocking their fingers together. Dozens of thoughts passed through his mind as he continued to struggle for words to settle the air. She glanced toward him from the corners of her glazed blue eyes as he cleared his throat with a closed mouth.

"Babe, they are all gonna like you...whether it's tonight, tomorrow, or after they have been around you a thousand times."

She turned her head slowly toward him, looking up at his eyes sitting eight inches above her own. She didn't speak but still begged for him to explain further. Case's next words would change the complexion of their two-and-a-half-month-old relationship from that day forward. Not knowing if he truly meant them, he rebelled against his own intuition and spoke them anyway, putting her hand now into both of his. Images of his father's warning to let things happen naturally swirled through his mind, perhaps a moment too late.

"They like what makes me happy. And that includes the one who makes me happy. Especially the woman I am in love with."

Lara freed her hands quickly and leaned into his full embrace, resting her head on his shoulder, and wrapped her arms around him as far as she could reach. She squeezed him tightly as a single tear rolled down her tan, previously troubled face. Her voice trembled in happiness as she said it back to him. "I love you, too" resounded loud and clear to Case, even though her words were muffled by her face being implanted deep into the sleeve covering his shoulder.

He held her tightly and kissed the top of her head and stared toward the wooden walls of the room with wide eyes, realizing he had said three coveted words prematurely in a desperate effort to resolve the situation. And there was no taking them back.

CHAPTER 9

A Wedding two Remember

• • •

"I LOVE YOU, TOO, BABE, but I gotta go – we have to get Scott to the church," Case muttered through his phone, standing in the middle of what would become Mr. and Mrs. Scott Notroh's living room later that day.

"That Lara?" Scott said, appearing out of the hallway.

"You know it was," replied Alan in a less than excited tone, feet propped up and folded over the corner of the recliner.

"Oh, yeah? What'd she have to say?" Scott spoke in Case's direction.

"I love you, Casey Wasey!!" interjected Ben in a loud, high-pitched voice. "Can't wait to see you later!"

Scott and Case chuckled simultaneously for a second or two before Case could finally answer.

"Just wanted to see how you are doin' on the big day!" said Case, escalating his tone with each word before finishing off his statement with a firm punch to Scott's shoulder. "I'm nervous about givin' this speech. So I know you're feelin' the heat today, buddy."

"Not yet," replied Scott. "I'm sure when it gets closer I'm gonna be nervous as anything."

"Bull," said Ben across the room before taking a seat on the tan love seat. "Your voice is shaking already."

Alan sat back further in the recliner, rattling off a text message to someone before looking up to join in on the other guys' conversation about the day's itinerary. "What is there to be nervous about? He's lived with her here for two years and they've been together since like 2nd grade."

"6th grade," Scott corrected him with a smile, the glazed look in his eyes giving away his understandable anticipation of his wedding day. "We should probably get over to the church soon. I don't want to get there after her and risk seein' her, ya know?"

"Looks like Keith is finally out here," said Ben, witnessing Keith's yellow sports car pull into the driveway through the bay window behind the couch.

"Yeah, man," said Case to Scott. "Wouldn't want that. We can leave as soon as these two characters decide to peel their asses off their chairs, since Keith is out here now. Is Mac meeting us there?"

"Yeah, he had to work this morning," said Scott, referring to the fifth and final groomsman in the party. He was a friend of Scott's from college who didn't hang out with the group on a normal basis. The crew got along with him well, but he lived about an hour away and wasn't able to join in on a lot of things they did together.

"So, let's get this show on the road," exclaimed Alan, sitting his large frame up slowly in the recliner. "Sooner we get him there, the sooner he can tap Marie on the honeymoon and we tap the keg."

All four friends laughed in unison at Alan's euphemism and lined up at the screen door, single file, moving slow as if they were cattle being herded through a fence. Keith, Case's college roommate, stood up from his car and kept one hand on the door.

"Too late now, Dubbs!" yelled Ben toward Keith, referring to him by his last name. "What's the matter? You don't have a damn watch?"

Keith's extremely calm demeanor and low voice defined him to the group and to all whom he came into contact with. He was the closest with Case: having lived with him for four years, they certainly had ups and several downs in their relationship, but Keith's part in the band of brothers about to make their way toward Scott's wedding was a necessary one. He was more than often the voice of reason, and never let the group get into too much trouble. He stood at 6 foot 4, and was as strong as an ox. When he, Case, and Alan would all sit in the same vehicle, it was shocking that their three large, muscular bodies didn't have to stop at weigh stations along the highway.

Keith moved his hand toward the long, dark, red beard which covered his face like a Viking and stroked it, flexing his arm in the process. Shaking his head toward Ben as if to intimidate him, Keith Dubbs didn't respond to the smart aleck remark with words.

"I was just playin' with ya..." Ben's voice slowed to almost a fearful tone.

"Jesus, Ben, what the hell are you scared of him for?" laughed Alan, walking past the group toward his Jeep which was parked furthest away.

"I'm not scared of him. Screw you, Klein!"

"Yeah, whatever," Alan said, turning completely around and back-pedaling toward his vehicle. "We all riding separate, I take it?"

"Scott is riding over with me since he's leaving in a limo tonight, Mr. High Roller!" exclaimed Case, grabbing his smaller friend around the neck with his entire arm and shaking Scott's entire body.

"I gotta drive separate unless you're bringing me back to my truck after the reception, Klein."

"Not happening, Ben!" yelled Alan who now faced away from the rest of the group, struggling to open the door to his Jeep.

"Well, if you can't get your door open now, I sure as hell don't wanna ride with you after you drink like a fish later," said Ben as he climbed onto the running board of his truck with the door open. "BEHHHHHHHH' sounded the truck's horn in the Jeep's direction at the same time as Ben's body hit the bench seat of the lifted truck. In response to Ben's obnoxiousness, Alan put his arm out the window, extending one finger in the truck's direction.

Case burst into laughter at the two bickering back and forth at each other. "Ben, buddy!... I don't think he's saying you're number one!!!"

The vehicles lined up in procession down the road connecting Jefferson with nearby Middletown, where the church waited for its groom. The Mustang was the last in line, carrying the best man and the man of the hour. For the amount of nerves that accompany any man on his wedding day, Scott was seemingly holding it together. Case was grateful for the opportunity to have one last conversation with his buddy before he crossed into a life of marriage. Although Scott and Marie swore that nothing would change when it came to their social life, Case knew it was inevitable. Maybe not right away, but things would slowly change. He savored every last second of their personal conversation on the way to the venue. Stone Manor was a beautiful setting in the woods just west of Jefferson. Scott kept the focus on his best man most of the way, attempting to elude his nervous system's efforts and stay at ease.

"So you are saying 'I love you' already? That's kinda fast, isn't it? It's been what? Three months?"

"Yeah, I guess it is soon. But when you feel it, you feel it," replied Case, keeping his eyes on the road in front of him.

"I mean it's awesome, dude, she seems like a good girl from when I've been around her. Just didn't know you all were moving that fast."

....

"You ok, dude?"

"Yeah, I'm good. Are you ok?! I'd be a wreck if I were you right now."

"I'm good, I'm good. I'm glad to have all you guys with me today. It's really great to have you all around to share this with me... But Case, you look like something is bothering you."

"Nope. Shipshape."

"Man, I know you. What is it?"

Case exhaled and glanced toward his friend longer than he should have, given the fact that he was driving. "It was too soon. And I said it first."

"Really? I figured that she did... That's cool. Like you said, though, man, when you feel it, you feel it."

"But I don't."

"Wait... You told a girl you loved her when you don't? Where's Case Metzger and who are you?"

"I dunno, man, it isn't that I don't feel strong feelings for her. I really do. I have fun with her. But after I said it the first time something wasn't right."

"What do you mean?"

"She was all upset, having a terrible day because she was away from Bailey and then there was this big, unnecessary scene when Ben almost hit her throwing a beer to me."

"Heard about that. Alan told me."

"Oh I am sure that he did. But anyway, what was I saying?"

"She was upset the first time you told her."

"Oh, yeah. Well, I just felt helpless, man. I wanted to make her feel better, and convince her that my opinion of her should be all that matters, but I couldn't put it into words. Before I knew it she was all over me saying it back."

"Well, did you tell her you think you said it too soon? But you do feel really strongly? Maybe you rushed it a little?"

"Wait until you see her face when I say it."

"Well, you gotta be honest, dude. You're the most honest person I know. Even when you shouldn't be sometimes. You don't sugar-coat things. You are Case."

"That's just it, man. I don't know that I am sugar-coating it. I think I'm just scared."

"Scared of what?"

"Well, Pop was right. He told me to be really careful. Because all at once it's like I have my own little family."

"I told you the same thing, man. I really like her so far, but just gotta let the cards fall where they will. Don't force anything."

"Says the man who is marrying his middle and high school sweetheart," Case chuckled.

"I'm a lucky guy. I know it."

"I know you do, dude. That's why it is impossible to not be jealous of you. You deserve today, man."

"Thanks, man. I can't say enough how happy I am to have you up there with me today."

"Wouldn't wanna be anywhere else in the world."

"And don't be jealous of me, man. Everything is gonna fall into place for you, too. Just be you like you always are. Everything happens for a reason. You never know. Maybe you said it at the perfect time. Maybe today is the day everything falls into place. Maybe today you see her and you feel that overwhelming feeling I have every time I see Marie."

"Yeah... Maybe," Case said, turning the Mustang sharply onto a backroad leading toward Stone Manor in the distance where the two could see lines of chairs set up on the lawn outside

"Maybe, maybe not. But trust me. You will get what you deserve, man. And it could be Lara."

"I am glad that you are so sure." Case took his hand off of the shift knob and placed it roughly on his friend's shoulder in the passenger seat and squeezed firmly, "Up, here it is, man, hope you are ready."

"Ready as I'm gonna get."

• • •

Scott and his groomsmen grouped together in a large room on the first level of the building, sitting around in various chairs and on the floor where they would kill the minutes leading up to the ceremony.

"One hour, Scott. Almost time!"

"Wait, it's 3 o'clock already?!" Scott exclaimed, leaning back against the wall next to their restroom.

"Yeah, buddy!" yelled Alan. "Ok, Case, go out and get it!"

"Get wh-hat? What are you guys g-getting?" Scott stammered.

"Something to help you out with that damn stutter you are developing!" joked Case as he buttoned the top button of his bright green vest, the rest of the group erupting into immense laughter while Scott sat on the floor, having not yet begun changing into his tuxedo.

"Yeah, man you need something to take the edge off. You've sounded like a five-year-old all day," said Ben, continuing what had become a roast of the groom.

"Oh, he's been like this all day? And I missed it? Son of a," said Mac, who had joined the group minutes earlier.

"Yep. He's been trying to hide it. But we all know that he's going to shit his pants again when he gets out there."

"OK, Alan, we don't need to go there," Case replied, walking out the door to fetch the bottle of Canadian whiskey and Dixie cups he had hidden in the back seat of his car. Before bursting into laughter once again, he repeated himself as he closed the door. "Really don't need to go there!"

Case was startled to see large groups of people already in attendance, some cutting through the building to greet Scott's and Marie's parents who stood in the large room Case was walking through to go to his car.

"Don't you clean up nice?" he heard a female voice say from behind him.

"He does, doesn't he? Goodness gracious."

Case turned around to see both Scott's and Marie's mothers amongst a group of well-dressed people he didn't recognize.

"Ha, thanks. Congratulations to you both. I have to get something from my car for him."

"How's he doing in there? Is my baby sweating bullets yet?" said Scott's mom.

"Ha getting pretty close. But we are taking care of him. I'll be back in just one second."

Case heard his name said a few more times behind him as he walked toward the front door of the building. Something along the lines of "That is Case, the best man," but he couldn't quite make out the sentences in the distance clearly.

As he shut the front door behind him and briskly jogged down the long set of steps toward the large gravel lot of cars, he saw a familiar vehicle coming to a stop near his car. The closer he got to his car, he felt his heart begin to beat faster. He had never seen her look so beautiful. She wore a dark brown summer dress and her skin seemed to be the perfect shade to go with it. Although the sun was beating down on his jet black tuxedo, he knew that the warm feeling coursing through his entire body wasn't from its rays, but rather was radiating from within.

"Hiiiiii!" he heard her say as he reached into his pocket. As he popped the trunk with the keyless entry on his key chain, the words of encouragement from his best friend echoed through his mind:

'Maybe today is the day everything falls into place. Maybe today you see her and you feel that overwhelming feeling I have every time I see Marie.'

"Hey, handsome! Did you hear me?! I said how are you?!"

He picked up the brown paper bag from the trunk and a half-full bag of Dixie cups and slammed the trunk shut.

"I'm great, Lacey. How about you?"

CHAPTER 10

Receptions

• • •

THE WEDDING CEREMONY PLAYED OUT just as Case had expected it to. A beautiful blue sky surrounded the 150 plus in attendance as he stood next to his best friend, as proud to be a part of the day as Scott was to be getting married. For moments at a time while the preacher talked, he even forgot that Lara and Lacey were in the audience. But for only moments. He glanced several times toward his family and Lara sitting in a back row, shooting smiles at them, then back to Scott and Marie, with his hand behind him. And finally to his long-lost friend, Lacey. He felt ashamed that he had lost touch with her. He felt ashamed that he had never mentioned one of his greatest friends to Lara at all. But at the same time, he knew why he hadn't brought her up.

She hadn't just slipped his mind. He had been trying to force himself to not think of her. He knew that his mind would travel to her regardless of how well things were going with Lara. They hadn't talked since before he and Lara had met, and, as awful as it felt, it was on purpose. He wasn't sure that he could put his feelings toward her behind him and move on toward someone else. Feeling uneasy about where the day could lead, he tried to vow to himself during the couple's vows.

This is Scott and Marie's day. Don't focus on yourself, Case. Don't let today become about you. I'm in love with Lara. And that's that. I think.

"You may now kiss the bride," said the preacher. Case's attention was pulled toward the newly married couple and he escaped his own predicament for a moment. The crowd erupted into cheers as Mr. and Mrs. Scott Notroh made their way down the aisle, walking together as husband and wife for the first time.

"'Bout time!!!" yelled Alan from beside the best man.

"Yeah!!!" followed Ben even louder than Alan. "Attaboy, Scotty!"

As Case and Marie's sister made their way through the center of the crowd, arm-in-arm following the newly-weds, he focused his attention straight ahead toward the horizon. In the distance, he watched the pine trees swaying slightly from the light breeze.

"That was beautiful, wasn't it?" said Marie's sister.

"Huh? Oh, yeah. Sure was. Been a long time comin'."

"I think we all need to go over and take pictures before the reception."

"Yeah, we will just follow them." Cased nodded in the direction of Scott and Marie heading back around the side of the building toward a large pond, with a dock that went almost halfway out onto the water.

They had made it through the crowd and were in pursuit of the newly-weds when Case saw an orange dress out of the corner of his eye. He knew it was Lara, and looked toward her. He wasn't sure if he was too far away for her to see him wink in her direction, so he blew her a kiss. As she mimicked catching it, she put both arms across her chest as if hugging herself, and turned to Lorrie Metzger and began to speak. Just as Case went beyond the building toward the pond, he saw Lacey approaching his parents to greet them. And Lara.

Case's thoughts whirled through his mind as the camera flash blinded him once again, posing with the rest of the group under the shade of a tall elm tree. The bridal party were all joking with each other, smiling and laughing. Meanwhile the guests for the day were all gathered towards a large pavilion in preparation for the reception. He didn't want to think about the possibilities that could become of Lara and Lacey meeting each other, whether good or bad. He imagined the context of their conversation, and it wrenched him inside knowing that both of them could respond with the words, 'Oh well, he's never mentioned you before.'

"What is your problem, Case?" rattled off Alan. "You in a trance over there?"

"No, sorry. I spaced out for a minute."

"Well, space your ass out over here with the rest of us," joked Ben.

"Ben, I WILL throw you in that pond. Get to stepping," Alan sounded off lowly, staring him down in the process.

Surprisingly, Keith joined in on the conversation. "Yeah, Ben. You aren't even drinking yet and you're already being annoying."

"What?? All I said was Case needed to come over here with the rest of us. You guys were saying it, too."

"Are you still standing there?!"

"Haha, guys, leave him be. He may be my older cousin, but we all know if he wants to get brave I'll toss him in the drink, too," said Case, beginning to catch up with the group alongside Alan and Keith.

"Well, as long as you don't throw Lara *a* drink. She might have a coronary," said Ben as he scurried toward the group, fearful that his three counterparts may actually come through on their offer.

Case was brought back to the night at the lake and how confused he had felt. Just as confused as he currently was.

"What's he talking about?" said Keith, looking toward Case with a peculiar look on his face.

As Alan chuckled under his breath, Case made it a point to not look to his left for any reaction. He didn't need to. He knew he was shaking his head.

"Nothing. He's an idiot. I don't believe we are related by blood sometimes."

With a simple "Hmm," Keith was satisfied with the answer given.

As the three finally joined the group and got into place for another picture, Alan spoke up over the muttering conversation between them all. "So, how many more of these are there? I'm gettin' pretty parched over here," he said, patting his round stomach over the top of the tuxedo jacket.

"Just like two or three more," said Scott with a seemingly permanent smile on his face. His day had finally come, and nothing anyone said or did could change it.

"Pretty sure your tank isn't on 'E', Klein?" said Case, cracking a smile for the first time in several minutes. "I'm sure the sweat on your forehead has enough alcohol to clean a flesh wound."

The group erupted into laughter at the quip, which would eventually be the bride and groom's favorite photo of the day. Case could not have timed his joke more perfectly, and Alan took verbal beatings even better than handing them out. As the group's chatter finally simmered down, Alan grinned toward Case, laughing in the process. "Where do you come up with stuff?"

"Never a dull moment with Case," added Marie.

"That's why he's my best man," replied Scott, joining hands with his bride. "This speech ought to be good."

"I don't know why you all are building this up so much. I am for sure going to disappoint all of you."

"Shut up, Case," Mac added. "I don't even know you that well, but I know I can't wait to hear this speech."

Case looked toward Mac, nodding his head at him as a respectful gesture, trying to hide the nerves that had crept into him over the previous few minutes. He had been so preoccupied with thinking about Lacey being there, Lara meeting her, how he felt when he saw Lacey outside at his car, whether or not he was really in love with Lara, amongst several others. He had neglected to even think about what he was going to say. 'Damn it, Case!' he thought. 'This is their day... Time to focus.'

As the group filed up in line to be announced to the party, Scott tapped an uncharacteristically quiet Case on the shoulder from behind. "What's wrong, dude?"

"Nothin', man," Case said over his shoulder, trying desperately to focus on the task at hand.

"You sure you are ok? You are being really quiet today."

"Yeah, I'm good. It's your all's day. Trying not to make an ass of myself."

"Well, you can still talk!" Marie said, fixing the train of her dress.

"I am talking."

"No, Casey. You are acting weird today."

"Well, I'm not trying to."

"See. You didn't even say anything about me calling you Casey!"

Case laughed softly. "I told you it's your day. I'm just kind of wrapped up in everything today. A lot to take in."

"Haha a lot for YOU to take in?" chimed Scott.

"Ha, yeah. Just so happy for you guys. I want everything to go the way you want it to."

"Well, you can start by being Case."

"Ok. I'll try that."

"And now I'd like to hand the mic over to the best man, Case Metzger," sounded through the large speakers. The bridal party stood at their seats behind a long table with fine china, flowers, and lit candles, atop a silk white tablecloth. All eyes moved toward Case as he took the microphone from the maid of honor. He took a moment to regroup his thoughts and tried to clear his mind. Glancing toward a table toward his right he saw his parents, Cage, Call, and Lara staring at him in anticipation. They all smiled at him and he returned a look, wrinkling the skin above his forehead and raising his eyebrows as if to say, 'Well, here goes nothin'.' In the few moments of silence before he began to speak, he continued to scan the room, admiring all of the faces focused on his own. To the audience it was mere seconds, but to him it felt as if he had been standing there mute for an hour. Lacey's expression was the last thing he saw before putting the microphone to his lips. She held her hands to her face as if she were in prayer, but her smile gleamed through them. Something in her eyes made Case suddenly feel at ease as he cleared his throat.

"Well, here we are," he began, turning his body toward the married couple next to him, then back toward the audience. "As Marie's sister said, I'm Case Metzger. And I would like to thank everybody for being here today to join us in celebrating Scott and Marie's wedding. I would also like to express my sincere jealousy that I didn't get be the first one clinking the glass with the knife," he continued, looking in the maid of honor's direction with a wink. "Always wanted to do that." The 150 plus crowd laughed briefly and came to a dull roar.

"I really don't know where to begin. I've been best friends with Scott since the day I met him. And I'm one of few of us out here today who can say he knew Scott before he and Marie got together. He is one of the most loyal people I have ever had the pleasure of being around, and he puts everyone else before himself. He knows how to make people laugh when they are having a bad day, he knows what to say when you need advice, and he can make you feel like you've known him forever within a couple minutes of meeting him." Case paused and scanned the room for a few seconds before continuing.

"He is great at everything that he does. Well, besides showing up on time, and driving.... and remembering directions.... and from what Marie says... Laundry and dishwashing.... but everything else he is great at." Case stopped his speech to join in with the laughter filling the air at the groom's expense, then placed a hand on his friend's shoulder and brought the microphone back up to his mouth. "But in all seriousness, Scott has been one of the greatest friends I could ever have asked for, and I don't deserve him. But Marie does. And if there is one thing he is great at above all others, it is loving that beautiful woman in the white dress next to him. I've been lucky enough to get to see them grow with each other since we were in middle school, and I know that he loves her more every day. There isn't anything that could happen that would ever make that trend stop. And from all of those experiences that I've been through with them, I've gotten to know Marie more and more. And I've gotten to see what Scott sees in her. We didn't always see eye-to-eye in the beginning... and that might be because she is a good foot and a half shorter than I am.... or it may have been because I was afraid she was stealing my best friend away from me. But as it turns out, she is the perfect match for Scott, and I know that if she could put up with having me and the rest of us on this side of the table for the last few years, she won't ever have any issues with Scott. I know I speak for all of us here when I say that I wish them both the best for the rest of their life together, and if any of us loves someone half as much as these two love each other, that we've found something worth holding onto. Now if everyone would please raise your glass, or whatever you have in front of you, I'd like to propose a toast..... because I know I have been talking a while and Keith and Alan want to eat soon."

Amongst the eruption of laughter, Case grinned toward his friends shaking their heads and chuckling, then raised his glass.

"May God be with them every step of their journey, and sustain the level of love filling these tables here today for the rest of their lives. To Scott and Marie. Cheers."

• • •

"Wow, dude. Did you memorize that?" said Alan, sitting down next to Case with a full plate.

"Ha – no, I didn't know what I was going to say."

"Really, dude? I figured you rehearsed," added Scott with a laugh from the center of the table. "I appreciate it, man, I liked it a lot."

"No big deal. I'm glad you liked it."

"I liked it, too," said Lara approaching the head table. "Congratulations, you guys!"

"Thank you."

"Thanks, Lara! Glad you could come!"

"Look at you looking all pretty as usual," said Case, bringing his glass up toward his mouth for another drink. "I see why you wouldn't let me see what you were wearing before today."

"Thank you, baby," Lara responded with a brightly lit smile. "You're going to come sit with us after you eat, right?"

"For sure. How's it going over there?"

"Good. Been listening to old stories about you."

"Oh, yeah? Hopefully nothing too embarrassing."

"Probably not for you. You don't get embarrassed too easily there, sweetie."

"Very true. But you're sitting with Mom and Pop... They do it pretty easily."

"Yeah, and I got to meet Wade and his girlfriend that you had talked about before. They are sitting with us, too. And Cage's friend, Nate."

"Steele? I didn't even see him over there."

"Yep, he's right there," said Lara pointing across the way toward their table where his parents sat in conversation with Cage and his closest friend, Nate Steele. Nate was a ladykiller to say the least. He was about six feet tall, with a jagged jawline, and jet black hair. He was chiseled from head to toe, and anything he draped over his body always seemed to leave every woman in his presence salivating. He was known affectionately by his last name, and nothing but. He was a great friend to Cage, and Case had always considered him as another younger brother. Many nights growing up, Cage would fall asleep early during a sleepover with Steele, and he would venture to Case's room to talk for hours about women, life and family, and they would laugh about Cage always inviting him over and then falling asleep.

Steele was the first to point out that Case always seemed to be the link between everyone, and Case never realized it until the night that they spoke about it. Cage's best friends, Steele and Eddie, were over at the house staying with him. Eddie was Cage's metaphorical twin. They looked nothing alike but spoke in the same tones, and looked at things in the same light that a Metzger by blood would. Case admired them both and could always count on them to protect his actual brother if trouble would ever arise. But on that particular night, Steele brought up the conversation of great friends and how they always seem to drift apart as life goes on. He spoke about how he saw that Case had several great friends and they never seemed to do anything together unless Case was involved. Case introduced most of them to each other after becoming great friends with them himself.

Seeing Steele for the first time in a long time suddenly made Case reminisce to that night. The nerves that had built up in him were settled for a moment, realizing that almost the entire wedding party knew each other because of him. He began to feel really good about his contribution to the day. He felt on top of the world. Like he had accomplished something. He had given a good speech, and his friendships had bloomed beyond his own scope. He didn't realize how long he had been sitting there patting himself on the back until Lara snapped her fingers in front of his face.

"Do you see him now?"

Case suddenly snapped back to reality, "Oh, yeah, I see him. Eddie isn't here?"

"Who's Eddie?"

"Cage's other best friend."

"Oh, yeah, I think I heard them talking about him like he was here. But I haven't met him yet."

"So did you get to here the schpeel about the 'Steele Cage' then?"

"Oh yes," Lara said, laughing. "They think they were made for each other because of their names," she continued sarcastically. "They are pretty funny together over there. And Steele is really hot."

"Who doesn't think so?" said Scott interjecting into the conversation.

"Oh yeah he is. Good thing he isn't a bit older or Scott wouldn't be sitting here with me," quipped Marie.

Marie and Lara both laughed in unison while Case waited for a break in the noise to continue. "He's a great guy. So is Wade, and so is Eddie. I'm glad you got to meet them."

"I thought Wade was kind of weird," Lara said, wrinkling her nose in disapproval.

"I'm weird, and you're with me...You just met him. How is he weird?"

"I don't know."

"Well, that makes sense..." said Case, perturbed at the comment about his tall, lanky, red-haired friend from high school.

"Well, hurry up and finish eating, I want you to sit with me."

"I'm trying to, babe. I will be over soon."

Sensing that Case seemed upset at something, Lara responded curtly. "Fine."

"What? I will eat as fast as I can and be over there with you."

"I said fine," Lara said as she turned and strutted angrily across the leaves of fresh cut grass, reflecting an orangish hue from the setting sun in the west.

As Alan watched Lara walk out of hearing distance, he leaned over to Case, who was eating his prime rib silently as conversations continued amongst the rest of the head table.

"Yeah, so who invited her?"

"Shut up, Alan. I don't care if you don't like her."

"Ha, but you don't even like her. You don't ever snap at a female like that."

"What are you even talking about?"

"Well, it was pretty clear she wants you over there, and now. Better put her first, bro, or she is liable to throw another fit."

"She doesn't know hardly anyone here, that's why she wants me over there. And what does that have to do with me liking her?"

"I know you, man. You don't get all short with someone you are enjoying the company of."

"Whatever you say."

"Want proof?"

Case sat back in his chair, laid his napkin on the table in front of him, and looked toward Alan condescendingly, crossing his arms. "Proof of what?!"

"How Case treats a woman who matters to him."

"What are you doing, a *Case* study?" he said sarcastically, mimicking a laugh.

"Nope. Don't have to. Here comes proof now."

"Proof of what, Alan??" said Lacey as she walked up to the table. "Congrats, guys! So happy for you!" she exclaimed to Scott and Marie at the center of the table. "Thanks for the invite. I'm glad I was able to be here."

"Glad you could, too. Hope Georgia's treating you well," said Marie.

"It is. Almost over, though. I'm done after next semester!"

"That's awesome," said Scott. "Guess you will be back here for good, then."

"That's the plan."

Case didn't even remember what he had been bickering back and forth with Alan about. He sat in awe at her beauty. Hearing her voice made everything negative go away. Nothing else existed. He was cognizant of the fact that she stood right in front of him, but his awareness ended there.

Lacey leaned on the table with one arm in front of Case and Alan. "So what were you two saying when I walked up? Here comes proof? You two are crazy."

"I said I need some 80 proof, and Alan said here comes proof because you were carrying two drinks."

"So you knew that I was bringing you whiskey?! How?!"

"That's really for me?"

"Yeah, I got a whiskey and Cola and I know that's your favorite, so I figured I would bring you one, too."

"Ha, well thanks, darlin'," said Case, surprised at his desperate attempt to cover up what they were talking about. Taking the cold drink from by her hand on the table, he looked toward Alan who was rolling his eyes and shaking his head slightly. "You were right, Klein. She was bringing me a drink."

"I was right alright."

"Well, do I get a dance later? Lacey said, puzzled by the awkwardness of the conversation between Case and Alan.

"You know we are gonna dance, Lace," said Alan.

Case began to feel sick to his stomach. Here she was, flirting with him as usual. And he was in a relationship with Lara. He wasn't sure how receptive Lara would be to him dancing with her. He didn't know what to say. He didn't know what to think.

Before he could speak, the audience was brought to silence by an announcement through the speakers.

"Excuse me, everybody, but if someone has a blue Honda Hatchback, your lights are on. Maryland plate number 4-2-1-C-A-L. Sorry for the interruption."

'Of course,' thought Case. There they were. Again. 'Why these numbers? Why can I not escape them? What are you trying to tell me?!' he desperately called out to a higher power in silence. 'This isn't coincidence. There's no way.'

No matter how hard he thought before this moment, no matter how much he tried to decipher why God would constantly torture him by making them appear and reappear, he couldn't help but always come back to Lacey. There was no escaping his thought that they would eventually be together. But he was with Lara. It seemed unfair to her. It seemed unfair to himself. 'What if these numbers mean nothing? And I throw away chance after chance because I'm hell-bent on something that is never going to happen? Then I'll just be a lonely, old man one day. Kicking myself for thinking into this too much. What am I saying? Lara's birthday is 2/1. I'm supposed to live for 2/1. That's what they mean. That's what they could mean. No. Lacey has always been 4 2 1. Her birthday is April 21. There's nothing clearer than that. Wait. Is there?

"Aggghhh!" exclaimed Case.

"What?" said Alan. "They said Honda Hatchback not a Mustang, you toolbag."

"Haha yeah, what's wrong, Case?" said Lacey. "They should have said attention – if you have a blue Honda Hatchback. Your car is junk."

"Haha yeah, and nothing, sorry. Got a lot on my mind lately."

"So not gonna dance with me, then?"

"As long as it's ok with Lara."

"Of course. I saw her over here. I got to meet her earlier. She seems nice. I'm glad you're happy."

"Pshhh," said Alan under his breath.

"What?"

Alan looked toward Case and then to Lacey, sticking out his bottom lip to notion that he meant nothing by the sound.

"Speaking of. I should probably get over there and see how she's doing. Thanks for the drink. I'll let you know about that dance."

"Ok. Well, yeah. I guess I'll talk to you later, then."

Case approached the table between his parents and placed his hands on both of their shoulders. "So, babe, they takin' care of you over here?" he said, looking to each side, first toward his mother then to his father.

"Oh yeah, son, we're introducing her to whiskey. She's never had the good stuff."

"She said you were over here tellin' tales, Pop."

"No. Never."

"Babe?"

Lara laughed hysterically to herself, almost spilling her glass on her dress as Steele steadied the table. She gathered herself and spoke up. "No, they are just telling me stories about you. Nothing unusual."

"See?" said Brett Metzger. "You know us better than that!"

"Good to see you, brother," Steele said, standing up from his seat across the table next to Lara. "You want to take my seat? Cage and I are going to go over and sit with Eddie and his family."

"Alright, well then, I will take your seat. Thanks for entertaining her for a while."

"Yeah, no problem, man. We will have to catch up later."

"Sure thing."

As Case sat down next to his girlfriend, his stomach felt even more uneasy. He took off his jacket and hung it on the back of the chair, and straightened his vest. "So, whiskey, huh?"

"Yeah, it's really good. Never liked it when I tried it before," Lara said.

"That's because she has never had the good stuff," Case's father boomed across the table. "Do you all need anything while we are up? Your mother and I are going to say hi to Scott and Marie."

"Nope, thanks, Pop," said Case, holding his half-full glass of whiskey and Cola in acknowledgment. "We're good."

"Get me another one of what you got before please," said Lara.

"Ok."

"Another one?" said Case. "How many have you had?"

"This is just the second one."

"Good Lord. Good to see you are having fun over here," said Case with a laugh.

"Well, what do you want me to do? I didn't think you were ever coming over here."

"I told you I was—"

"Who was that girl up there talking to you and Alan?"

"Huh?"

"Don't act like you weren't talking to that pretty blonde up there."

"That's Lacey."

"She said that you two are best friends."

Case had never been so happy to be sitting at an empty table. He didn't want to have to defend himself in front of the rest of them. Even though they were surrounded by several others, he knew nobody else was paying attention to their conversation. And he was thankful for that if not for anything else in that moment.

"So you know who she is and then you ask me who she is anyway?"

"Don't change the subject, Case." Lara's tan face had gotten a shade brighter through the blood gathering behind her complexion. Case could tell that this conversation was not going to go over well. He tried desperately to think of a way to mitigate the situation, but knew there was no way around it.

"Yes, we're great friends. But I haven't talked to her in like four or five months."

"*Sounds* like you are great friends."

'I'm busy, she's busy. I'm sorry, am I missing something? Why do you sound so angry?"

"If she is your best friend how come you have never talked about her before? Why am I finding out about her from your mom? Your parents raved about her for ten minutes after she came over and talked to us."

"I don't know. Like I said, we haven't spoken in a while. She is still in school down in Georgia."

"Well, I find it really odd that you are such great friends with a hot blonde, and you never mention her."

"Because I haven't? She has never come up."

"Have you ever dated her? You said you only had one serious girlfriend before me."

"No. Babe–" Case paused and put his hand on Lara's leg over the soft fabric of her bright orange dress. "I've never dated her. She doesn't like me like that."

'Uh-oh,' he thought. 'Wrong response.'

"Oh, so if she did like you like that you would have, or would be dating her right now."

"We are just friends!" he responded in an escalating tone. He didn't want to lie to her about Lacey. So he began to bend the truth. "I had a thing for her at one point, but we never dated. We've always just been friends. You have friends that are guys and I don't accuse you of anything."

'Recrimination. Another bad move,' he thought immediately after speaking.

"Well, I never had crushes on any of my guy friends."

"Babe. We are just friends. And I am in love with you. So what else matters?"

"Your family loves her. You're apparently as close as friends get. She's beautiful. She's so nice. I mean, she gave me a hug and she just met me. She is your type. I don't want to have to compete with someone."

"Who's competing? And YOU are my type," Case said, pointing a finger in Lara's direction. "Now give me a kiss."

Lara sat up slowly in the chair and leaned in, pecking Case's lips, and then sat back in the chair and crossed her arms. Case scooted her chair closer to his so that his folded legs were flush with hers and put an arm around her shoulder. "So where did Wade go?"

"He said he was going to move his car."

Case's uneasy stomach had evolved into one resembling extreme sickness. He hadn't lied to Lara, but still didn't feel good about what had just been said. They were just friends, but his feelings toward Lacey had never gone away. He had tucked them away, and not speaking to her allowed them to be buried beneath the surface, only to re-emerge at the worst possible time. He knew that he did in fact love Lara. But it was only a fraction of the feelings that he had toward Lacey throughout the years.

As he and Lara sat alone, Scott and Marie's first dance came on the speakers and they watched together beneath the moonlight. Watching them dance, he began to feel better about everything that had transpired. He felt he might actually be destined to be with Lara, and God was just testing him. Then he also thought about when he had first introduced Kylie to her, and how she didn't hardly react at all, and showed no emotion or discomfort with Kylie and his friendship. Could she tell that there was more than Case let on? He wasn't certain why Lara saw such a threat in Lacey's friendship, but deep down he knew.

Wade and his girlfriend returned to the table after the newly-wed's first dance, and seemed to ease the tension that had grown at the table. He and Case reminisced about playing poker and basketball together the summer before, and struck up a conversation about committing to do the same in the near future. Lara had livened up and didn't seem to be upset anymore once Case's parents rejoined the table shortly after. They joked and carried on for the length of several songs, while several others gathered at the table to congratulate Case on a well-delivered speech earlier and catch up with his family.

As another slow song began to play, Case watched as couple after couple began making their way to the dance floor in the center of the large, grassy area to the right of the tables. The faded hardwood beamed reflections off light from the DJ's setup.

"I better go dance with your mother before somebody else comes and steals her away," joked Case's father as he excused himself from the table, taking Lorrie Metzger's hand and leading her in stereotypical fashion across the freshly trimmed grass onto the dance floor.

"Do you want to go dance, babe?"

"I'm not much of a dancer, maybe in a little bit," Lara responded.

"Alright," Case said, leaning back in his chair and sipping more of his second whiskey and Cola concoction.

"I'll dance with you, big boy," joked Wade, batting his pale white eyelids quickly in Case's direction, which earned him a love smack from his significant other sitting at his side.

Case just laughed at the gesture and set his drink down on the table, watching as Wade escorted his girlfriend down the same path his parents had just taken.

"I'm going to call my mom and check on Bailey," Lara spoke and she backed her chair rigidly along the cool, damp blades which served as the floor beneath them.

"Alright. Tell her Case says hi," Case remarked with a wink, pushing her chair back under the table for her. "Hurry back."

Case watched as she glided through the dimly lit night sky away toward the building in the distance to escape from the noise of the reception until all he could see was the light of her phone against his ear. Sitting at the table by himself, he caught a glimpse of Cage and Eddie laughing together by the dance floor while Cage seemed to be acting out a scene from a movie or television show. Case took another drink from the glass, this time emptying it to just remnants of ice and watered-down Cola before setting it back down. He spotted Alan by the bar ordering another beer and decided to go join him for another drink until his date was to return.

Standing up from the table and adjusting his vest again to keep his white dress shirt from being revealed at the bottom, he rolled his head in a 360-degree angle. His body felt like he had been asleep for eight hours. The way his body creaked and cracked made him realize how long he had been stagnantly sitting at the table without joining in on the night's festivities. He turned his torso to the right in a stretching motion and then back to the left. As he started around the table toward the bar he heard his name.

"Case!"

Lacey's voice was even more recognizable to him than his own. "Yes, ma'am?" he replied before turning to locate her.

"Where'd your girlfriend go?"

"She's on the phone with her mom."

"Oh, ok. So what did she say?"

"Say about what?"

Case felt the smooth skin of her palm on his as she grasped his fingers and pulled him toward her slightly.

"About our dance. C'mon."

Case looked back toward the building out into the darkness and took a deep breath. He set his drink down on the empty table to their side, gripping her hand back softly.

"Alright," he murmured in a voice just louder than a whisper.

Lost in the moment, he followed her lead toward the slow melody that moved with rhythm through the cool summer sky, not looking back to the table where Lara had returned to her seat.

CHAPTER 11

Four Days

• • •

"YOU HAVEN'T TALKED TO HER since when?!" Kylie said, dropping her sandwich onto the Ziploc bag on the table in surprise.

"Since Sunday morning," Case said with a blank look on his face. "I might as well say Saturday night because she barely would talk to me the entire night back at her house."

"I don't know if you noticed, Case." Kylie paused, staring at him across the patio table in front of their building. "But today is Wednesday. How do you just not talk to your girlfriend for three or four days?"

"Ask her," he responded. "I've tried to talk to her like twenty times a day, but she doesn't answer."

"Well, what on God's green earth did you do? I thought you said the wedding was good."

"Yeah, the wedding was. Lacey being there wasn't."

"Case. Case. Case."

"What?!"

"You're still hung up on her?! What happened?"

"Nothing happened."

"Yeah. Because nothing leads to Lara not talking to you since Sunday."

"Ky – nothing happened. I didn't do anything wrong."

"So what is the deal?"

"She's jealous of Lacey. She says that she doesn't measure up to her. That my family likes her more. That she's more my type."

"Jealousy is such a wasted emotion... When I met her I didn't get the feeling she was the jealous type."

"I didn't either. But she sure as hell flipped out this weekend because of my being friends with Lacey."

Case spoke toward the table as he fiddled with his water bottle, opening and closing the flip top. Kylie knew he wasn't telling her the entire story. There had to be more to it, and she would dig until he submitted.

"Case."

"Yes. Kylie?"

"You never look at me when you talk. What else happened?"

Case picked up the water bottle and squirted the remaining liquid into his mouth and washed it around his mouth for a few seconds before swallowing. As he swallowed he looked toward the waste bin to his left and tossed the water bottle toward it. Clanging off the side, the bottle landed by a group of four women walking with lunch bags toward a larger table along the patio. The heavy-set woman in the middle stopped and picked it up, discarding it in the trash can at her side.

"Sorry about that. Thank you," Case said with a wave.

Kylie's stare toward her friend was never broken. She still peered in his direction, leaning in with a facial expression that didn't require accompanying words.

Case finally looked in her direction and stared toward the sky with a deep breath.

"What, Ky?"

"Well?"

"She went away from the table to call and check on Bailey, and when she came back I was dancing with everyone else on the dance floor."

"And by that you mean you were slow dancing with Lacey, I'm sure."

Case, being startled by her uncanny ability to decipher the story from a female point of view, closed his eyes for a few seconds and shook his head, yes.

"Well, people dance with other people besides their spouse or girlfriend all the time. It doesn't mean anything. Did you dance with Lara, too?"

"Tried to. She wasn't interested after that."

"Well, yeah, I'm sure she is just jealous that you danced with her first. She will get over it. If she doesn't, well, that tells you something, doesn't it?"

"Yep," Case said quickly as he gathered the remains of his lunch and placed them in his bag, trying to hurry their lunch hour along. Kylie sat still, soaking in the entire situation that Case had just spelled out for her. Something still didn't sit well with her. She couldn't quite put her finger on it. As Case began to push his chair out from the table she stopped him with another question.

"I still don't get it."

"Get what?"

"I mean... I get the silent treatment... I use it all the time. And it is quite effective."

"Really? Do you?" Case snickered sarcastically.

"But three. Basically four days? Just because you danced with her? I eat lunch with you basically every day and she doesn't care. At least you've never said that she does."

Case spoke under his breath and he stood up from beneath the umbrella of their table, pulling his white sunglasses down from the crown of his head to cover his eyes. The sun beat down on the back of his neck as he pushed in the chair. Its blazing light did not penetrate through the umbrella, but by the expression on Kylie's face, it seemed to be. She sat with squinted eyes, puzzled by everything, as if she couldn't figure out a simple question of logic.

"Wait. Case."

"Huh?" he said, stopping to look back toward her. He had already began toward the doors to the building, leaving her sitting alone steps behind. "Um. I said that's because I told her about you." After speaking more clearly this time, his eyes froze looking toward the door as his body turned toward them once again.

"Hold up one second, Mr. Metzger," Kylie said sternly, halting his footsteps in an instant.

He didn't have to turn around to see that her expression was a perfect hybrid of disappointment and anger toward him. He heard her heels clicking against the rock patio stones quickly in his direction until they stopped at his side.

"You mean to tell me."

"Ky–"

"No. Case. You listen to me."

The light off one side of her face reflected a bright white light that was clear even through his sunglasses. Her arms crossed in front of her and one hip popped to the side, Kylie could be seen by everyone within sight as a stereotypical upset female.

Case didn't want to hear what she was going to say. Somehow he knew she would make him feel worse than he already did. But her words always had purpose. The truth hurt. He was wrong for not telling Lara about Lacey from the beginning. He knew that. But he was about to hear it resound from the last place he would want to. Well, almost the last place. His father and especially his grandmother spoke in similar tones to Kylie. Ky found ways to make her words hit home, just like they did. The same trait that made Case confide in Kylie was also the trait that made him resent her at times. He hated being wrong. He hated that she was always right. But, deep down, he knew he needed to hear the verbal lashing that was in store. He had avoided the topic with his father, and since he had missed church on Sunday being at Lara's, he hadn't seen his grandmother, Cindy Metzger. She was sure to pick up the non-verbal cues from him that something was awry. Just as Kylie was doing.

"You mean to tell me that you didn't mention her at all before Saturday?"

Kylie knew his silence meant 'no,' and continued to spout off toward him, not even pausing for air.

"This same girl that you've been friends with for I can't even remember how long. This girl that you consider your best friend. The same that I heard the life story of for the first two months I knew you. Was never once mentioned to your GIRLFRIEND!?"

Case felt 2 inches tall. He didn't care how many people were seeing him be reprimanded for his wrongdoing. He had made a mistake, knowingly. He knew he had to apologize. He knew that keeping her a secret would eventually blow up in his face, but he wasn't sure if it was too late to salvage. He listened carefully for a glimmer of hope in Kylie's voice. He needed to know if she thought it was too late, or if he could bury the hatchet with Lara. Kylie's opinion meant more than he would ever let her know.

"I wouldn't talk to you either!" Kylie's escalated voice sounded. "Do you know sketchy that looks? Do you realize that your actions just scream 'I'm hiding something'?"

Two men walking back into the building held the door open for them as they stood in an awkward silence.

"Thank you, we will be a minute, though," Kylie said toward them pleasantly before reverting back toward her friend who had unexpectedly upset her. "They weren't rhetorical questions, Case. I want to hear you say that you know why she is that upset. And how lucky you are that she didn't just flat out drop you."

"I know."

"You know what?!"

"It was dumb, Ky. I was scared. Scared that this would happen if I told her. You said yourself before how much I light up when I talk about Lace. I didn't want to screw up my shot with Lara by her thinking that there was something there that wasn't."

"So by not mentioning her at all, that was supposed to avoid the entire situation altogether...?" Kylie questioned, unfolding her arms and flailing them around in front of her face as she spoke.

"No. I don't know. I wanted to be honest with her. I really did. I was scared that she would think that I still had feelings for her if I brought her up too much, or if I didn't mention her enough."

"You mention me with great ease. You mentioned Scott. You mentioned Alan. You mentioned Lincoln. You mentioned everyone else without a problem. She never thought that you had feelings for any of us. Did she?"

"No," Case said followed by a subtle laugh. "I could never have feelings for Alan like that, though, he's a little big for my taste."

Kylie didn't laugh, but shook her head instead. "Case, joke all you want, but we both know what you did was wrong. Yeah, it has to be tough. You have always had Lacey on this pedestal, and those feelings will always be there. They may fade some, or flare up from time to time, but it's just like your first love. It felt good, and feels good to think about from time to time, but you have to let it be just that. There's no problem with you having had feelings for her, or even thinking about those feelings from time to time, you are human. But if you just bury them or hide them in the closet... they will never go away. You will fight them your entire life regardless of who you are with."

"There are so many things that remind me of her, Ky. Sometimes several times a day. I'm scared that they won't let me love Lara the way I should. So I tried to push them away."

"Case. Things remind me of Ty all the time. That will never change. By you never saying anything to Lacey about how you felt, it left those doors open. You will always have to battle them because of that. But you can't let it hold you back. Don't think that those doors had to shut for you to walk through another one."

The words spiraled through his mind. He didn't know how, but what she said made sense. It was as if his world had been turned upside-down by her words: a backwards version of all the thoughts that had spun around his brain for the last few months, and especially the last few days. He felt at ease for a moment before remembering Lara hadn't been returning his calls or texts. He took out his phone to check to see if by chance she finally had. Be she didn't. As he looked toward the top of the display he saw that they had been outside longer than they should have. 1:24PM.

"Good God, Ky, it's almost 1:30: we have to get back inside."

"Whoops. Let me get my stuff from the table," Kylie said as he heard the clicking of her heels once again.

"Wait! Ky?"

"Yes?"

"So what should I do? Do I keep trying to call her?"

"She'll answer when she's ready," Kylie said with confidence loudly across the patio.

"So you think I can save this thing, then?"

"I think you can do just about anything."

Case pulled out his phone as the day wound down, contemplating whether or not to send a text. The clock on his computer screen flipped from 4:20

to 4:21 as he looked up at his emails before looking down at the phone at his lap again. Seeing the numbers, his mind was made up.

I really miss you and I want to see you, can I come over after work?

He set the phone on the desk, and tried to focus on the monitor in front of him. He looked back and forth toward the cellphone amongst several papers on the desk and back toward the screen. His antics were causing his pace of response to the inquiries to slow to less than half-speed. He suddenly felt a presence behind him and spun in his chair to see who it was. Standing at the entry to his office was his boss, Jennifer. She was in her fifties and had short, graying hair. She was a thick woman who wore the most eloquent outfits with several accessories each day. She was extremely good at what she did, and expected the same of her employees. Case, worried that she may have noticed a slip in his work that day, cleared his throat and spoke up. As he spoke, his attention was drawn toward the short, vibrating sounds of his phone on the desk to his back.

"Hey, Jenn. What's up?"

"Everything Ok, Case? You seem startled?"

"Yep. Shipshape."

"Alright, well, let me know if we're putting too much on your plate. You know you are doing twice as many inquiries per day as everyone else. I hate to pile it on you, but you're the best on the team. We don't want to underutilize you."

"Oh. No, ma'am. My caseload is fine. I was going to ask you for some more, actually."

"See what I mean?" his boss chuckled. "Anyway, I just wanted to check in on you before I left for the day: haven't seen you much today."

"Sorry. Just trying to hit my numbers. Haven't been very social this week."

"Well, keep up the good work." She paused. "The management team sees how important you are to the company, and how dedicated you are. You are definitely an asset for us, Case."

"Thanks. Just doing my job, want to the best I can."

"And we appreciate it, I can never say it enough, Case. Just continue down the path you're on. You have learned and applied things at an incredible rate."

"I don't know about incredib–"

"The average responses in a month for each member of our team is 380... Do you know how many you've done already this month and it's only the 19th?

"I'm not sure, I can look if you want." Case started to turn toward his monitor, not only to look for his month to date numbers, but also because he wanted to glance at his phone to see who had sent him a message. He was stopped in mid-turn by his boss's voice.

"Four hundred twenty-one," she said. "That is astounding. We have run quality reports on them as well, and you are scoring above the rest of the team with almost twice the efficiency."

421 was all he heard. His memory traveled back to his conversation earlier with Kylie just before seeing Lacey's smile appear and disappear in the backs of his eyelids as he blinked. He shook his head rapidly side to side as if he had just been hit swiftly across the face, and then envisioned Lara's gaze back toward him the first night in his car in the moonlight of the parking lot.

"I'm shocked as well," Jenn joked from the door frame, laughing at his body language in response to what she had said. "With numbers like that, I better start watching for my job," she continued jokingly.

Case laughed with her and finally submitted to the temptation of turning to grab his phone from the desk with his right hand. He heard her speaking as he stared down, reading the text message.

"I'm out for the night. See you in the morning, Case. Keep up the good work, I see a bright future for you," said Jennifer as she knocked twice on the frame of the door before exiting out of sight down the hallway.

Yes, Please come over. I miss you, too, and Bailey really wants to see you.

As he registered the words his boss had just spoken as she left, he spoke softly to himself as he clicked out a response to Lara's text.

'Me, too...Me, too.'

CHAPTER 12

Time four bed

• • •

FOR THE FIRST TIME IN his life, Case began to believe wholeheartedly that the numbers that had followed him all his life meant something other than the beauty down in Georgia. It had been months since Scott's wedding and the summer was winding down. He couldn't remember the last time he saw the numbers pop up, much less the last time he thought of Lacey and himself getting together. Something in him had changed the day he spoke with Kylie outside at work.

Maybe it was her words. Maybe it was an internal epiphany. Maybe he finally gave up on his dream. Maybe the thought of losing Lara changed his thought-process. Case didn't know what had changed, but he didn't even realize it had changed. It was as if the numbers never meant anything else. He wanted them to mean Lara, so therefore they did. But they also would trail off to the point he wouldn't even notice them anymore. 4, 2, and 1 had disappeared from his life; he had forgotten about them.

The summer had its ups and downs, petty arguments, and disagreements, but all in all, things were going well. Bailey's social skills had increased tenfold, and she was slowly becoming a smaller version of her mother. Case seemed to cave to her every move, and he often found himself wishing that she had been his own. Lara had graduated from college and found a full-time job in Virginia, and seemed much more pleasant toward everyone in general. Her quality of life radiated from her smile. She had almost everything that she had ever wanted, and things were the way they were supposed to be for her. No more dramatic scuffles. No more heartless men in her life. No searching for a job. And most of all, no Lacey.

Case had tried to apologize for what had transpired at the wedding, and for not bringing Lacey up in conversation, but Lara wanted no part of it. When he brought it up, she discarded the conversation as if it never happened. She didn't want to talk about it, and life was better without even thinking about the existence of Lacey, and if Case never spoke her name again it would be too soon. Case remembered her saying that night after work, "I don't like her. And that is that." She went on to conclude: "I don't care if you are friends with her, but I don't want to hear about her. Ever."

"She is one of my best friends, babe. She is going to come up."

"No, she won't."

"So if we talk I am supposed to just not say anything..."

"Yep."

"So, let me get this straight. You are ok with me being friends with Lace, but I'm not allowed to talk about it."

"Yes. I thought I was pretty clear."

"Well, babe... I don't think it's healthy for our relationship for me to have a friendship with someone and not ever talk about it." Case exhaled. "That feels like keeping secrets from you even when it's not."

"Well, if I asked you to stop talking to her, would you?"

Case's eyes wandered in every direction but hers, trying to decide if it was a trick question before responding. "I wouldn't appreciate being asked that either. That's like asking me not to talk to Scott. Or Alan."

"You wouldn't. Just say you wouldn't."

Case sat on the deck outside of her parents' house in silence, just looking back at her leaning against the sliding glass door.

"Exactly. But if you never talk about her, then it will be as if you don't talk to her at all to me."

"Isn't that what started this? You wouldn't even let me apologize earlier for not ever bringing her up. And now that's what you want?"

"Alan doesn't like me... so why is this a big deal that I don't like her?"

"It just doesn't...Never mind."

As he watched Lara walk through the doors to the deck inside to wake Bailey from her nap, that would be the last Lacey was referenced in their conversation. It didn't feel right to Case, he knew it would eventually cause a problem. Or several. But the memory of that night fled from Case like a bird for the winter.

Lara and Case had brought Bailey to a small beach by her mom's house in New Market for one last visit to Lake Linganore for the toddler before the summer ended. It was late Saturday afternoon, and Bailey would sit along the edge of the still lake playing with the sand for hours on end. The summer air had chilled just slightly as it does in the early weeks of September, and the couple lay upon towels watching her play from feet away as the sun began to set, listening lowly to the Bluetooth speaker at their side.

"Dakota and Michelle asked if I could come for a girls' night tonight downtown."

"Oh, is that who just text you?" said Case, propping himself up on the towel by his elbows, before moving his sunglasses to the top of his head. As his eyes adjusted he leaned toward her and placed one of his hands on her towel like an invitation to continue.

"Yeah, I haven't gone out in a long time..."

"We just went out like a week ago with Scott and Marie?"

"You know what I mean, Just the girls."

"Ha yeah, I know. So go. It will be good for you."

"Mom isn't home tonight. She went somewhere with my stepdad."

"I was wondering where she was earlier when we stopped there to get stuff... but what does that mean? Because she's not home you can't go? You don't live there anymore."

Lara had moved out earlier in that summer after landing her job in Virginia as a junior accountant. Case was proud of her for getting out on her own with Bailey. The two had spoken about moving in together, but Case ultimately decided against it, much to Lara's chagrin. She didn't understand why he didn't want to live with her, and he spent countless hours explaining that he needed to save money in order to be comfortable moving away from his parents' house. But he had basically moved in anyway, spending several nights a week there, sometimes only going home for enough time to grab more work clothes and a DVD or two. Lara was convinced that he just didn't want to move in with her, and was making excuses not to do so, and she was partially right.

Case did need to save money, and he wasn't in great financial shape despite his success at work, due to frivolous spending and extremely high student loan and car payments. He also was extremely cautious due to his father's warning. They had been together for more than two seasons, but Case still felt it was early to be living together, and liked things the way they were for the time being. He wanted things to happen naturally, and not to rush into a new living situation. He didn't want to move in and then have things fall apart and then have to run home with his tail between his legs to a choir of 'told-you-so's.' He was intrigued by the future, and the possibility of moving in together, but still knew deep down that it wasn't a good idea this early. At least that was the reason he had convinced not only her of, but also himself.

"Well, I don't have anyone to watch Bailey."

"What? Am I not lying right here next to you?"

"Well, I didn't know what you were planning on doing. I figured when I said I wanted to go out you would run off to Alan's to drink beer and play cards like usual."

Case was perturbed at the comment, dealing internally with the hyperbole of an assumption she had just made. But he decided not to rebut her comment, knowing that more than once he had gone out with his buddies, only to have her subtly upset the next day for having been left alone.

"No. If you want to go, I will stay with her. Me and the squirt have fun. You're acting like I've never watched her alone before."

"Ok... well then, I will tell them to pick me up," Lara said with a teeth-baring smile, looking down toward her phone as she typed a message.

Case looked over toward Bailey in her own world of sand and plastic buckets and shovels, and felt a warm sensation through his body. He suddenly felt excited to have a night alone with her, like father and daughter. He stood up and put his white T-shirt back on and brushed the sand from his trunks.

"You want me to go tell her it's time to get ready to go?"

"Hm?" said Lara, lost in her phone and in the thought of having a night on the town with her friends for the first time since meeting her Prince Charming.

"Do you want to get ready and go now? Sun is gonna be down soon."

"Oh. Yeah. We can go."

"I will go peel squirt from the sand, she's not gonna want to leave."

Lara shook her head in agreement and began to place items in their beach bag, bidding farewell to the water and the sand for the last time of the summer. As Case walked toward Bailey, Lara heard his flip-flops crunching softly through the sand and him speaking to her. She was surprised when she saw that Bailey was not crying, and not upset, but rather was helping him place the different items into the sand-covered bucket. The still lake rippled as a gentle breeze warmly flowed from the trees in the distance toward them, being the last to leave the beach. Bailey held the oversized pale in one hand, and placed the other in the much larger hand of Case.

"Let's go get Mommy," Case said in a high whisper, swinging her up into his grasp as she laughed.

"I get her!" said an excited Bailey, laughing from being whipped into the safe arms of her father-like figure.

"You hear that, Mommy? We're gonna get you. You better run!"

Case jogged swiftly in Lara's direction, Bailey laughing cutely in anticipation as she bounced in his arms while they ran, causing the sounds of the voice to go up and down like a roller coaster. Lara smiled at the two charging toward her with the sun setting behind them through the trees, reflecting in broken beams off the water. Before they knew it, the sun had disappeared completely and was replaced by a full moon as they pulled into Lara's apartment complex.

"Be good for Case, ok, baby?"

"Ok, Mommy," said Bailey, sitting on the living room floor in her pajamas.

"Come give me a kiss."

"Ok!" said Case, as if she was speaking to him.

Lara laughed and he put his arms around her in front of the apartment door.

He kissed her softly on the lips, brushing her hair behind her ear, and pulled back abruptly. "Don't let all those guys drool over you without buying you a drink, k?" he said sarcastically with a chuckle before pulling her close once again and rubbing his rough face against hers softly and kissing her on the neck.

"Not in front of Bailey!"

"What?! I didn't do anything...yet."

"I will text you when we are on our way back," said Lara, releasing from his embrace and placing a hand on his chest.

"Baby... Do you want to give Mommy a hug before I go?"

Bailey stood up, carrying a small blanket and two dolls in her arms and walked toward the door into the arms of her mother.

"Bye, Mommy," she said as Lara picked her up and squeezed her tightly.

"Be good. I'll miss you."

"We will miss you, too, babe. Have fun, I'll see you when you get back," said Case, taking Bailey from her arms, being careful to not let any items fall from her arms. Lara turned and opened the latch to the door and began to close it behind her before being stopped by Case's voice just prior shutting it completely.

"Babe?"

"Yes?" she said, peering her head through the opening. He let Bailey down and the sound of her small feet scampering back toward the living room filled the small apartment.

He approached her slowly and put a hand on her chin, and pulled the door open once again before whispering, "I love you."

She closed her eyes and kissed him and returned the endearment as she pulled away to walk toward the running car awaiting her across the parking lot.

"Be careful!"

"I will," she said, not turning to look at him as she walked in quick steps toward the bright lights of the car.

"Bailey, are you ready to get in bed?"

She shook her head 'no' and continued to play with her dolls, mimicking a conversation to herself. Case knew she needed to go to sleep soon, but was enjoying watching her. So much to the point he didn't have the television on, or even play music in the background. He smiled at her and decided to let her play for a few more minutes.

"Case?"

"Yes, squirt?"

"You play with this one?" said the small version of Lara, holding up a small doll depicting a tall, blonde woman in a dress.

"You want me to play with you?"

She shook her head yes, and Case dropped to his knees and crawled next to her on the carpet.

"You're the mommy and I'm the daddy, Ok?"

"Haha ok, squirt, but we need to go read a book and get in bed soon, ok?"

Case lay upon the floor, holding his head up with his bent arm, and speaking in an emphasized high voice to emulate a woman's tone. Several minutes had passed without Case even realizing it. It wasn't until he saw the cute girl yawn while crawling toward a pile of other dolls to retrieve another toy for their scene.

"Bailey, I think it's time for bed."

"I want to play."

"You are tired, aren't you? Case is tired. Let's go get in bed ok?"

"But I want to play," she pleaded as her tired face changed to one of disappointment. Case could see her tired eyes preparing for tears and held his breath, not wanting to see her cry. He knew his soul fell apart every time she cried, and he was overwhelmed with a feeling of helplessness. Like she was his own spawn, his goal for her was immense happiness, but he knew that letting her do what she wanted wasn't the right thing to do.

"I'll tell you what. I will lie down in your bed with you and we can read a book."

"I want this book!" she exclaimed, grabbing a book from the shelf as they walked in her room. Her mood had changed in an instant, and Case felt good inside now that she seemed to have accepted the barter.

"Ok, we can read that one. Come'ere," he whispered, sitting down on her small bed and rubbing the blanket beside him.

Her short, quick steps rattled across the carpet as she leaped into the bed beside him.

"Case..."

"Yes Bailey-bear?"

"Can you read in the dark?"

Case chuckled at her cute comment and smiled. "Sometimes, sweetheart, but not when it's really dark."

She lay back and looked at the picture of the cats and dogs on the front of the children's book. "Really dark?" she asked.

"Haha yes, squirt, you have to have some light to see," he said as he stood up and turned on her nightlight.

"I don't like it really dark."

"That's why Case turned on your nightlight sweetheart. See?" he said and he turned off the overhead light to her room, leaving only shadows created by the spinning light plugged into the wall.

"But you can read now?"

"Sure can," he said as he crunched his body onto her small bed.

"I will turn the pages."

"Alright, sweetheart, you can turn the pages," Case said as he moved his legs uncomfortably onto the floor at his side to be sure not to break the frame of the bed. He opened the book and kissed her softly on her forehead. "Ok, you ready?"

She yawned and shook her head up and down. Case's heart melted at the sight of her two-and-a-half-year-old face stretching in exhaustion. He was amazed at how much she had grown since meeting her and how she had transformed into a small girl who spoke in full sentences. She had developed her own personality and was extremely bright. He felt lucky to be able to spend his Saturday night with her and couldn't imagine anything better as he lay in the dim light, reading the words to her slowly. She would turn the page before he finished reading and would point to different characters, stating what they were.

"Yes, That is a puppy. Good job, Bailey."

"He is a biiiig puppy."

"Haha yeah, he is. What color is he?"

"Yewwow."

"Yell-o. Can you say Yellow?"

"Yewwow."

"Close enough," he snickered as she turned two pages at one time. Case realized that he had to paraphrase what was happening on the smooth sheets of paper in order to tell the entire story, and he did just that as she closed the book.

"The end!" she said loudly, taking the book from him and throwing it at her feet.

"The end," he repeated. "Sweet dreams, squirt."

"Case?" she said again.

"Hm?" he said, yawning himself, leaning his head back on the hard, treated wood of the bed frame.

She rolled over and lay her head on his shoulder and put her small arm around him as far as she could.

"I wuv you."

What was left of his heart from being slowly melted down all evening immediately liquified in his chest. Her small, frail arms could barely hold more than a blanket and two dolls, or a beach pale, yet they overwhelmed him. He felt paralyzed by them and by the sweet and innocent words in the spinning glimmer of the nightlight. It was a feeling like he had never felt before. One he never wanted to end. And one that couldn't be replaced.

The words registered in his head immediately, but it took him several breaths before he could put them together. "I love you, too, sweetheart. Night night." He fell asleep with her small head on his chest, curled up closely to his warm body stretched off the side of the bed. In what would normally be an uncomfortable position, he slept peacefully like a giant, next to the smallest thief in the world, who had stolen his heart.

CHAPTER 13

A Night two Remember

• • •

THE BALCONY OF LARA'S APARTMENT was small, but suited just right for Case and Bailey's morning full of toddler conversation and finger-painting. They sat upon a small, two-person patio table on the fourth floor of the complex, and the balcony faced the normally unbusy streets of New Market. Sunday mornings in this part of Maryland more closely represented an old-time western town with little to no movement. If a tumbleweed were to scoot by on the vacant streets beneath them it would have been odd to Case, but certainly would have fit the mood. The late-summer morning sky was clear and crisp. The blue of the sky and the white of the clouds swirled together like Bailey's paint on the paper in front of him. He thought to himself for a moment how things seemed to be going too well. Life had taught him not to get too comfortable with how his life was going, whether it be good or bad, as the other was always waiting around the corner. Something about this morning was different. Something didn't sit right. The feelings he had felt the night before as he fell asleep with Bailey on his chest had given way to an unwanted feeling of emptiness. A warning shot from above. His gut was almost never wrong, at least not that he could remember. His emotional intelligence was stellar. He had developed an uncanny ability to translate the mood of a room into his own telling of the future, whether it be long- or short-term. The stale air of the morning was thick in his lungs as he began to trail off into his own world while Bailey sang and painted atop the table in front of him.

'Why am I feeling like something is wrong?' Case thought to himself and sat up in the chair quickly to catch the bottle of finger paint that tumbled away

from Bailey off the end of the table. Placing it back on the table at her side gently, he continued.

'Last night was great...Lara got to go out with her friends... I got to spend time with Bailey... Bailey told me she loved me as if she were speaking to her own father...'

"What is it?!" he said aloud.

Bailey stopped smearing the paint on the paper with her tiny hands and looked toward Case.

"Huh, Case?" she questioned innocently. Even sitting atop the table she still sat below him. She peered toward him with a puzzled look and wiped at her face as a gnat circled her. The brown, red, and green colors of the paint created a new color smudged on her cheek.

"Nothing, sweetheart," Case said calmly, taking a paper towel and rubbing the puddle of paint from her face, leaving two thin lines of green on both edges of her small cheek. "Are you hungry? Do you wanna have some cereal and go see if Mommy is awake."

The mentioning of her mother brightened her face more than the reflections of the sun beaming off of her tiny smile as she shook her head yes.

"Ok. Let me wipe off your hands. – Hang on, squirt!" he said to the toddler and she turned and tried to descend from the table on her own.

"We have to get you cleaned up first, ok? Can't be getting paint on everything."

"Ohhhkay," said Bailey as she shrugged her shoulders and sat limp and still on the clear top of the table covered in just about every color from the bottles of paint to their left. Case found it adorable that she shrugged her shoulders impatiently at her age as if she were a stereotypical teenager upset with her father because she couldn't have what she wanted.

"There ya go, kiddo, do you want Lucky Charms?" Case said, sliding open the door to the balcony, and she scurried into the living room like an excited puppy.

"I want da cooky ones!" she yelled loudly, climbing onto the couch, grabbing her blanket and baby doll on the way.

"Talk softer please, k? I don't think Mommy's up yet."

With a wide-eyed nod, Bailey agreed and began to whisper as Case turned toward the kitchen. "Case."

"Yes, dear?" he whispered in return.

"Can I watch the mermaid movie?"

"Yes, Bail, you can watch it, I'll put it in."

The overwhelming feeling that something was wrong filled Case again as he knelt to place the DVD in the player.

'Why do I feel like this?' he pondered.

"There ya go. Mermaid movie's coming on," Case said toward Bailey lying back on the couch, almost entirely engulfed in its cushions and her blanket. "I'm gonna get your cereal: you want the cookie ones, right?"

She shook her head up and down with her eyes lost in the screen in front of her.

"Ok, be right back."

Searching for answers, Case found none in the milk or the cereal as he placed them on the counter. He continually told himself that he was crazy. 'Things are finally going great for you. Don't just expect something to go wrong.'

His continued urgings toward himself were to no avail, and he still searched for why he felt the way he did. For as much as he knew how great things were going, he also knew that when he felt the way he did, a storm was sure to follow.

As he put the bowl of cereal on the coffee table in front of Bailey in the living room, he heard the shower in the master bedroom start.

"Mommy must be awake," he said to Bailey and walked back toward the kitchen to put everything away. Then it hit him like a ton of bricks.

'What time did she get home?'

'Why didn't she wake me up to come to bed?'

'Why wouldn't she?'

Case made his way toward the bedroom door a few minutes after hearing the shower stop. Lara stood beside the queen-sized bed draped with dark purple sheets and a purple and white checkered comforter. She had a pair of Case's shorts on, rolled up to the point where they would no longer fall off of her waist, and a white tank top. He could tell her hair was still soaking wet beneath the towel that held her hair up, standing up directly on top of her head.

"Good morning, beautiful," he said as he walked slowly in her direction, intending to give her a kiss. A kiss that would hopefully be accompanied by words that would make the empty feeling inside him disappear.

"Morning," Lara responded distantly, removing the towel from her head and bending forward to dry her hair further. Case loved the way her hair appeared an even darker brown when it was wet, but his focus was drawn away from it in this moment.

"How'd you sleep, baby?"

"Fine."

"Bailey's having breakfast, we didn't want to wake you."

"Good."

"I'm not really hungry so I just made her some cereal. But I can make you something. Are you hungry?"

"No thanks."

Case's uncanny ability to feel oncoming moods prior to their arrival stirred within him. The feeling in his stomach twisted and turned with each short response. He knew that there had been times in the past when he had looked into his intuition too far, but something told him he wasn't this time. He couldn't ask her what was wrong: he knew she would say 'nothing' and speak to him even less.

'What could I possibly have done?' he thought quickly. 'I was here all night. What is she being abrupt for?'

He approached her as she stood up from drying her hair, rubbing the towel back and forth between her hands in a motion as if warming her hands in the cold. He gently grabbed her shoulders and stared into her eyes, which appeared more empty than the feeling in his stomach. She seemed to be looking through him, like he wasn't even there.

"God, I love your hair when it's wet, babe. It is so sexy."

"Thanks."

"Where's my good morning kiss?"

Lara leaned up with her eyes open wide, looking toward the open door to the bedroom and pecked him quickly on the lips. As he tried to pull her close for a hug, she walked past him back toward the bathroom silently. Case, looking puzzled with a blank look on his face, pursued her path toward the restroom. Standing in front of the large mirror, still foggy from the heat of the water that had only stopped minutes ago, she pulled her toothbrush from the ceramic holder on the sink.

"So what time did you get home?"

"I dunno," said Lara's muffled voice between the strokes of her toothbrush.

"O....K...?"

"Well, did you have fun?"

"Yep."

"Good... Glad you had fun."

'OK, what the hell is going on here...?' thought Case as he leaned on the frame of the door. Something is up with her. Whatever I did, I must be making it worse now. This isn't the Lara I've been dating.'

The heat from the bathroom was not the only thing making him sweat. It was as if the feelings within him had escaped and filled the entire apartment. He gathered his thoughts carefully before choosing his next words, since his significant other had appeared to have evolved into a human form of a time bomb.

"Well, I am gonna go out here and sit with Bailey... I guess you can tell me more about it later..."

The silence pushed him over the edge.

"What's wrong?"

"Nothin'."

"Don't tell me nothing's wrong, I've been talking to you since I came in here and you've said like eight words."

"What do you want me to say?"

"Uh, the things you normally say to me in the morning when I stay here... Good to see you, baby... How was Bailey for you last night... Anything."

"How was Bailey last night?"

"Don't act like that. Tell me what's bothering you. You are obviously mad at me for something."

"I'm not mad."

"Oh, you just turned into a mute last night? Don't want to talk to your boyfriend…"

"Keep saying things like that, Case, and I will be mad," she replied sternly, trying to pass him in the doorway. Case stood firmly at the door with his forearm against the frame, determined to find the reason she was being curt with him.

"Saying things like what, Lara? I apologize for saying good morning and asking how your night was," he said in a sarcastic tone. "How rude of me."

"Stop being an asshole."

"Excuse me? I'm not the one being evasive."

"I'm not being evasive, Case!" she raised her voice slightly. "Now get out of my way, I am going to see my daughter."

Case removed his arm and leaned back against the wall as she moved past him.

"Well, are you going to tell me why you're acting different today, or am I going to hear about it after I leave to go to church?"

"I'm not acting different."

"Yes, you are. You are avoiding conversation with me. What did I do?"

She stopped as she reached the bedroom door and nearly closed it.

"You didn't do anything. Stop yelling. You know I hate it when you yell in front of Bailey."

Case chuckled to himself in disgust at her statement. "Who's yelling? I'm calm. There's no way she has heard anything that I've said."

Lara rolled her eyes toward him and shook her head. "Just stop, Case."

"Stop what? Just tell me what is wrong… Did I forget to do something? Were the lights on when you got home? Did I leave the seat up? Why are you treating me like a stranger?"

Lara's face and the silence as she stood with her hand still on the door handle spoke to him more than she had. As she turned to end the conversation and open the door, he spoke again.

"Wait a minute."

"What, Case!? Can I go see my daughter now?!"

"What happened last night?....Why don't you know when you got home?... How much did you drink....?"

"I only had like three drinks."

"Yeah, three drinks. Ok. Well, what happened that is making you treat me like this?..."

"Nothing."

"So what, do I need to call and ask Dakota what you all did last night for me to know what is wrong?"

A few long seconds passed. Case crossed his arms and stood tall awaiting her response.

"Well?"

"We just went to like...two bars and these guys kept following us around. They wouldn't leave us alone."

Case cleared his throat. "So did you tell them to leave you the hell alone? Why didn't you call me if you had guys bothering you?"

"You had Bailey, it's not like you could have done anything. And they weren't bothering us. They were really nice."

"So you dragged around these guys as your drink ticket I'm guessing...-- No," Case interrupted his own statement. "I can't stop every guy in a bar from talking to you. What happened...? You wouldn't be acting all covert unless something happened."

...

Case's voice began to escalate at the lack of response. "Lara... tell me what happened! Is there a guy under the bed or something?! You need to tell me now before I start to get really angry. You're not telling me anything!"

"One of them kissed me, ok?"

Case closed his eyes in disbelief and took a deep breath, calming himself to the point where he could speak. Surprisingly, the tone of the skin upon his face had not become red, but rather a pale white like he had seen a ghost. The feeling in his stomach paralyzed him in his shoes. He couldn't move.

"Kissed you...You didn't kiss him..."

"No! He wouldn't leave me alone. He said that he needed a kiss or he else he wasn't going to let us leave."

"And Dakota and Michelle just let this happen.... you let this happen...."

"They weren't at the table when he did it. They went to the bathroom and by the time he came back he was gone."

"But you let it happen. At no time it crossed your mind to let this guy know your boyfriend was at your apartment asleep with your daughter!?"

"I told him I had a boyfriend, but he just kept saying that he didn't believe me."

Case leaned his hands forward and ran them through his hair, bringing them to a stop and the back of his neck where he locked his fingers together and closed his eyes.

"If I had a ring it would have never happened," Lara said through tears rolling down her face.

Case snapped from his daze immediately. "WHAT DID YOU JUST SAY?"

"If we were engaged and I had a ring, then he would have seen it and he would have never done it, but we're not."

"You've got to be kidding me, Lara."

"It's true. Guys wouldn't try to hit on me if I had a ring."

"That's bullshit. And you know it! I can't believe you just said that! YOU let a guy kiss you. YOU let him buy you drinks. YOU didn't make him stop. YOU put yourself in that situation. and now you're telling me that it's MY fault?!"

"No, I didn't say it was your fault," she cried, stuttering through her words as she wept.

"THAT'S EXACTLY WHAT YOU JUST SAID!"

Case spoke in full-blown screams now. He was hurt in more ways than one, and was no longer allowing his thoughts gather before shouting them. Lara continued to cry as she leaned against the closed door, where she had now dropped to a seated position against the bottom of it. She desperately tried to stop him from leaving the room as the tables had turned from only minutes before. A five-minute dialogue had felt like an eternity to both of them. The reality of what he had just heard began to set in with Case, and suddenly he became calm. The sounds of the cartoons playing through the walls filled the moments that were not already filled by his deep breaths and the sniffles of her crying.

"Look. If you think that having a ring on your finger is going to stop any bar-hopping asshole from hitting on you and trying to take advantage of you...then you want a ring for the wrong reasons. And that's certainly not the reason I would ever give you one. I'm going to church."

Lara had sprung to her feet as he attempted to open the door above her body below him. Her cries to get him to stay didn't make him pause for the shortest of seconds. She held his upper arm in her tight embrace as he opened the door and begged him not to leave.

"It was my fault!"

"Baby! Don't go!"

"Please!"

"Baby! You can't go!"

The cries behind him in the hallway echoed through the apartment, but they were drowned out by the thoughts in his own head. He stopped at the couch where Bailey had leaned over to see what the commotion was, innocently holding the spoon for her cereal against her chin.

"What's wrong with Mommy?" Bailey said, looking up toward Case's swollen, red eyes.

"She doesn't want Case to leave, sweetheart. But I need to go, sweetheart."

He kissed her on the forehead and picked her up and hugged her as a single tear fell from his face onto her pajamas.

"Why don't you go give her a hug. I will see you in a while, ok?"

"Ok," said Bailey as he set her down, feet first on the carpet. He heard her quick footsteps trail off behind him toward her mother's bedroom and he closed the door behind him to the apartment, locking it behind him.

CHAPTER 14
Proverbs

• • •

THE METZGERS' CHURCH WAS NOT unlike any other Christian church. It stood tall with a brick front and a white steeple. The building itself was extremely large, and the parking lot stretched out beyond the length of the cemetery to the west. The property was lined with sycamores and ran parallel along Route 180, one of three main roads in the small town of Jefferson. The road forked a half-mile past the church where one could continue into downtown Jefferson, or north toward Urbana or New Market on the other side of Frederick County.

Case's Mustang rumbled as he tore into the parking lot, several minutes late for the 10:30AM service. As he came to a stop in the same corner spot he always parked in beneath the tallest tree in the line, he pulled the emergency brake back with immense force to the point where it could not go back any further. He was searching for something. An image. A familiar face. An idea. Anything to take his mind of what the morning had already delivered. He felt thankful that the news he was hit with this morning came on a Sunday. For if there was any place in the world that could take his mind to another place, and away from the hurt, it was here.

He forced a smile toward the last greeter as he entered the building. Everyone else had taken their seats and the sound of the opening hymn dwindled down beyond the walls to his right in the sanctuary.

"Better late than never, Case," whispered the older man who was tasked with greeting the church members as they entered. The man smiled and shook Case's hand as he walked up. "Good morning, sir. Good to see you," the man concluded as he released his hand. He closed the door to the sanctuary behind him and he disappeared into a pew beyond the clear glass window in the shape of cross toward the top of the door.

The Metzger family had been going to Jefferson United Church for generations prior to Case's memory, and they had been sitting in the same pew in the back atop the balcony since it was installed. Case climbed the steps to the swinging door at the entrance of the balcony and stopped just prior to entering. He said a silent prayer to himself with closed eyes and took a deep breath.

Since he could remember, one of the most interesting things about Sunday mornings was who he would see when he pushed the door open. It was like the faith lottery. There were sure bets, like his parents and youngest brother, Call. Cage was a 50/50 shot ever since he got his license years ago. Then there were numerous members of the church softball team that Case was in charge of. Several of the team members were close friends of Case's, some of whom he convinced to join the church just so they could play. Pastor Currington had told him that any reason to get people to join the faith and to participate in the church's activities was a good one, so Case had rolled with the idea.

The faith lottery door would sometimes swing open to reveal several of the players, a few, or sometimes none. Case's cousins, aunts and uncles were also a possibility, as well as random faces sitting in the Metzger section. But there was one thing that was constant. Grandma and Pappy Metzger were always there. The odds on their attendance were a sure thing. And on this morning, Case couldn't wait to swing the door and find out whose company he had won.

"Welcome and good morning," he heard Pastor Currington address the crowd from below as he walked in. The congregation still stood as the opening hymn had brought them to their feet. The announcements of upcoming church events echoed through the sanctuary off of the stained-glass windows and 50 foot high ceilings. Case's focus shifted from what Lara had done for the first time all morning when he noticed that the pews normally filled with Metzgers and friends were empty, with the exception of his grandma Metzger. He quickly tried to recollect a reason his parents wouldn't be there, and tried to fathom the idea of his grandfather not standing beside his grandmother.

It was the first day of September, but Grandma Metzger's smile was like 2 in the afternoon in the middle of July. It warmed Case's soul as it always had. Even as the inevitable thoughts of Lara kissing another guy crept back into him, seeing her made him feel at home.

He batted his Sunday bulletin against his leg and he joined her in the pew. He could see the words 'How are you?' and 'Good to see you' in her eyes without her speaking.

"Hi, Grandma," he whispered.

Being polite to Pastor Currington and all the members of the church, she didn't speak, even though her whispers could not be heard from a distance without great effort. She simply smiled again and placed a hand at the center of Case's back and rubbed softly. Taking her non-verbal cue, he focused forward down onto the announcements that were coming to an end as another hymn began.

As disappointed as he was on this morning that his parents and friends were not there to help him get his mind off of Lara, there wasn't another person that he would have rather picked to be by his side in the pew, had he been given a choice. Her words of wisdom had righted his ship several times before, and her proverbs and short life lessons were engrained in his heart.

The first verse of the hymn harmonized throughout the congregation of over fifty, and Case stood next to his grandmother with hands in his pockets. Even with her by his side the feelings of rage and utter sadness thundered from within. His eyes began to well up, and it took all of the energy he had not to allow a tear to develop and fall from them. He had slept peacefully beside Bailey the night before, but his eyes suggested otherwise. They continued to swell right up, and held two large bags beneath them. His face was as pale as the white button-up shirt he wore, and if it weren't for his hands in his pockets, the pulsation of his flexed forearms would have been noticeable from a mile away.

'How could she do this?' he thought, shaking his leg and tapping the end of his foot against the floor. 'Why would she do that?' 'Do I not make her happy anymore?' 'Did I ever?' 'What do I do?' 'Do I break up with her?' 'Should I have left?' 'Did I overreact?' 'What about Bailey?' 'I can't leave her.'

Case squeezed his eyes shut to hold back the salty liquid gathering around his pupils. All of the possibilities of where to go from here, what caused him to be in the situation he was in, and all of the thoughts coursing through the channels of his brain made him feel like he was in an overcrowded room. It was like the thoughts were actually speaking to him, and all speaking at once for that matter. A feeling like 50 people were all trying to tell him something at once, and he didn't know who to listen to.

The whisper from his left made all of the thoughts go silent like a movie theatre's lights dimming down to start the show.

"What's wrong, dear?" said Grandma Metzger.

Case knew he must have been really causing a scene as he stood there when he heard his elder speak while the service was going on. Rarely would she take her focus off of the service to engage in any sort of conversation, whether it be long or a simple greeting.

"Nothing, Grandma. Why do you ask?"

"If you don't want to say, I understand, child."

"I'm sorry I'm standing here sulking and interrupting church, Grandma. I thought I was going to feel better from being here."

"Well, your eyes look like they are ready to help bring a bumper crop. You looked troubled since you came in the door."

"I just don't know what to do, Grandma. And I don't know if talking to anyone about it is going to make things any better."

"Well... sometimes it doesn't. Sometimes time is the only thing that makes things better."

"Yeah," Case whispered in response and dropped his head. His grandmother placed her hand on his back again and didn't continue to probe for him to speak his troubles, for she knew he would spill them if he felt it necessary and wouldn't provide any comfort.

As the congregation sat down at the direction of the pastor, the thoughts in his head began to engulf him again. The airwaves of the pastor's sermon made their way to his ears, but were one of only several hundreds of words that Case seemed to hear and think at the same time. He breathed in and out in deep, long breaths throughout the duration of the sermon, and his grandmother's concern for him grew larger.

Case glanced toward her to see if he was bothering her focus on the good word of the morning, and she smiled back yet again. His mind cleared only for a second, maybe shorter. Long enough for him to remember that his parents were out of town for Call's chAlanger baseball team, explaining their absence. A single moment of clarity felt good to him and he desperately sought more concrete ideas and thoughts. Absolution was all that made him feel an inkling better when he felt down like this, and he had run to the only absolution he knew. God and family.

He forced himself to utter another whisper to his grandmother, despite the fact it would interrupt her focus. He knew that she felt his heartache through the hurt in his eyes which had migrated to her own eyes like a flock of birds landing in the branches of neighboring trees.

"Where's Pappy?" he whispered, hoping that a question or phrase spoken about something other than his fractured heart would bring another moment of clarity.

Out of normal character, and due to the situation at hand, she responded.

"He came to the early service this morning. He had to go to Pennsylvania this afternoon to help your Uncle Jimmy with something."

"Oh," he said, turning forward to try to focus on the words the pastor spoke. Even though he had been unable to decipher the scripture of the message to the point due to not being able to pay attention, he had tuned in and out to enough to gather what the pastor was speaking about: parenting, guidance, and the importance of direction in a child's life.

As the service ended, Grandma Metzger stood up slowly and hugged her grandson. She squeezed him gently as the side of her head rested firmly upon the center of his chest momentarily. He felt a portion of his troubles fade into her as if she had taken them through her embrace.

"Why don't you come to lunch at the house today, Case?" she said as she pulled away. "If you don't have anything else planned. I know you have softball today."

"I'd love to Grandma," he replied. "I am going to run home and get my gear first, but then I will be right over."

"It will be nice to have you over," she smiled.

"Might be just what I need right now."

"If you make it there before me, you know the door is already open."

"Why wouldn't you be there first, Grandma?"

"My leg isn't doing so well, I don't know how much longer I will be able to make it up here on Sundays. It took me a great amount of time today."

"Are you sure you don't want help getting down?" He gently grabbed her shoulder in an offer of assistance.

"No, child, don't be silly. I will manage. You run along. I will see you in a little while."

The tires of Case's Mustang slowly became covered with stone dust as the shocks of the vehicle were tested on the long driveway of stones to the farm. The big, chalky, red-brick farmhouse where his father had grown up lay at the end of the drive, and despite her warnings, his grandmother had arrived there before him. The shingles atop the roof appeared to be peeling off of the house and the shutters desperately needed painting. He had taken his mind off of Lara and Bailey as much as he could, and given the circumstances, he felt much better than he had before. He didn't know whether it was because he was in familiar surroundings with one of the most important people in his life, or if it was because he had become apathetic of the situation. Or somewhere in between. Not thinking about it and forcing it aside helped, but he knew it wouldn't heal anything.

The warm aroma of a fresh loaf of bread baking in the oven made its way to his nostrils as the creeky, white screen door slammed shut behind him. Despite anyone's effort to keep it from doing so, the door would always give away one's location. The rusty spring attached to the door would pull the door quickly and slam the wood of the door to the frame.

"There he is," she smiled as he walked into the kitchen and sat down at the antique dinner table that had been in the family for ages. He forced a smile onto his face as he replied, looking not toward her, but to a picture of her and his pappy atop the new refrigerator. The picture was from years earlier, but it suddenly reminded him of his own relationship woes. The happiness radiating from the picture brought a rush of jealousy to him. The joy on his grandfather's face was what he had always desperately wanted for himself. And the comfortableness and satisfaction of Cindy Metzger's expression were what he wanted his counterpart to feel.

"Here I am."

"Just going to make us some sandwiches, hope that is ok."

"You know I love that bread. You could make me an air sandwich as long as it's on your bread, Grandma. Although I'm not very hungry right now. My stomach is bothering me."

"Well, you are still a growing man. You need your strength. I know you will eat, you are your father's son," she chuckled.

"That I am," Case said as he looked out the window in the corner of the kitchen. Through it he noticed the several lines of bird feeders along branches of the oak trees immediately outside the farmhouse. The were also poles mounted in the ground holding contraptions with bird food.

Since he could remember visiting his grandparents, the bird houses and their frequent visitors were always there. Peering out the window toward them always whisked him away to a time when he was five or six years old. He and Cage would sit in the corner pointing toward the different birds, smearing their fingerprints onto the old window in the process.

"What one is that, Grandma?" Cage would say.

"Yeah, Grandma," Case would follow. "What kind is that one? I really like that one."

"That's an oriole, Cage," Grandma Metzger would reply. "That's a swallow." "Oh, you like the hummingbird the most, Case?"

She knew them all. Every single one. Birdwatching was her niche. Her passion. She knew everything about every winged animal to perch itself outside the window. Both boys would stare in awe as their grandma would open the window and feed them from her hand. She always tried to have her grandsons do the same, but the birds would always fly away. They called to her.

They loved her. It was as if she had been a bird in her past life, and she spoke their language. The whistling and emulation of a bird's call she could create were uncanny.

"Looks like it's done," Case heard his grandmother say, snapping him out of his daze of childhood memories.

"Grandma, when did Cage and I stop asking you about the birds?"

"Oh, I imagine you all were around ten when you lost interest," she chuckled. "You all sure did love to sit with me back when."

"Yep, good old days," Case said, straightening up his chair to the table and she set the hot loaf in the center of the table. The slices were cut by hand, but might as well have been cut automatically by machine. Her old yet steady hands always made the perfect slice. As Case slowly placed a couple pieces of fresh breast meat from a turkey who probably walked the coop on the east side of the farm only weeks earlier, he continued his thought.

"I miss those days. When nothing hurt." His voice lowered, reflecting disappointment with where the fork in the road of his life had brought him.

"What do you mean, when nothing hurt, child? Do you want tea or water?"

"Water, please." Case paused. "When I was a kid, feeling hurt meant Mom or Dad didn't let me do something I wanted to do, it wasn't this sick feeling I have in my stomach. It wasn't feeling empty. It wasn't not knowing which way to go. What decisions were right."

"That is true, you miss those days once you get bombarded with responsibility, don't you?"

"Sure do," Case said, forcing himself to bite into the normally delicious sandwich. It had no taste to him today. Nothing seemed to matter except what had happened the night before leading into this morning. No matter how long he escaped the feelings, they came back.

"What is making you think about that, dear?"

"Oh, nothing, Grandma. Just don't know what I'm doing wrong, what I'm doing right, what to do in general." Case exhaled deeply, lost in thought. He couldn't even look her in the eye when he spoke, for fear of breaking into tears.

"Well, you know I am here. Whatever is bothering you, you know I am here for you."

"I know. I don't want to talk about what happened. I'm afraid it will make me feel worse."

"I understand, you said that earlier. But I'm not just an old advice giver. I might be getting a little long in the tooth, but my ears still work," she said as she winked at him with a smile. "Something tells me this involves that pretty girl you have been seeing."

"It does," Case said reluctantly, forcing down the bite of his sandwich. "She did something that is hurting me pretty bad, Grandma. But I want to forgive her. I don't want to give up on us."

"Well, you don't have to share what it is, child. I know you will make the right decision regardless. You are a Metzger boy. You know what you can and cannot control. And that God will take care of the rest."

Case forced another smirk, which was short-lived, pushing the other half of his sandwich forward on the table to signify he couldn't eat anymore.

"I think I know what is right," Case said slowly, closing his eyes and opening them rapidly to keep his tears from developing once again. "But I can't imagine us not together. I don't even want to. And what makes it even harder is Bailey is involved."

"She is a cute little girl," Grandma Cindy remarked, taking his plate to the sink and handing the other half of the sandwich to their German shepherd, Arnie. "Having her involved will complicate things, but you mustn't think of only her, or your mother. No matter what has happened, remember that you cannot make anyone else happy without being happy yourself."

"Making them happy makes me happy, Grandma.... Making others feel good is what makes me feel good."

"Like I said, you are a Metzger. It comes with the territory."

"I know, I know," said a frustrated Case, wanting his grandmother to give him the answers to life. "And I don't feel happy right now. But I don't want to give up. I can't just leave them alone. Especially Bailey."

"They must have gotten along fine without you before you came along. And they would if that is what needs to happen for you to be happy. You need to figure out what is best for you, and if that is what is best for them as well, then you know what path to take."

"But Grandma, I'm the realest father figure Bailey has ever had... I can't just take forever to make up my mind what is best. I need to know now. I don't think I can go without seeing her. Without seeing her play, without feeling the love from her little smile."

"I know how you feel, child. I know you love her as if she is your own flesh and blood. Like she is your family, because that is what she has become. I know how much you love her, and I can see it in you. But only you know what is best. And whatever choice you make will be the right one, I have faith in that."

"I wish I did," Case said, barely keeping back his insecure feelings inside from swelling through his heavy eyes. "I see her as my own daughter, and I don't want to think about the possibility of things ever being over. I never have until now. I just don't know what to do."

Grandma Metzger sat back down at the table and wrung her hands, making a consoling face with her eldest grandson. "Let God guide you, Case. He won't give you anything you can't handle," she said with a long pause before uttering a phrase she had said his entire life, "Faith isn't faith..."

"Until it's all you're holding onto," he joined her in unison, sniffling as he concluded.

"Pastor Currington was speaking right to both of us this morning, then, wasn't he?" she said.

"What do you mean, Grandma?" Case said, puzzled by her statement.

"His sermon about the children we love, whether they be our own, a stepchild, a neighbor's child, an innocent child you see around town."

"I could barely think in church, I couldn't even comprehend his message. I heard him talking about children and I think about how children touch us in so many different ways, but that was really all I heard."

"You got it, Case," she said. "I couldn't help but think about how I've seen my children grow into being parents of their own, and how I'm even seeing you in a bit of a parenting role. But his message touched my soul even deeper this morning. It made me realize how we love our children, and won't ever let them go, even if we don't see them as often."

Mesmerized by what his grandmother had said, Case felt guilty for not having been able to focus at the service earlier that day, and wished that he could have listened more. He wished he could have focused.

"God puts each child in each of our lives for a reason, they teach us to be strong. They teach us to set an example. And they teach us what we won't let ourselves learn otherwise. Remember that, Case. Regardless of what happens, young Bailey has taught you more than you may ever realize, regardless of your time with her."

"Thanks, Grandma. I know she has. I need to get over to the field for softball soon, though. Thank you for talking to me, I feel a little better."

"I love you, Case. I'm always here. Good luck at your game."

"Love you, too, Grandma, I will see you later," he said, drudging toward the screen door through the living room.

"If you start to feel lost, read the fourth chapter of Proverbs as Pastor Currington suggested," she said, catching up to him and handing him her study Bible.

"This is yours, Grandma. I have one at home."

"No, you take that one, I will get it back from you."

"Alright, I will bring it to you later this week."

The screen door slammed behind him as he waved toward her waving back at him with her brightening smile. As he unlocked the door of his car, he thumbed through the Bible and opened it to Proverbs 4, which had been the focus of the sermon. The yellow highlighter in his grandmother's good book brought his eyes to one verse in particular, as he read while sitting down in the car. He felt his heart stand up in his chest when he saw the number of the verse, and quickly rubbed his eyes to make sure he was seeing correctly. In an instant, the numbers that had disappeared from his life suddenly held significance again. A reel of his photographic memory flashed before his eyes between each word as he read. First seeing his grandmother, and then Cheyenne. Then Lara. And then Bailey.

And finally, Lacey.

His eyes focused as he read once more prior to starting the vehicle, Proverbs 4:21, 'Let them not depart from thy eyes, keep them in the midst of thy heart.'

CHAPTER 15

Four, Two, One

• • •

THE AFTERNOON DRAGGED ON AS Case's mind wavered. He had hardly been able to pay attention at his softball games that afternoon. If it weren't for his being the coach, he probably would not have gone. His body felt weak. The ball felt as though it weighed a hundred pounds when he would gather it in his glove and throw to first. The world was carrying on, but Case didn't want it to. He wanted to rewind. He wanted time to stop. He wanted to forget what he had been made privy to early that morning before church.

The only thing that made his mind clear was the look of the clouds for a few moments between games of his double header, and the fact that Lincoln had showed up to play.

His long-lost friend, who had lived with his family during a few of Case's college years, had moved to Connecticut. The two kept in touch when they could, but spoke on what seemed to be a quarterly basis. On a normal day, Case would have been extremely thrilled to have seen him, but his emotions were elsewhere. He wanted to clear his mind. He didn't want anyone to know anything was wrong. But it was inevitable. Especially through the eyes of Cage and Lincoln.

"Nice snag out there, sugar," smirked Lincoln as the softball team commenced to the dugout after the middle of the sixth inning, smacking Case on his rear end.

"Thanks, man."

"What, I get no love?"

"Sorry, thanks, you sexy beast," said Case in a less than ecstatic tone, attempting to cover up the gloom of his day.

"That's more like it!" Lincoln laughed. "What's up with you? I mean I know I've been gone a while, but you don't seem yourself. You haven't cracked a joke about me all day."

"Nothin'."

"You say nothin'..." Lincoln paused. "Good enough for me."

"No, no, Lincoln, you're right," Cage interjected as he sat down on the bench in the dugout and wiped his brow. "When Case makes a play like that out there we don't stop hearing about it for like two months and he didn't say a word."

"I do not, Cage."

"Um... yeah you do," Cage exclaimed before continuing in a deep voice, sarcastically mocking his older brother. "You guys remember that one time I dove and caught that ball at Utica Park? Yeah, I jumped right through the chain link fence."

"Shut up, Cage, I've never said that."

You could barely understand Cage's words through his own laughter and the noise of the surrounding echoes of laughter from the rest of the team whose attention was drawn toward Cage as if he were a stand-up comic.

Cage calmed himself before continuing his mockery. "My name is Case and I hit the ball 500 feet because I'm the coach and I run this sh–"

"Cage! Shut your damn mouth. Or I'm gonna knock you 500 feet... and through the chain link fence."

"Ohhhhh," the team sounded in unison.

"You're up to bat anyway, you little jerk."

Cage ignored the crowd as he made his way toward the batter's box and away from the conversation continuing along the bench.

"Gotta give him credit, he's got your voice down pat," snickered Lincoln, patting his friend on the back.

"Yeah, well, I guess he can take a shot at me once in a while. He knows I'll knock him around if he pushes it too far."

"Ha, yeah, that he does.... Nice shot, Cage!" Lincoln remarked and he watched the ball soar over the right fielder's head as Cage sped around second base.

The normally upbeat Case was the only member of the team not on their feet as Cage stood up from his head-first slide into third base.

"That's how we get it started!" yelled Lee onto the field. "Way to hit the ball!"

The loud words of encouragement coming from all angles of the field were merely background noise to the band of deep thoughts playing in Case's head. He wanted desperately to talk to someone about what happened, but didn't want to face the fear that someone might tell him something that he didn't want to hear. He loved Lara and Bailey, and the thought of not seeing them anymore brought his life into perspective over the last few hours. They had become his life. He didn't make decisions without considering their wants and needs. His hunger to be a provider had been fulfilled for over a year now through making them happy. Seeing them smile. Surprising them with a gift. Hearing the words "I love you."

Case gripped the bottom of his jersey and brought it toward his face to wipe away the sweat and to dry his eyes in the event that a tear snuck through. He unconsciously yelled out the next three people in the line-up as he looked at the faces of his players individually, searching for the perfect person to talk to about everything if he could bring it into words.

At the end of the bench he saw Alan's large silhouette along the dirt before he actually looked at him. 'Alan hates Lara,' he thought. 'He is just gonna tell me to kick her to the curb regardless.'

Just as Case finished his thought, Alan's voice bellowed across the field toward Wade who was now hitting. "Come on, Wade! Don't be a pussy this time!"

"CHURCH softball, Alan," Case said to him loudly through the backstop and shook his head. The comment got no reaction from Alan besides a swig out of his water bottle, although his inappropriate comment soon brought Case's attention to Wade.

'Wade wouldn't tell anybody else,' he thought. 'But I've never talked to him about that kind of stuff before... it would be really out of left field...but maybe...' As Case heard the aluminum bat smack the ball, he saw it slice right past the pitcher and skid through the grass into center field. Wade jogged swiftly into second base with a stand up double and Cage crossed the plate in what might as well have been a walk.

'Maybe Wade would be perfect to talk to...' thought Case, looking out through the heat at the tall, linky, freckled redhead standing on second base. Just then, Wade looked toward Case and placed his fingers at his mouth and stuck his tongue out of his mouth, waving it back and forth quickly. For the first time all day Case laughed, more so at how ridiculous his previous thought was than at Wade's antics. 'Well, then... not having that conversation with him.'

"Your bark losing its bite over there, cuz?" said Ben from behind him, wearing a clean uniform. Ben was on the team but hardly ever played, even when Case would try to put him in. He wasn't athletic at all, and really only came to the games to join in on whatever heckling took place, even if most of the time it was at his expense.

"What are you talking about?" Case said over his shoulder at the sound of his cousin's voice.

"Everyone can usually hear you yelling every time the team does something good. And you're just sitting there saying nothing."

"I'm fine, just got a lot on my mind."

"Well, come have a cold one after the game, we can talk a while."

Inside, Case said to himself, 'Yeah, right... I'm not talking to you about any of my problems. You're just gonna say whatever you think I want to hear,' but chose different words to speak aloud.

"Yeah, maybe. We will see."

"What?" Cage said, still out of breath from running the bases seconds earlier as he invited himself to the conversation.

"Who was talking to you, Cage?" said Ben, laughing to himself.

"I don't know, no one I guess. Just was seein' what you guys were talking about. Surprised Mr. Badmood here was actually speaking to you," Cage remarked, referring to his older brother.

"I got your bad mood," Case quipped.

"Well, we are only down by four now." Cage changed the subject quickly. "Good."

Case stretched the seconds of the moment in his thought of speaking to Cage about the entire situation which lay in front of and behind him. Behind closed doors Case valued his brother's opinion, but knew he would be biased. He knew beneath all of the picking between the two that Cage loved him as much as he loved anyone, but Cage would be behind any decision that he would make regardless. Case's middle brother was better-suited to conversations of confirmation. He could make the decisions that Case made feel more concrete, but only after they had already been made. Case felt awkward about going to his younger brother for any type of advice in the first place, being that Cage was just that, his YOUNGER brother. Case wanted to set the example for him. He didn't want to show vulnerability. He wanted to be the rock that a younger sibling needs, and he hadn't yet realized how much great advice can come from someone with less years. And the brief thought of discussing his conundrum with Cage passed before it really came.

"Did Lincoln tell you he's moving back?" Cage muttered as he placed his batting gloves below the bench at his feet.

"He is?"

"Yeah, I figured you already knew?"

"No, he didn't say anything to me yet. Back into Mom and Dad's?"

"No, apparently, this girl he is dating now is from here, too. They met up in Groton, he said, and they are moving back down here to Jefferson."

"Hm, well, that's a surprise."

"Yeah, it will be nice to have our leadoff batter here again," Cage said, loud enough for Lincoln to hear as he took a few practice swings by the opening in the fence.

Lincoln didn't speak, but instead made a slight smirk toward the Metzger brothers sitting at the bench. By this time, Case was totally zoned out from the game. As he stared off in the distance in Keith's direction behind the backstop, his mind was far from clear. 'Not Alan. Not Wade. Not Ben. Not Cage. Not Lee. Keith??'

Keith had been on the other end of many deep conversations back in college when he and Case had been roommates. He was logical. His thoughts were always clear. He would have an honest opinion.

'I would do all the talking,' Case thought to himself. 'Keith is a great listener. He will be straight to the point with what he thinks. I can talk to him about this...but just not now. He won't say much: I need someone to bounce my own feelings off of.'

The final out of the inning broke Case's focus. The team members grabbed their mitts and returned to the field and he followed them. He was the last onto the clay-colored dirt covering the infield, and he broke into a light jog toward center field where he played between his brother and Lincoln.

"This guy came our way last time!" yelled Lincoln toward Case.

"Yeah, I gotcha," Case said back across the blades of light green grass that sat still in the heat.

"Ball has been carrying. Give 'em a step or two!" added Cage from right center.

The three moved in a back-pedaling motion toward the fence that stood 300 feet from home plate as Keith released the pitch. The ball bounced past the new church member playing catcher and each player watched him chase the ball. The sun had begun to make its way below the trees off in the distance to the west, but its rays still burnt bright. The muggy air made the field feel like a sauna for the players as they anxiously awaited the next pitch.

Case heard his teammates encouraging Keith on the pitcher's mound with every pitch, but his thoughts continued to wander elsewhere. The next pitch was hit hard right back at Keith, but he was able to snare the ball before it passed him.

"Whoooo!" yelled Lincoln who was left field. "Let's go!"

In an effort to try and rouse himself out of the funk looming over his head, Case yelled as well. "Nice play! Two more! Here we go!"

"Case is awake out there! Uh-oh!" screamed Lee sarcastically from third base. The sound of his voice traveled through the valley for what seemed like miles. Case stuck his thumb up in approval and chose not to respond to the remark as the ball bounced quickly in Lee's direction. Case watched him from the outfield and he threw the batter out by a step at first.

"One more! Then we hit!"

"What are we down by anyway, Lincoln?" Case said through his new-found focus in the field.

"Four, I think!"

'Ok. Down four,' Case thought. 'Need this out, we got two down.'

All at once, Case had joined the game. He didn't know if it was the fact that it was the last game of the season nearing the end that pulled him in. Or if God had finally made him clear his thoughts. But he didn't notice. He didn't care. As two more pitches were thrown, he realized that he went a few moments without thinking about Lara. Something else did matter, even if it wasn't as much. But it was enough for now. For this moment.

"Ball four! Take your base!" the umpire's voice carried to the outfield.

"We're Ok, Keith! Still got two here!"

Keith nodded his head toward the outfielders in acknowledgement as he prepared himself for another batter. Case assessed the situation at hand as he tightened the Velcro of his glove. His mind would go back to Lara, but only for a moment. His attention was drawn toward Lincoln jetting toward the foul line to try to catch a fly ball. He watched as the ball soared just out of Lincoln's reach.

'What have we got?' Case continued as he normally would during the course of any game. He constantly reminded himself of the situation so he could play accordingly. First, he always thought of the score, what they were up or down by.

'Down four. Ok. We can come back from that. That's nothing. We just can't let them score any more.'

He thought quickly and precisely. He knew that he didn't have much time in between each pitch. 'Alright, we can stop them. We got two outs. Need this last one.'

'Where am I throwing if this ball comes to me?' he questioned himself rhetorically.

'One man on. He's on first. Solid single, I go to the cut-off man, anything in the gap I'm looking toward third.'

"Let's go, fellas!" Case boomed across the field awaiting the next pitch. The pitch landed for a strike and a full count. This time, when the ball was thrown back to Keith, Case quickly summarized his early thoughts and repeated them to himself. Over and over. So he wouldn't have to think about what to do. Until he no longer had to think at all.

'Down Four. Two Outs. One man on.'
'Down Four. Two Outs. One man on.'
'Four. Got two. One man on.'
'Down four. Got two. One on.'
'Down four. Got two and one.'
"Four, two, one."
Case stood frozen in his cleats.

The aluminum bat made a noise closer to a hammer striking wood as it collided with the ball. Case begged his feet to move. The felt like they were stuck in quicksand. In cement. In shoes made of concrete. The numbers struck him as they always had before. When they always took him back to Lacey. Before Lara ever came along. They made time stand still. They slowed his heartbeat. Then sped it up. They made his body feel hot. And sent chills down his spine.

He watched the ball as it moved in slow motion toward him. Seeing its trajectory, he forced his legs to finally move. Moving more swiftly with each stride, his eyes stayed on the ball, while his feet moved quickly beneath him. He brought his elbow higher as the ball began to drop like the sun in the distance beyond the trees. His glove stretched out above his head while continuing in a dead sprint toward the edge of the field.

Cage screamed at his brother as he jogged toward him, watching as Case got closer and closer.

"Fence! Fence!"

Three sounds followed Cage's desperate warning toward his brother. The first was rawhide clapping against leather. The second, bone and flesh against metal.

The third sound was followed by silence. The third sound was Cage's voice again. A helpless cry. The sound waves of his voice pierced the ears of everyone on and nearby the field. The lone syllable which escaped his mouth held tones of both anger and concern. The sharpness of his scream, as Case's body lay motionless on the ground, cast a cloud of fear over the field.

CHAPTER 16

Two my senses

• • •

LINCOLN SNAPPED HIS FINGERS REPEATEDLY in front of Case's face. The players looking to the outfield stood still, waiting for signs of movement. A signal that he was ok.

"Case."

"Case."

He lay on the ground motionless, with the exception of his stomach rising and falling subtly with his breaths. Somehow the bright yellow softball still rested firmly in his glove. A bright red scratch went from the side of his eye through the blonde hair of his eyebrow. Surprisingly, the rest of Case's body appeared to be unharmed. His large frame had collided with the 10-foot-high chain link fence at full speed.

"Case. Buddy, can you hear me?"

He lay still with his eyes closed.

"Case, quit messin' around, can you hear me? Do I need to call an ambulance?" Lincoln said, expressing his concern more in each word. A few seconds of silence passed and Lincoln looked up toward Cage standing overtop of them.

"Cage, go get your phone."

"Get his phone for what?"

Cage had turned to run in toward his phone when he heard his brother's voice. He turned around quickly to make sure he wasn't just hearing things.

"How you feelin', buddy? Don't be scarin' me like that."

Case finally opened his eyes to see Lincoln knelt at his side.

"I'm fine, how's the fence?"

"I think it's gonna be ok." Lincoln laughed. "You need a hand to get up?"

"Nah, just let me lie here for a second."

"Hell of a snag, though."

Case sat up with the help of his hands pushing down on the grass. He lifted his glove up to see that the ball was still in it and laughed to himself. Shaking his head side to side quickly like a dog after a bath, he popped to his feet. Taking the ball from his glove with his right hand he lobbed it underhand toward Cage.

"Let's hit the ball."

Case spent the remainder of the game focused on why the numbers had returned. He never thought about them anymore. Maybe they had remained, but he no longer noticed them. What he once thought was his destiny being signaled to him had faded into the darkness, only to reappear twice in one day. The Bible. On the field.

Am I trying to see them again? What is going on? Am I seeing them because I can't stop thinking about what to do with Lara? It hasn't even been a day!

The team packed up their jerseys, bats, and gloves and filed out to their vehicles one by one, inquiring about their next game as they left.

"When's our first play-off game?" Alan said, holding his bat bag across his burly chest. He adjusted it with his dirt-covered arm and continued before Case had a chance to answer. "Do you know yet? When will they tell you when we play?"

"Not sure... I would guess by Tuesday since it's next weekend."

"Word. Well let me know, I will be there."

"Alright man, I'll see you later."

"So you don't know when we play?" gestured Wade.

"Ha, no. I will let you all know when I know."

"Alright, bud. Let me know if you and Lara want to have dinner or something this week."

Case's look toward Wade was sharp. But he quickly remembered that nobody knew his situation. Sitting alone on the bench, he looked down toward his bag and away from Wade. Overcompensating for the angry look he had just sent in Wade's direction, he spoke softly as he enunciated his words.

"Ok, man. I will call you. Good job today."

"Thanks, bud, see ya."

Moving slower than his teammates, Case remained on the bench. Placing each of his bats in his bag in what could be super-slow motion, the lone person left within sight was Lincoln. Case stood up and swiveled his torso from side to side to stretch, and winced in pain. His entire body felt sore and throbbed along with his heartbeat. He hadn't realized the excruciating noise that expelled from within him as he stood in dim light that remained. The sun had retired beyond the trees and the lights surrounding the field were not on, but a midsummer glow filled the air. Case could see only a small slice of the moon hanging in the sky, but he could see in each direction for miles. The same vision provided by the reflection of a still pond in the night had set down amongst the field. If it weren't for the pain Case felt both mentally and physically in this moment, he would have been in an extreme sense of serenity.

He closed his eyes and sat back down, hoping to see the answers he sought in the darkness beyond their lids. As he exhaled deeply, he heard footsteps through the gravel coming in his direction. Startled by the noise, he jerked his head to the left.

"You ok, old man?" said Lincoln as his figure cleared into Case's vision.

"I don't know."

"Took quite the spill out there," Lincoln muttered, joining Case on the bench.

"Yeah, didn't hurt as bad earlier."

"Adrenaline, man."

"I guess."

"I knew you were fine. Nothing keeps Case down."

"Ha, nothing, eh? That's funny," Case returned, following it with a sarcastic laugh.

"Brings me back to my original question. You ok?"

"Just sore. Like you said. I'll be fine."

"You ain't changed one bit, have you?" Lincoln smiled, removing his visor and lightly tapping it on the metal bleacher over and over like a nervous tick.

"Huh?" Case responded, confused by the statement.

"You think you're the only one who can tell when something's wrong? Unless you turned over this new quiet leaf, something is bothering you."

"That obvious, huh?"

"If you tell me it has something to do with Lacey, I'm obligated to finish that fence's job."

"Lacey?"

"Yeah, you got that same look on your face you always did back at the warehouse when we would talk about her. That 'I wish I had the guts to do something but I don't' look."

"I don't know what you are talking about, P'. I talk to Lacey about as much as I have talked to you in the past year. Time has flown. It didn't seem like you were gone that long."

"Ha, life happens, right? But I'm back now. I expected you and her would have finally gotten together by now. Just seemed like you always would."

"Last I heard from her, she was dating some guy from down at school on and off. But no, until today... I hadn't even thought about her at all..."

"Never thought I'd live to hear you say that."

"There was a point that I didn't either, but no. Not her this time."

"Ok then. What is it? I know it's about a chick. You didn't have to confirm that, because I can already tell."

"Well...How much time you got?" Case said jokingly.

"For my brother Case? All the time in the world..."

"Well, P. I need someone to help bring me to my senses."

"Tell me everything. You know I'm all ears. We have a lot of catching up to do as it is."

"Alright," said Case, taking a deep breath and staring out into the now pitch-black sky filled with the shimmer of bright stars. Redirecting his focus back toward Lincoln straddling the bench on which they sat, he could still see him clearly at a close distance.

"So remember the girl I told you I met last winter at The Hollar right before you moved away?"

CHAPTER 17

Fourgiveness

• • •

Lincoln and Case had caught each other up on over a year of absence from each other's presence in just under four hours. They spoke of Lara. They spoke of Bailey. They spoke about work. Lincoln spilled the news that he was back in town living with a woman who was now his fiancée, named Winn. Surprisingly, Case found himself engulfed in laughter a few times as they reminisced about the old times they used to have when they lived under the same roof. On the other hand, Case was not surprised by his friend's understanding of his current conundrum. Lincoln had not been aware that Case and Lara were dating, and had to dig deep into his memory bank to recall the only conversation they had about her prior to their current conversation. He faintly remembered Case's mentioning of meeting a girl on her birthday, but had not been privy to the events that had taken place over the last year and a half. Nonetheless, Lincoln's stream of advice had not changed from what it had been before. He only gave you as much of his opinion as you desired. Nothing more. Nothing less.

As their dialogue moved from the bench to standing behind the backstop, and finally to sitting on the tailgate of Lincoln's new truck, Case felt stunned by his friend's perfect interpretation of his story. It was as if Lincoln were there through it all. He understood what Case was going through somehow, and Case was somewhat shocked that his own thought-process was being conveyed through Lincoln's words.

"Look, man. Bottom line. If you think she loves you. And you love her. And you love her daughter. It's worth a second chance, isn't it? Let the water go under the bridge. You always talked about forgiveness. Hell, you had that big poster on your wall that said something about forgiveness."

"Father forgive them, for they know not what they do."

"Yeah, that." Lincoln paused. "I'm just saying I think that if you have made it this far, why not give it a real chance? If it isn't meant to be, you will know."

"You realize you sound like me right now, right?" Case joked.

"Ha – well, we became brothers for a reason. Trust me, man. Give it another shot. Something will hit you like a ton of bricks either way. Good or bad."

"When did you get this way, P'? We always were close and had talks, but you didn't used to be this deep. At least not that you let people see. Maybe a few times."

"When? Winn."

"Win-Win?" Case said with a questioned look on his face, wrinkling his nose and squinting.

"Yeah. When I met Winn. She is it, man. She changed me. For the better. I'm still the same old P', but I see things clearer than ever. She makes me want to be the Lincoln Parks that I am today. And that's why she's the one."

"Ohhhhhh. Well, P. I am happy for ya. I can't wait to meet her. She must be somethin' else."

"That she is. And if there's a chance that Lara makes the same change in you, it's worth trying to get through. I mean she has obviously changed you."

"Changed me how?"

"There was nothing in your life that I ever saw that made Lacey an after-thought. If she had that kind of effect on you, she changed you. Whether that is for the better, I guess we'll see."

"Guess so."

"Alright, man, well, I'm gonna get to the apartment before Winn sends out a search party, it's gotta be past midnight. Let me know how things go."

"I will. Thanks, brother," Case said as he hugged his friend. "I appreciate everything. Glad you're back."

As Case followed the tail lights of Lincoln's truck through the dark and foggy park, he felt good for the first time all day. It was as if he had a conversation with himself, and had justified everything in his life. Lincoln made a great point: any female that could make him give up the idea of him and Lacey fading off into the sunset together was one that he couldn't give up on. Not without a fight.

The confidence in his decision that he had made to forgive Lara made him feel at ease for the ride home, and carried him all the way to his bed where his exhausted eyes would finally rest. His justification of everything seemed to make perfect sense for the moment. But in the same moment, he had failed to realize that Lacey's disappearance from his life was not at his own will. The feelings had a shadow cast over them. She had been slowly erased from his memory, and it was no coincidence. For nothing grows in shadows.

Lara jerked open the door as fast as she could when she saw him through the peephole and jumped into his arms. She kissed him as if it was the first time.

"Case!" yelled Bailey, running to the two of them in the doorway from the living room of the apartment.

"Hey, squirt! Whatcha doin'?!" Case said through a voice muffled by another kiss from Lara.

"Mommy, Don't kiss him when he is talking to me," Bailey said in as stern a voice possible from a three-year-old. Case laughed out loud as he held Lara in one arm and placed the other on Bailey's blonde hair.

"It's alright. She just missed me."

"I didn't think you were going to ever come back," stammered Lara as she squeezed him tightly around the neck.

Case gently loosened her grip as he made his way into the living room. "I missed you girls, too. I'm sorry for overreacting."

Bailey looked at Case, confused from his words. "Overreacting?" Lara discounted what he had said all together, suppressing his ability to speak once again with another kiss.

"So how was work today?" Lara said pulling away from his lips.

"Same old, same old. They keep saying that a promotion is around the corner, but I think they are saying whatever it takes for me to stay where I'm at even longer."

"You'll get there, Casey," reacted Lara with a hint of empathy in her words.

"Please don't call me that, you're gonna get Bailey star–"

"Casey!" screamed Bailey as she looked up at them on the couch while playing. "Is you gonna play with me?"

"Is I?"

Bailey nodded her head in agreement, looking down for a moment to confirm that her toys had not run away before peering back in Case's direction with wide eyes.

"Well, I wanted to talk to Mommy some, but I will, ok?"

"Okay."

"We will be right back, okay, baby?" Lara said, untangling her legs from Case's on the bright red couch. She batted her eyes quickly in his direction, pulling desperately upon his arm to remove him from the couch and drag him back to the hall.

"Ouch!" yelped Case loudly as she yanked his arm. Startled by his reaction, Lara's face grew pale. Case looked first down at Bailey who stared up at him innocently, scared by the emotion that had escaped from him. Lara's face looked less innocent, and she waited for an explanation for the outburst.

"Sorry, wasn't trying to scare you and Mommy, Bailey," Case said in a smooth and calm tone. "Case hurt himself playing ball yesterday, he is just a little sore."

"What happened?" Lara said quickly. "Are you sure you're ok?"

"I'm fine, I ran into the fence when I caught a ball."

The explanation was enough for Bailey, who had migrated closer to the kitchen floor at the edge of the carpet, where her dolls were having their own conversation.

"Well, did you go to the doctor? Is that where you got that cut on your head?"

"No. I'm fine. And yeah, it caught me across my face and my shoulder." Case stretched out the collar of his white T-shirt to reveal a deep purple bruise that engulfed almost his entire right shoulder. Seeing the discoloration of his skin made Lara quiver.

"Babe! That is disgusting! You need to get it looked at. You're going tomorrow."

Case pulled the shirt back to the base of his neck, once again covering up the natural tattoo that made it difficult to see the permanent ink upon his skin. In an instant he was standing up. Simultaneously checking to ensure that Bailey wasn't paying attention, he placed his hand upon the bottom of Lara's chin. Rubbing her soft skin between his finger and thumb, he inched closer to her concerned face.

"Listen. Wounds heal. All of them. Every single one."

"But–"

"Shh," he whispered, closing his eyes and gently pulling her in the last bit. Their lips but a half-inch apart, he repeated in a whisper, "Every single one."

Case suddenly felt a sense of inner pride that he was able to express 24 hours of feelings in just a few words. The double entendre appeared to have been heard by Lara with no confusion. As quickly as he had drifted out into a body of emotions the day before, the look in her eyes pulled him back to shore. He stared into them intensely, like he could see his future self in her gaze. He blinked slowly once, and as he opened his eyelids once again it was as if her eyes were a shade of darker blue. Something he had never seen in them before.

"Ar-Are you staying tonight?" she said with a slight stutter.

"If that's ok."

"Yes, please."

"Then I'm here all night," Case responded with a wide smile, like all the world was right again.

"Ok, I'm gonna go plug my phone in."

"Alright."

Case redirected his attention toward the little girl playing 'house' with her toys in another world.

"I love you more."

"Nuh uhhh. I love you more," Bailey spoke on behalf of her dolls, mimicking a deeper voice for the man.

"Whatcha doin' over there, Bail?"

"The mommy and the daddy are tallllking," she responded without looking in his direction, drawing out her words as if irritated. Case laughed to himself and leaned back on the couch. He closed his eyes for a moment and smiled, grateful for his most recent breath. Reaching into his pocket, he pulled out his phone, and began to type a message to Lara in the other room.

'Get back in here. Missing you already. And I love you more.'

Case heard the sound signaling that his message had sent as he looked back toward Bailey.

"Bailey, do you still want me to play?"

Bailey responded but he didn't hear her. The sensation that filled his body as he read Lara's almost immediate reply caused his ear canals to shut down. He read it once again. And again. He rubbed his eyes and shook his head and read one more time to make sure he wasn't crazy. Or seeing things.

The fifth and sixth times reading it over, it was evident the response wasn't meant for his eyes. Clearly an accident. The seventh time brought sadness, and the eighth anger. His thumbs typed out a response seemingly on their own. Case stared down at the conversation for a few seconds before willing his body to his feet, despite the weak feeling that had crept into his legs.

C: *'Get back in here. Missing you already. And I love you more.'*
L: *'Yeah he definitely bought the whole thing. He is out playing with Bailey right now and he is acting like everything is fine. You were right he believed that all we did was kiss. I'll talk to you more about it tomorrow.'*
C: *'On second thought – I think I'm gonna leave. Don't text me. Thanks.'*

CHAPTER 18
Falling two pieces

. . .

"WHAT DO YOU MEAN, YOU broke up?!" Cage screamed surprised over the phone. "What the hell happened?!"

"Guess she didn't love me anymore."

"You just said you broke up with her..."

"I did."

"So... what, Case? You sound like you're not doing so well. Do you want me to come home from school and we'll talk about it?"

"No. You just went back last night. You stay where you're at. I'll be fine. I guess." Case's voice sounded as if the life have been literally pulled from his body. He lay still in his bed. The tears had not yet come. The shock of his nervous system had held them back like a dam until now. It took only the sound of Case's voice to convince his brother what he had to do.

"No, Case. You sound like shit. You would come see me. I'm coming home. It's not that far."

Case responded through the pain and the immense feeling of helplessness that was inflected in his voice. She had broken his heart. Once and for all. There was no decision to make. He was done. But the pain didn't care why it happened, or why Lara kept texting him. She had to know there was no return. The well was dry. He had not an ounce of forgiveness that remained.

"Do what you want. You're going to anyway."

"I'm leaving in five minutes. I will be home in like an hour."

The minutes that Case had his eyes closed seemed like hours. No sound was in the air. No movement. The empty house that would always seem to creak and settle in the slight breeze just outside the foundation was lifeless. Despite his less than emphatic attempt to stop his brother from coming home to comfort him, he could not wait to see him. He couldn't wait to see anyone who wasn't Lara. Each minute brought about a new prayer that he sent above, which seemed to have no answer.

Is this what I get? Why does this have to happen to me? Snap your fingers, God. Make me feel better.

His decision to forgive her the previous night could not have been a worse one. The feeling was much different than he had remembered. When Cheyenne broke his heart it had healed relatively quickly. He didn't feel the same then as he did now. This was total emptiness. This was a feeling like never before. The picture he had painted in his mind of his future family included Lara. And Bailey. He found himself quivering for breath as he abruptly came to a conclusion that he hadn't already. No more Bailey.

She had become HIS daughter, too. He clenched his eyes together hard to fight the new flood of tears that had formed for a new reason. The realization that he would no longer be able to play with her. No longer be able to watch her grow up. His heart wouldn't be melted again by her smile, or by her innocent "I love you" while putting her to bed. There was nothing left to melt anyway. Lara had taken care of that.

The thought of losing Lara suddenly wasn't at the eye of the pain he felt. It was Bailey. She didn't do anything to deserve this. She would have so many questions. As far as she would know, he left. He was gone with no explanation. No explanation outside of what Lara would tell her.

What would she tell her? Will she even remember me as she grows up?

Case stood up from bed and cleared the tears from his face. His eyes hurt from being overworked, and he looked as though he had developed pink-eye in both pupils. Worse than that, his stomach felt as though he had been punched. After all, his heart had just been destroyed. The pieces of it that Lara had not obliterated through her actions felt as though they had been infected with poison and had dropped to his stomach. There was a hole where his heart used to be. He sniffled twice and screamed deeply aloud in the empty house, "WHYYYYYY?!"

"What did I do!?" he bellowed to himself between sniffling to retain what little bodily fluids that hadn't already escaped through his eyes. He punched the drywall to his left as hard as he could, leaving a hole through it. He put his hands to his side and leaned forward against the wall. The scent of freshly exposed drywall hit his nostrils as his forehead rested above the crumbles of Sheetrock. His entire body hinged against the wall. He brought his arm up beside his head and rattled the wall twice, but this time with not as much force. He heard Cage's footsteps echo down the stairwell as his entire body collapsed to the floor.

Cage recognized that he had never seen his brother like this. Not with Cheyenne. Not with any girl. Not ever. He was witnessing a new emotion. One of sadness. Sadness with disappointment. Disappointment with disgust. Disgust with anger. Anger with helplessness.

Cage grabbed Case's arm as he lay on the floor. "Case. Really? Get off the floor."

"You have no idea how this feels, Cage. I just want to feel nothing right now."

"It goes away, Case. You know that." Cage paused. "You got over Cheyenne. You don't even think about her anymore."

"She didn't cheat on me, either," Case struggled to find the breath to speak.

"Wait, what?" Cage questioned.

Case's words reflected off the cold concrete floor at his brother's feet. "You heard me." The tears had stopped. The gauge was empty. A sensation similar to a bitter defeat at the end of a long journey found its way from Case to Cage. They both felt it. Case's pain coursed through his brother like it was contagious.

Suddenly Cage took his hand away from his brother's arm upon the floor, stood up straight and closed his eyes. His arms flailed behind his head in disgust and stopped behind his neck.

"I didn't know, Case... You didn't say anything. I'm sorry, man."

The sound of Case's deep breaths were his only response, sounding like the strong winds of a storm.

"If she did something like that, you don't want her, Case. She doesn't deserve you. I thought you just broke up with her because you argued all the time. I really didn't see that coming."

"You know you should be a therapist," snarked Case as he sat up and leaned against the dresser.

"Sorry."

"It's whatever. Like you said. I'll be fine right? I won't ever think about this after a while," Case bellowed sarcastically toward his brother.

"You know time heals everything, you've told me that so many times."

"I don't think I'll be forgetting any of this ever, Cage. This cuts pretty deep."

"But you're Case! You're my big brother. You always figure it out. Always."

"Not this time. I have no idea what my life is now. I'm lost. I'm alone."

"You are not alone. I'm right here."

Case shook his head condescendingly, wrapping his arms around his bent knees.

"I always have an idea of what to do. Where to go. Why something is happening. Until now. None of this makes sense to me. I have no idea why this happened. What I do now. Nothing."

"You get off the floor," Cage said, "and you hold on for dear life."

"Hold onto what? There is nothing to hold onto anymore, Cage. You think something is one way and you come to find out it is the opposite. You fall for someone and let your guard down. You get away from who you were and become this bumbling idiot. Sitting on the floor in your room. Crying over something that you would have seen coming a mile away if you didn't change who you were!"

Case's words escalated back into tears as he began shouting. He had no idea why he was yelling at his brother, but he couldn't stop himself. It felt good to release his emotions in the company of someone else.

"So tell me, Cage! Why don't you just solve it all?! That's what you came home for, isn't it! Tell me! Tell me what in hell I am supposed to hold onto now! What exactly do have to fall back on?!

Case buried his head in his arms and his entire body pulsated as he wept. Meanwhile, Cage had a tear of his own escape and run down his cheek. Cage wanted desperately to take away his brother's pain, as he had done for him so many times before. But how?

"Case., he said quietly, almost in a whisper.

"WHAT?" Case sternly responded toward the ground.

"When is the last time you went over to Grandma and Pap's?"

Case jerked his head up in confusion, nearly hitting it on the dresser behind him. He squinted in his brother's direction and bit his lip firmly. "Cage. What the hell are you talking about?"

"When?" Cage said calmly once again, unbothered by the harsh tone of his brother's reactions.

The enunciation in Case's voice represented that Cage had pinched his last nerve. And the look on his face was transformed to one of aggravation for the moment. A change from the sadness and gloom seconds before.

"Yesterday, Cage. Why are you asking me that?"

Cage knew that he was about to jolt his brother to his feet and could be subject to a brutal brotherly beating if he didn't get to the point quickly, yet he remained steady in his explanation.

"Well, when you walk in the side door, Grandma's got a sign hanging there at the end of the hall. You remember what is says?"

Case stared blankly up at his younger brother standing above him, realizing in that moment that Cage was no longer just that. In this moment, Cage was the brother, the friend, the person that he once was. What he needed to become again.

"Well... do you? What does it say?"

"I know what it says, Cage," he uttered under his breath, conceding that his brother had given him the answer he screamed for moments before.

"Well, you asked me what you had to hold onto. What you had to fall back on now. So tell me what it says."

A minute of silence passed before Cage spoke once again. "Well, even if you aren't going to say it, I know you know what it says. I'll leave you alone. Come upstairs if you want to talk some more."

Case heard his brother's light footsteps fade up the stairwell as he stood. With closed eyes, he envisioned the white craft sign that hung from a rusty nail in his grandparents' house with black lettering and a blue cartoon angel with no face painted on its edge. A sign that stated: 'Faith isn't faith until it's all you're holding onto."

CHAPTER 19

One thing

• • •

THREE DAYS HAD PASSED AND Case's entire body still ached. One would have thought that it was due to his body slamming into a chain link fence days before, but it was not. It was from his heart slamming on the brakes. Lara's actions were his biggest obstacle to date.

Somehow he had come to grips with what she had done. He had faith that everything would be ok. But time still stood still. He forgave her inside. But he still wasn't himself. Something didn't sit right about the entire thing. Initially, he ignored all of the incoming text messages apologizing for what she had done. He didn't want to think about her. Not at all. Even though it was impossible, for she had became his life over nearly a two-year span, he forced his mind away from her.

As the texts continued, he couldn't bear another one.

I told you to not text me. You did this. Not me.

Lara. Stop texting me. I do forgive you. But I can't forget.

What is wrong with you? Please stop talking to me.

Lara! I am not responding to any more of these. You made the bed. Now lie in it. With whoever you want. I will come leave the key and get my stuff one day this week.

No matter how many responses he sent, they wouldn't stop. The thought crossed his mind to change his number, but left as soon as it came. Strangely, the texts made him angry but left him feeling satisfied somehow. They were what was keeping him from the ledge. As promised in his last message to her, he wouldn't talk to her again for quite a while. Nonetheless, the familiar tone and accompanying vibration of his phone became a routine in his life following the break-up. He tried to get back to what he considered normal. Somehow his work didn't suffer, and he received a promotion that same week and had become a manager. In Case's mind, work helped. Staying busy there felt normal. Having people who now reported to him made him feel more important in the workplace than ever. His time spent there had been a godsend. He channeled his focus in the right direction between the cubicle walls, but when he left the double doors each night, there she was. Not literally, but in his mind.

Every night as soon as he walked through them, he would pull out his phone and call her to see if she had prepared dinner, or if she needed anything. He would ask how her day went. If there was anything she needed on his way there. How Bailey's day was...

Bailey.

The hole where his heart once was was still hollow, and had yet to regenerate at all. The hurt that he felt from what Lara had done and what he was forced to do was nothing compared to the feeling of weakness that nearly knocked him to his knees each time he thought of Bailey. The smell of the grass that struck him as the door opened reminded him of those calls, which of course led to his thoughts of the cute little blonde girl who had stolen his heart. The crisp air brushing his cheeks took him to watching her run around the playground in her winter coat, smiling and laughing. The long walk to his car reminded him of her endless questions as he held her little hand when they walked anywhere.

A single tear fell down his face as he sat down and looked in the rear-view mirror. Her toddler seat was no longer there. He couldn't ask her what kind of ice cream she wanted from the front seat. He couldn't see the elation in her face when she screamed, "Chockwhit!" He wouldn't see her again. He wouldn't get to see her grow. He wouldn't witness how much smarter she got each day. Nothing. Ever. Never again. These thoughts were what wouldn't allow him to move on. What made him restless.

The sound of metal clinking together as Case placed the keys in the ignition of the silent vehicle were interrupted by a loud slam against his passenger window.

"Case!"

He quickly wiped his face of the tiny dampness across his cheek and put the window down.

"Yes, Ky? Can I help you?"

"That how it is now? You became Manager Metzger and you don't let people know when you are leaving?!" she said, leaning into the window, her brown hair softly waving in the light breeze.

"No. Sorry. Haven't been talking to really anyone unless I have to, if you didn't notice."

"Well, I'm not just anyone... How are you holding up? Alan told me what happened."

"Yeah. I'm ok as I can be, I guess. Sorry I didn't tell you myself."

"It's ok. I get it. I'm glad you found that out now and not later on. Everything happens for a reason."

"Thanks. I know," Case replied less than emphatically, implying with his tone that he didn't want the conversation to continue.

"Just forget about her! If she did something like that, she definitely doesn't deserve my Case."

"Ha."

"Well, since you got the promotion and are Mr. Big Shot now, I think we should celebrate tomorrow night at The Hollar."

"Kylie. Tomorrow is Thursday. There is this thing called 'work' on Friday."

"I didn't say go crazy. When Alan texted me the other night, that is what he was asking me. If I would be able to come Thursday night to celebrate with you guys."

"Us guys? Wouldn't it be kind of important for me to be invited to my own celebration?" Case said, rolling his eyes and pulling the keys from the ignition in the process. He had hoped that his demeanor and tone had sent a signal clear enough for him to leave him alone for now. It did not.

"Well, I told him I think it is a great idea." She paused. "You deserve to celebrate a little."

"Since when do you talk to Alan other than when you're with me anyway?"

"Ever since he knows I am probably the only one who could convince you to come." Winking at him, she stood up from the car and backed away a few steps.

Case forced a smile, which she was sure to know was less than genuine, and shook his head. He put the keys back in the ignition and didn't speak. Putting the window back up while he placed the shifter into reverse, he heard Kylie's muffled voice through the glass.

"See you tomorrow night!" she yelled, smiling from ear to ear. She knew that she had been successful, and that Case couldn't tell her no. He gave her a slight nod of the head and raised his hand to her in acknowledgement as he drove slowly past her silhouette walking in the darkness beyond the parking lot lamps. Case thought to himself that the best part of the conversation that he just had was that he didn't hear the text messages come in through his phone as it rested in the cup holder. At the stop light, he unlocked his phone to see his notifications screen was full. Seeing they were all from Lara, he didn't even read them. He deleted them, maneuvering his eyes up and down from the phone to the stop light between each one. As the light turned green, he made the left toward the highway and tried not to look toward Bailey's favorite ice cream place. But the green neon sign lit up with 'Ruby's Ice Cream' shined so bright that it reflected throughout his car, and into his heart.

• • •

Case felt awkward and selfish for not putting off an aura of thankfulness and pure joy sitting in the middle of the large booth at The Hollar. He felt even more awkward peering across the empty tables to the spot where he and the crowned girl had first met. He looked away from it and stared down at his drink, blocking out the sounds of jovial conversation surrounding him. Swishing the ice of the whiskey and Coke in a circle, he was lost for a moment, forgetting where he was. He would much rather be sitting at home alone. At least there he wouldn't be perceived as rude for wandering off in his own mind.

"There he is! Congrats, man!"

Case barely heard the voice but paid no mind. Odds were that whoever's voice it was, was indeed talking to him. He didn't care. Quickly Case justified his ignorance of the voice to himself, assuming someone else in the bar was there in celebration of something.

In all truthfulness, he recognized the voice. It was Ben. And the real odds of someone else celebrating something were slim to none. The only people in the bar that night whom Case didn't recognize were an older, gray man playing darts in the corner with what one would presume was his wife, and a stocky twenty-something bartender he had never seen before. The bar was empty, besides the handful of his friends.

"Shut the hell up and sit down.... Congrats again, buddy!" He heard Alan's voice boom beside him as Alan's elbow dug into his side with the comment.

"You realize I don't even have to look over there to know who just walked in, right?" Case's voice echoed, pausing his glass right before his lips as he spoke.

"Huh?"

"Ha, Klein.... You are only a dick to one person in this world. So, even though I didn't look to see who was talking, what you said gave it away."

"Yeah. Sorry, man. Not sure who even told him to come out tonight," Alan smirked in Ben's direction adjacent from him, knowing he had spoken loud enough for him to hear.

"I'm sure you did. As much as you bust his chops, you can't stand it when he isn't around."

"Yeah, you're right, Case."

Case, befuddled by his friend's response, stared toward him. Surprisingly, he had sounded serious.

"I can't stand it when he isn't around. Because if he's not around, then his sister's not around. And God Almighty, she has got some tig ol's!" Alan erupted into immense laughter, which could be heard throughout his large gulps of beer.

"Klein... Jesus... that's my cousin."

"You know I'm just playin', Case," smirked Alan, winking and making a suggestive noise as he snapped his index finger toward Ben.

"You all need another drink over here?" said the raspy voice of Glen, their favorite bartender.

"I'm good, Glen, thanks," blurted Kylie, sitting across from Case.

"I'll take another one. Babe? You want anything? Coke? Water?" said Scott attentively.

"No," Marie quickly reacted. "I told you that before."

"I apologize for asking."

"Whatever."

"O....K.... Alan?" said Glen, wiping a bar towel between his large, grease-stained hands.

"Buuuuuuuuuuurgggghhhhhhhh," belched Alan at the top of his lungs, holding his empty mug toward the sky, immediately drawing laughter from the entire group. Marie's serious look toward her husband was gone in that instant.

"Got it, buddy. What about you, Case?"

"Good for now, man, thanks."

"You alright, bro?" Glen nodded in Case's direction.

"Shipshape. Celebrating," Case said with a sarcastic smile and a thumbs-up.

"Congrats. On whatever it is. Well, I'll be right back, let me know if you all need anything."

"Thanks, Glen!" exclaimed Marie, almost immediately followed by Ben, who had gotten his own drink from the bar and was sitting back down.

"Why didn't you tell him why we're celebrating?" said Klein.

"What's he care about my job?"

"Job? Screw your job. We're celebrating you dumping that hoebag."

Case showed no emotion. He didn't feel any either. Besides, he knew that Kylie or Marie would almost instantaneously reprimand him for the comment. It wasn't if, it was who.

"Alan!" screamed Kylie, reaching across the table to firmly smack his arm.

"What? You don't hear him arguing, do you? She was useless."

"You don't need to talk like that. They have literally only been broken up like five days."

"Yeah, Alan. Don't be an ass," added Marie, her voice streaming past Case in Alan's direction. She placed her own arm on Case's and rubbed gently. "I'm sorry about what happened. AND that Alan is being an asshole."

"He's fine. You're fine. I'm fine. Doesn't matter, right?" Case said in voice slightly above a whisper.

"Look. I'm sorry I'm not sorry. I'm not gonna apologize for Lara being a conniving bitch. He knows I couldn't stand her. I chAlange any of you to tell me one thing good she brought to him!"

"Alan, easy," said Scott, suggesting to him with his eyes to change the subject. Seemingly saying *'Case is right next to you, dude... cool it.'*

"No. I'm sure he agrees," Alan continued loudly. "I'm waiting. Somebody give me one thing. And I will never talk about it again."

The silence that came over the group was one of shock. They couldn't tell if it was how Alan had felt the whole time about Lara and he was venting it now, or if the beer had begun talking.

"See?! Silence. I rest my case. And *our* 'Case,'" Alan gloated, taking a long drink from the fresh mug Glen had just set in front of him and putting his arm around Case's neck. Case's body moved from his long-time friend's gesture, but his eyes didn't. Staring down at the table next to his drink, the group could tell that he was hurting. As the awkward silence waited to be broken, the group randomly exchanged uncomfortable looks with each other. The silence was broken by Case's voice, this time clear and gentle.

"Bailey."

"What?" said Alan, removing his arm from Case's neck and adjusting his pants in his seat of the booth.

"Bailey."

"What about 'er?" Alan said, confused.

Case didn't know if he really didn't understand, or if he was too drunk to hear anything. So he chose not to say anything else.

"What's he talking about?" Klein looked quickly around the table, realizing that Case wasn't answering on purpose.

"He said Bailey. You heard him. You said you would shut up about it forever if someone gave you one thing she was good to Case for. And he just gave it to you," said Kylie sternly across the table top.

"Oh."

Despite his great friend's words and actions over the last few minutes, something had hit Case. He knew what he needed to do to start feeling better. He stood up from the booth seat to the side of the table.

"I gotta get outta here. Thanks, guys, for comin' out. But I have to go take care of somethin'.

"What? Where are you goin', dude?" said Scott, shifting with the paradigm of the conversation.

"I just gotta go do somethin'. I appreciate you all inviting me out, and getting me a few drinks. But I need to go."

"Well, alright, man. Drive safe."

"See ya, Casey! Congrats on your job!"

"Thanks, Marie, I'll see you all later," Case said calmly, knocking his knuckle on the table in acknowledgement to them as he walked toward the door.

As he walked out, he heard the bickering behind him.

"Look what you did, Alan! You pissed him off and now he's leaving."

That wasn't it at all. After all, the entire conversation had somehow brought him an idea that would provide him with some closure, which he desperately had been calling out to God for.

CHAPTER 20
Something four Bailey

• • •

CASE WATCHED THE BROWN AND yellow leaves spiral to the ground one at a time like they were taking turns diving as he lifted the pencil from the paper. The words had spilled onto the perforated sheet with great ease. With each word he felt his back get lighter and his eyelids heavier. He had always been much better expressing emotion through written words than verbally, but this time was different. No corrections. No erasing. No crumbled papers next to the wastebasket. Just a single sheet of paper, and the granite color that the pencil left behind as his right hand slid across it.

"Hey, Case, what are you writing?" Case heard his mother carrying in bags of groceries through the front door.

"Oh hey, Mah. Nothing."

"You look awfully focused there. Your head didn't even move when I opened the door."

"Yeah, just can't write fast enough."

"Hmm. Well, can you give me a hand out here real quick? Or will that break your concentration?"

"Of course."

"Sorry, it's just really starting to get chilly out here," said Lorrie Metzger, holding open the French door for her son.

"It's no big deal, Mah. I can spare a minute or two, and yeah this is really cold for September."

Case grabbed the plastic grocery bags with one arm and slid them up his other wrist, both attempting and succeeding to gather them all at one time. His mother rolled her eyes toward him and shook her head.

"You don't have to get them all, Case. I can help, you know?"

"I know. I got it. Just get the door."

His mother fled quickly up the steps of the front porch to open the door once again. As Case climbed the steps with five or six bags on each arm, he heard his phone chime from the kitchen table faintly in the background.

"Case! Your phone's ringing!"

"I hear it, Mom," Case responded as he backed through the doorway, barely closing it with a swift kick behind him as he maneuvered toward the kitchen. "It's just a text. Did you see who it was?"

"No. I just heard it beep and it lit up."

"That's what phones do, Einstein," Case joked toward his mother. She wrinkled her eyes, and stuck her tongue out at him in an act of mimicry. Case continued in a joking but condescending tone as he placed a box of cereal in a high cabinet. "Just hit the button on the front and tell me who it is, please."

"Alright, alright," she said from across the countertop, picking up the phone, appearing to examine it like a foreign object through the corner of Case's vision.

"I can figure it out. Just give me a second."

Case laughed out loud. "I'll be done putting all of these away before then."

"It's good to have my Case back, I will say that," she said with a smile.

"What do you mean?"

"You and Cage. And your father. All you ever do is pick on me. But you haven't really said much for the past week."

"That's helping with that," he said, nodding toward the paper and pencil lying upon the wooden dinner table.

"Writing? Really? What did you say you were writing?"

"I didn't."

"Oh. Well, it looks like a poem."

"It's not a poem, it's a letter."

"Letter to who?"

"Don't worry about it, Mah. Who texted me?!" he said through a chuckle while he emptied another bag into the cupboards.

...

"Mom, who was it?" he stared at her, slightly concerned.

"Lara."

Case's eyebrow's raised and the wrinkles of his forehead became defined through the glare of the kitchen light above him. "That's not funny."

"It is from her."

He let the bag of dish soap and other cleaning supplies free from his grip and they rattled loudly on the linoleum floor. 'What the hell does she want?' he thought to himself, and the words soon followed.

"It just says 'Can we please talk? I'm sorry. Can we pleeeeease talk?'"

"She already knows the answer to that," Case said sternly as he swiped the phone from his mother's hand. He subtly shook his head as he unlocked the phone once again and held the screen close to his face, confirming the message his mother had relayed seconds earlier. He looked toward her in disgust at first, but his expression changed quickly. Staring down toward the phone, he noticed the paper and pencil sitting on the table once again and felt a sense of relief.

"You going to send her one back?" Lorrie Metzger broke the silence.

"Yeah, I am."

"You know what's right."

"I know I do. I'll be downstairs," muttered Case, grabbing the sheet of paper and writing utensils from the table and pinning them to his body between his ribcage and elbow.

As he walked down the unlit stairwell to his basement bedroom, the light of his phone created a glow off of the unfinished drywall surrounding him. He flipped on the light, keeping his focus on the small screen as he typed. He finished typing out his text before sitting down at his desk and throwing the device onto his bed to the left.

Her interruption was unexpected, as the messages begging for forgiveness and another chance had stopped days before. He thought they were over. Case still thought of the way things were on a normal basis, but was determined to establish a new normal. A normal that once again would be without her in his life. And the letter in front of him was his ticket there. He was convinced. Somehow, he knew it would help him turn the page. He knew it was what he needed to do. He knew it would one day be appreciated.

The chimes of his phone buzzed through the room like an annoying cricket, but he kept his eyes toward the desk, rereading each line as he spent another 45 minutes writing. He thought about erasing a few things for a few more minutes and writing something different, but ultimately felt a great satisfaction with the stationery in front him.

Case grabbed the phone from the bed and typed out another message before placing it in the front pocket of his sweatshirt, soon adding his keys and the paper folded in half, entitled ~Bailey~.

"Where are you headed, Case?" said his mother as he opened the front door, allowing the cool wind of the early evening to draft through the house momentarily.

"I'll be back in a bit."

"Will you be late?"

"No."

"Alrighty. Be careful."

His father sat in the recliner, watching a baseball game on the TV in the corner of the room, and continued the conversation before Case could exit.

"Case!" his voice boomed.

"Yeah?"

"Stay strong. We're behind you."

"What d'you mean?" Case said in a fast-paced tone.

"We're just behind you, son. No matter what. Remember that. Be careful."

Case just nodded his head in agreement silently, not letting the emotions come through in his expressions as he closed the door behind him.

● ● ●

The night had grown even colder by the time he reached the door to Lara's apartment. The metal handle vibrated loudly, buzzing with each firm knock of his hand. It was a few seconds before she opened it, and he looked down at his watch as she did. It was almost nine o'clock.

"Hey," she said softly, standing there in her pajama pants and one of the shirts that he had left there.

"Hi. Sorry it's late. But I told you I was going to bring this back and I never did," he said, holding out his hand with the key to the doorway in which they stood.

"Thanks," she said faintly, taking it from his hand and crossing her arms, her slender body hidden inside the oversized shirt.

"Your stuff is in front of Bailey's room. I put it in a box for you."

"Alright," he said in a clear voice, attempting to keep the awkward dialogue to a minimum. "I'll grab it and let you get back in bed."

"Sorry I'm wearing your shirt. I always wear it to bed. Just forgot," she said to his back as he walked toward the bedroom to grab the box.

"It's whatever, you can have it," he whispered as he neared the end of the hall, nervous that if he spoke louder he would keep Bailey awake. As he got close to it, he realized that the light to her room was still on, and the door was open. For a moment he felt excited. She was still awake. He would be able to give her his gift and see her once more. Knowing she was normally in bed by now, he peered in the room toward the bed as he bent over to pick up the box.

She was nowhere to be seen. Clutching the box with both arms, he looked back toward Lara at the entry to the hallway with a puzzled face, not saying anything.

"She's at Mom's," Lara said, looking more and more unhappy and depressed with each passing moment.

"Oh." His heart sank in more than one way. He knew this was her fault. She did this. He forgave her once in his heart, but she lied. She cheated. But seeing her like this made him feel guilty. He knew his actions were not the cause of the situation in which they both stood, but right then it felt as though they were. He couldn't stand to see anyone like that, regardless of whether they should or not.

And then the one thing he had planned to do, which had kept his sanity for the last couple of days, he would not be able to do. Bailey was not there. He had envisioned having one last conversation with her. Reading her the letter, even though she wouldn't understand. But that was out the window.

Suddenly, the look of his father's face just before he had left home a half-hour earlier entered his mind. And the thought of his family being behind him gave him strength. He knew he couldn't drag it out anymore. The plan of giving the letter to Bailey hadn't played out like he thought it would. But not much ever did. What he had pictured would not become reality, like when one imagines what a new vacation spot will look like, but never does. But that didn't mean that it wasn't right. The real version could be just as good. It could potentially be better.

He tightened his lips and breathed in through his nose, setting the box down just before the front door as Lara stood like a statue, almost emotionless.

"I'm sorry, Case," she uttered to him with her arms still crossed as he dug into his sweatshirt pocket for the letter.

"I know you are." He paused, pulling the folded paper out. "Look, I don't want to step on your toes, but I brought this for Bailey. You don't have to give it to her if you don't want to. It's up to you."

She took the paper from his hand and sniffled as though crying, and wiped at her nose with her arm like a child.

"Of course I will give it to her."

"Thanks, means a lot," he said. "Well, take care of her. And yourself. I'll see you when I see you."

"You, too," she said, as he pulled the door open, grasping the box between his arms and somehow freeing his hand enough to close the door behind him.

As he placed the box in the trunk of his car, maneuvering his softball bag to make room inside, Lara unfolded the letter.

> *Bailey–*
> *The first thing I want to say is that I am so proud of you... I have had the great honor of being a part of watching you grow into the cutest and smartest little girl I have ever met. I know that you can't read this right now, and you wouldn't understand even if someone read this to you, but I thought that after all the time that I have spent with you and your mommy that you deserved to know why you don't see me anymore.*
>
> *Your mommy and I have gone through a lot lately, and I'm not sure when or if you will ever see me after today. Some things happened and Mommy and Case can't be around each other anymore, and it has*

nothing to do with you. When you are old enough to read this by your-self you probably won't even remember me, or even have any pictures of you and me together. But I want you to know how much I appreciate having been a part of your life. Everything you have taught me without even knowing it. You may not be my daughter, but I love you as if you are. Even if Case never gets to see you ever again, I cannot imagine that ever changing. For every day that passes from the day I am writing this letter, I will have thought about you 100 times, and how you are do-ing. What you are learning in school. What you want to be when you grow up. If elephants are still your favorite animal. If you still hug your mommy every night before bed. If you remember me, and all of the smiles we shared together.

I'm sorry that I won't be there when you finally learn to wink back at me before I leave the room after reading your night-time story. And I'm sorry that your mommy and I couldn't be the family that we were, and the family that such a special little girl deserves, but I promise that you will someday have something even better. I know this because I know this, and I have no doubts that you will grow from an amazing young woman into an adult. I don't know if I will ever have a daughter of my own, but if I do and she is half as smart, cute, and curious as the girl this letter is addressed to, I will have been spoiled by God yet again. I have never done anything in my life to ever have deserved to spend one day with you, much less for two years. But I was given that chance. And it was for a reason.

This letter to you is not only to thank you for your innocence and everything I have learned from such a young person, but it is for me. It is the end of a chapter of my life, and the start of a new one in yours. But the beauty of this book we call life is that we can always turn the page back and remember the good times of the past, no matter what the present brings. And even if Case is a stranger in your eyes as you read these words, this is my gift to you. To let you have one lasting memory of the love that I have for you. To know that somewhere in this world, no matter where it

*is, Case still loves you and wants you to have everything you deserve. And
he knows your God will give it to you, because God gave him Bailey for a
short time to teach him how to be the man he should be. I love you, Take
care of your mommy.*

 Love,

 Case

Lara wiped the tears from the page and placed the paper in one of her daughter's books on the shelf, as she heard the Mustang pass through the light and fade away into the night beyond her balcony door. The light of her phone blazed across her face in the darkness of the living room and her tears continued as she could no longer hear the distinct rumble of Case's car.

Despite knowing how he would feel ahead of time, Case still felt as if somehow everything was his fault. He shifted through the gears emphatically as he weaved in and out of the two lanes of wet highway. The rain seemed to leave the windshield as quickly as it came, and the thought of turning on his wipers never crossed his mind. The field of vision in front of him couldn't possibly be any more blurry than the glaze of hurt upon his eyes. The one street light of Jefferson turned green just in time for him to hang the right turn toward the Metzger household just a few miles away.

The house was dark as the front door creaked open, and the unexplainable guilt from within him began to make Case shake with anger.

I know this isn't my fault. Why do I think it is? he thought.

"Case!? That you?" he heard his mom peek around the corner.

"Yeah."

"Everything ok?"

"Yeah. I'm going to bed."

"Ok. Night night," said Lorrie Metzger.

Case heard her soft footsteps glide across the hardwood back to the master bedroom as he opened the basement door to retire for the night. As he changed into his sweatpants, and lay down in bed, he still fought the feeling of guilt that had come about. It felt unfair. It felt as though something wasn't right. As he rolled over underneath his cold sheets in the darkness he heard the vibration of his phone and saw the light reflect off the wall poster in front of him. He sat up in bed and grabbed the phone from the table.

This doesn't have to be it, read the text from Lara.

"You've got to be kidding me!" Case said aloud, slamming the phone onto the soft surface of the bed, returning the state of the room to complete darkness and silence. Case decided quickly that it was time to turn to prayer. It was time to ask God for help. His own efforts weren't getting him anywhere. Ignoring the text messages hadn't made him feel better. Being with his friends hadn't made him feel better. Writing Bailey the letter worked for a short time, but the feeling that accompanies uncertainty had only taken a short vacation.

> *God,*
>
> *I know I am ungrateful at times. I know I don't talk to you enough. I know I take you for granted. But I can't get through this alone. Well, I mean I know I am not alone and that you have been with me the entire time, but I need something. Something to push me forward. Something to tell me that I'm gonna be ok. Something more. I need a sign that I am going to get past this and become the man I need to be. A man you would be proud of. And with everything that has happened, I'm starting to doubt that I will ever be that. I don't know what to do. I don't know how to be Case without them anymore. I know I'm asking too much. I know I deserve to feel like this because I don't always do the right thing. I go against what you've taught me on an hour-to-hour basis. But I'm begging you. Please. Show me it's gonna be ok. Show me--*

Case's silent prayer was interrupted by the vibration of the phone once again. He exhaled deeply and spoke aloud to himself.

"I need to ask for these texts to stop is what I need to ask for." He shook his head as he picked up the phone again. "What's she gonna say next?"

Lacey Sewell (10:42PM): *Hey, stranger :) How's life?*

CHAPTER 21

Flash Fourward

• • •

I N THE YEAR THAT HAD passed since Case left Lara for the last time on a cold and rainy night, he slowly became a new version of himself. He spent most nights with his friends at first, and then work began to take over. The rush of being in a position of power overtook him, and the efforts that he put forth in his love life, or lack thereof. He was held in high regard by several areas of the firm, and most of his subordinates enjoyed working for him. Case treated them fairly. He stayed calm in unsettling situations. He was smart. The answers he didn't have he would eventually find.

Nonetheless, he still found time for a female in his life. For the first time he had begun to fear that he would never find love that was true, and in a self-fulfilling prophecy was doing just that. He went out on several dates, sometimes several different women in a week-long span. He would always find a reason to not give them a second date, or a reason they weren't what he was looking for. If the girl made him laugh and smile, or if she seemed interested in similar hobbies as himself, he would talk to her a bit longer, almost always over the phone or by text. But sooner or later every bridge would burn and Case would add another item to his list of things he knew he wanted in a counterpart; and ultimately to the longer list of things he didn't want.

Most weekend nights were spent at The Hollar with Alan, and sometimes Cage, who had finally seen enough summers to drink legally. Glen would have the glass or the mug full by the time the swinging doors shut behind them, and each glass would be dry by the time he would watch them walk out – more often than not with a couple girls who had just enjoyed their first night in the small-town watering hole.

"Never gonna meet a chick worth keeping in this place," Alan would say like clockwork.

"What about her?" Cage would add.

"Cage, you wouldn't know what to do with that," Alan always chuckled.

Case was himself, but afraid to fall again. Afraid things would go bad. Afraid he would open up too quickly. Afraid his work would suffer. Afraid he would miss his chance with Lacey.

'What chance with Lacey?' he thought each time. 'Somehow she has stayed single for over a year since she has been home. And all you do is think about what you could say to her.'

"Case! Why are you staring off into space?! Look what Cage just pointed out over there."

"Huh?" Case snapped back to reality.

"Your brother sure can't talk to a woman for anything, but he can pick 'em out in a crowd." Alan nodded to the crowded portion of the bar by the dance floor. "Little ditty in the pink and white."

"Yeah, I see her."

"What's your problem? You seem like you've been in a daze these past couple weeks?"

"Nothin', man. I was just thinkin'. Give me a freakin' break."

"Well, you haven't taken anything home in a while," Alan snickered.

"And you have?!" Case exclaimed.

"That's beside the point. Cage has been with the same girl for what, like, three years? He is still prospecting with me."

"Shut the hell up, Klein," Case remarked, taking a swig from his beer.

"What's more important than that anyway?" Alan joked, watching as the group of girls began to dance to a high-paced country song with one another. "Look at 'em go."

"Nothin' really, work said something about they might want me to take over the Carolina office sometime in the future. Kind of like a two-year plan or something like that. Was thinking about that–"

"That's awesome."

"I guess."

"What do you mean, you guess? Makin' big moves, son!"

"Yeah, I've never really thought about ever leaving here. This is what I know. Everything I love is here."

"Listen to you. You sap. What happened to the Case that was reeling in a different girl every other week and making sure they had a friend drunk enough to at least entertain me while you ran off God knows where?"

"I dunno, man. Just hearing them say that's what their plans are for me. It triggered something. I just thought by now I'd be settling down with someone. Makin' a family."

"That will come. Now let's go see if those girls want to practice makin' a family." Both Case and Cage chuckled at the comment, taking a drink from their glasses in the meantime.

"But seriously, man. What if I did leave?"

"I'd miss you man," added Case's younger brother. "But you'd be back, it's not that far and we would come visit. And you would be back around all the time, I'm sure."

"Hey, toolbag. Didn't you say this was in like a year or two, if it does happen anyway?"

"Yeah."

"So, what does it matter? You got your own nights to be a stick-in-the-mud and think about all that."

"Just hard to imagine not being able to just come see everyone whenever I want. Mom and Dad. You guys. Cage." Case paused. "What if something happened to Cage? I don't think I would want to be down the coast. He's one of the things that keeps me going."

"I know what this is about," Alan smirked. "Yeah, your parents, us, Cage, everybody you know around here. The things you are used to doin'."

"Yeah," Case perked up, excited that Alan finally seemed to be showing a hint of compassion with the whirlwind of thoughts in his mind.

"We both know this is about Lacey."

"It is not," Case responded sternly.

"Bull," said Alan. "Not sayin' all that other stuff ain't true. But she is every bit the reason you are overthinking this.

"What are you talking about, Klein? You're crazy."

"I'm crazy?! You are the one who never stops talking about her. And hasn't stopped talking about her since like middle school," Alan bellowed between gulps of a tall beer before mocking his friend.

"Guess what Lacey and I talked about at lunch today? Lacey did this. Lacey did that. Lacey and I are knitting a sweater together." He continued in an impersonation of a feminine voice. "Case is the best guy friend ever, because he wants to be with me, but is too much of a pussy to ever, ever, ever ask me out on a real date."

"I don't sound like that. And neither does she," Case said defensively, staring over his shoulder to halt his brother's laughter from the display Alan had just put on.

"It's whatever, dude. I'm not the one who buys the same holder ticket every Saturday night because he says it's his 'lucky number'."

"It is my lucky number."

"Zero Zero Zero Four Two One obviously is your lucky number.... seeing as you have never won with it once."

"I don't have to explain myself to you. Or anybody."

"No, no," Alan continued condescendingly, "you don't have to. It's pure coincidence that Lacey's birthday is April 21st, and even more coincidence that you have told me the story that you met her on her birthday."

"You knew about that number popping up randomly before that."

"No I didn't. You never talked about it before then."

"I've always seen it!"

"Are we really arguing over a goddamn number right now?" Cage chimed in.

The comment stopped them both in their tracks, and it was like it had never happened. Glen walked over behind the bar in which they sat, signing if they were good or if they needed another with hand gestures. They both gave him the thumbs-up for a refill, realizing that they knew each other's voices extremely well, having been able to hear one another over the band which had started back up.

Still desperate to prove to his friend that he was wrong, Case declined the offer to buy the 50/50 ticket drawing when a waitress brought it over.

"What do you mean, Case? You always buy this number. I saved it for you like Glen told me to."

"Not buying one tonight. Thank you, though."

Alan rolled his eyes at the entire situation, placing the frosty mug down on the bar and wiping his lips before standing up from the bar stool.

"Let's do this," Alan said, smacking his large palm on the corner of Case's shoulder upon his white and red flannel button-up. "You are wearing the party shirt after all."

• • •

The liquid courage had taken its toll on the three of them, and throughout the bickering, Case had lost count of the glasses that had been placed in front of him. He hardly remembered talking to the girls the next morning when he awoke much too late for church.

He checked his phone for messages and rubbed his still-tired eyes as he arose slowly from his bed. Knocking firmly on his brother's bedroom door a few times, he quickly became irritated at the lack of response and opened it anyway.

"You go back to school today?"

Cage opened one eye with his head still on the pillow, staring at the shadow of his older brother in the doorway.

"No, Tuesday," Cage said in a groggy voice, having just been woken. "It's fall break."

"Well, did I do anything stupid last night?"

"Case. Let me sleep, can't we just talk about that later?" Cage rolled over in bed and out of the beam of light from outside the room his brother was letting in.

"Nope. Because I have three messages from a number I have never seen before," Case said as he turned on the light. "And two of them aren't very nice. Listen to this one," he continued, reading the third message verbatim aloud to his brother.

"Have fun alone at your mommy and daddy's house..." Case read, pausing before finishing, "...you drunk asshole..."

"Yeah – don't sound good. Any ideas?"

"Yeah, I have an idea. Less Crown and Cola. And less telling girls you still live at home," Cage said, bursting into slow laughter, not awake enough to fully enjoy the rare put-down of his older brother.

"You and Alan kept on yelling at each other after the holder won, and then you just started being mean to those girls you two were talking to for no reason."

"After what?"

"The ticket that you always buy. You all were arguing over how you always buy the same number and Alan was saying how you buy it because of Lacey and so on. And it won last night."

"The one night I didn't buy it."

"Yep."

"Ain't that somethin'?"

"Yeah, well then, you and Alan yelled some more and then Glen told me to take you all home."

"How'd you drive? You can't drive my car."

"I didn't. You did. You both did. Neither of you would let me."

"Oh.... and this 'mommy and daddy' comment?"

"Not real sure how that got brought up. But once you and Alan made up by treating those girls like dirt together, they seemed to take a liking to making comments about you living at home. And about Alan being huge."

"Awesome...."

"Yeah, never seen you like that before ever, Case. I didn't know what to do."

"Guess I let my thoughts get the best of me."

"Guess so. But you kept bragging about some date you have next weekend with some girl from work when she gets home from vacation. Said you had gone out a couple times before. I don't know. You kept saying a lot of stuff that didn't make sense to me at all."

"Oh, yeah. I am supposed to go out with this girl Heather next Friday. Why the hell was I talking about that?"

"You're asking me?"

"It was rhetorical, Cage."

Case couldn't shake the thought that his number had finally won. Fittingly, on the one night that he didn't buy it to make a point. He stood in the doorway shaking his head at everything.

"Can't believe 421 finally hit."

"It did," Cage interjected his brother's train of thought. "You were livid. Couldn't believe someone else won with your number."

"I should have known it was gonna win this week. I saw it–"

"You saw it every single day this week one way or another. The clock. The ratios you saw at work. The license plate on the highway. I know. You told me like ten times last night."

"Oh."

"I'm your brother, Case. I know that number surrounds you. You've told me. We've met."

"Alright, smartass – just seems like I have been seeing it a lot lately. It's like haunting me."

"Maybe it means what you think it means."

"Maybe it doesn't, Cage."

"I'm just sayin'."

"Right, well, are you watching the football games with me today?"

"Yeah, if you let me get some more sleep."

Case pulled the door shut, and pulled his phone from his pocket once again, deleting the messages from the 687-0421 number that had been sent to him the night before. 'Guess I better call Alan', he thought, punching in the number on the touchpad and walking back toward his room.

CHAPTER 22

Two times the limit

. . .

THE AUTUMN SEASON HAD LEFT Jefferson early, and swirling winds accompanied the flurries that came with the coolness of the month of November. Seasons seemed to be the only thing that ever changed for Case. Every day had become a mundane routine. He would awake early enough to go to the gym before work, always ultimately deciding to hit the snooze button for another hour and push it off until the end of the day. Wake, work, gym, watch TV or surf the internet for a bit, sleep, do it all again. Case often wondered if his life was supposed to be this way. 'Maybe this is my purpose,' he would think to himself, while fighting the stop-and-go traffic on Interstate 70. 'Maybe I'm meant to be alone. Not lonely. Just alone.'

He would often chuckle to himself after thinking such thoughts, knowing that he was only thinking in such a manner with hopes of his luck changing. But the same sequence would always occur. Going on a second or third date at the weekend with someone new didn't even excite him. Watching his beloved Green Bay Packers on Sundays and the occasional lunch with Lacey was the only thing he looked forward to. He and Lacey worked within minutes of each other, yet only saw each other in person less often than Case made it to the gym prior to work.

As he drove toward the gym on a late-November night, he pulled his phone from the console, and found Lacey in his recent contacts list. Staring at the red light standing out in the dimness of the early night in front of him, his car sat at a stop behind a purple car that looked just like hers. But he knew it wasn't. With each echoing ring through the speakerphone, he smiled wider.

Simply waiting for her voice was enough to make him forget his day-to-day troubles. He loved the way her voice made him feel through the phone, and how he could hear the way she said something even when it was by text. He became attached to the memories of their conversations, and there was always something that stuck out in his mind every time.

"Hiiii!" he heard her say as the light turned green.

"Hi."

"How's life?" she questioned, as she did every time they spoke.

"It's alright."

"Just alright?"

"Better than bad, right?"

"I suppose. But I want to hear you say your life's going great!"

Her upbeat voice always seemed to lift him along with it, and his answer to the same question would be different after each of their conversations.

"Well, when it is going great, you will be the first to know."

"That's more like it. I can hear you smiling, you know," she said.

"Oh, can you? Well, I can hear you smiling, too."

"Guilty as charged." She paused. "So what's up?"

"Nothing, was just on my way to the gym and saw a car that looked just like yours. Figured I would see if you want to do lunch this weekend."

"I have a date on Saturday, but maybe we can do Sunday? No never mind, the Packers are probably playing," she corrected herself.

He laughed, knowing she had him pegged better than anyone. But the first part of what she had said had finally registered.

"Oh a date, huh?"

"Yes, this guy from work has been begging me to go out with him. I finally gave in. I figured it wouldn't hurt. In all honesty I should have said yes a long time ago. I have kind of had a thing for him since he started."

"Well, you'll have to let me know how it goes," he said, knowing that truthfully he wanted to hear about nothing of the sort. Unless, of course it involved how her escort had crashed and burned.

"Okayyy. He seems like a good guy. Although I am kind of leery about it. He won't tell me where he is taking me."

"You've told me a dozen times you like to be surprised. You love spontaneity."

"I do. But that doesn't mean I don't worry he's going to take me for a picnic in a cemetery or something like that."

"I'm sure that is what his plan is," Case remarked sarcastically, pulling into his parking space in front of the gym, taking the phone off speaker and pushing it to his ear.

"Better not be taking me to a cemetery," she laughed.

"Never know, we've had fun together doing dumber things than sitting in a cemetery eating peanut butter sandwiches."

She caught her breath from the laughter and spoke through the handset once again, "Now if we go on a picnic. No matter where it is. You know I won't be able to not laugh when he pulls out a peanut butter sandwich."

"From his Longaberger basket his mom gave him."

"Case!" she shouted, bursting into laughter once again.

"What?" he said rhetorically, "I was just saying he might sweep you off your feet..."

"It's possible." Her voice calmed down once again, before being cut off by him finishing his thought.

"And into the six-foot hole he dug before you got there."

"Case, that's not funny!"

"If it's not funny, then stop laughing."

"I can't. So what about you? Any new women you haven't told me about?"

"Yeah, supposed to go out with this girl again tomorrow night, actually."

"Again?! You mean someone is making it past the first date?"

"It's the fourth date, actually," he said in a clarifying voice.

"Ohhh, excuse me! How am I supposed to know? You never tell me about any of them until after you are done with them."

"You make it sound so dirty."

"Ha, well, it's true. You haven't been serious about anyone since Lara."

"I know what I want. And I know when what I have isn't it. Is that a bad thing?"

"No. That's a good thing."

"It sure is," he said, looking at his reflection in the rear-view mirror, shaking his head at himself. There she was. On the other end of the line. And talking to her was easier than anything else in his life. He was Case when he talked to her. Never anything more. Never anything less. And in that moment, he knew why most girls never made it to a second, third, or fourth date. They weren't her. They didn't make him feel like that. Like he did sitting in his cold car outside the gym, sharing silence over a phone with her that, for whatever reason, wasn't awkward. She made him feel alive. She made him feel like he had more of a purpose. Yet, for some reason he couldn't figure out, he was never the one taking her on a date. He was the one she was telling about it, and how amazing it was. Or amazingly awful. And as he watched the clouds turn shades of pink and orange in the distance, this talk had found its way to his memory bank. Whenever he would see the clouds change colors from the setting sun in the future, it would bring him to this night. This conversation. This feeling of utter happiness, yet complete emptiness. The same way each time he would look down to see his shoe untied, it took him to the night of Scott and Marie's wedding. How beautiful she looked when he looked up after tying it before they danced. The same way that the sound of a wind chime took him to her parents' porch, where they sat talking into the hours of the night on summers off from college.

All the memories were identical. They made him feel good, and they made him feel bad. For, as happy as he was in each of the moments of his past involving her, he could never convince himself to take the leap. For the fear of things changing. For the fear of denial. One way or another, things could never be the same if he did. His opportunities were sure to dwindle to nothing, if they were existent at all. But there was always down the road. Down the road at some point he would find the courage to change things for better or worse. At least he had always thought so.

This time felt different. The road had forked, and he didn't turn. He stayed the path he had always been on, and something told him that the 'road closed' sign was just ahead. The pit of his stomach suddenly felt as if he had been punched. Continuing the conversation for a few more minutes revealed that she was genuinely excited for her upcoming date, and that yet another guy would become in her eyes what she was to him. He was careful not to let the resentment show through his voice, as he continued to downplay the entire ideal.

The feeling loomed over him like a thick fog for the remainder of their conversation and throughout the next 24 hours into his fourth dinner date with a woman named Christina, whom he had met through a mutual friend at work. She was interesting, smart, and even somewhat funny. They had enjoyed their first three dates together, but Case treated her poorly on the fourth night, not listening to her stories and dazing off into his own thoughts instead. Not laughing at her jokes, and giving nothing but forced smiles. Yet another failed attempt at a relationship. No one measured up. To make matters worse, he knew that he was making her feel uncomfortable. He knew that there were a thousand other ways to let his date know that he wasn't interested in their courtship continuing, yet he couldn't stop himself.

When she stormed away from the restaurant before the bill even arrived at the table, Case felt like he had hit the bottom. Not only had he wasted a woman's valuable time for four dates and two weeks, but also the one thing in his life that had always given him a glimmer of hope, for some reason, fell dark. He left cash on the table that he knew was sufficient to pay the bill, finished his beer, and walked toward the entrance as he loosened his collar. For a November night it was unusually warm, and he didn't even bother to put on his coat as he sat down in the car. He didn't care if it was chilly or warm. He didn't care about anything really, as he peeled his wheels and directed the Mustang toward The Hollar.

"What's goin' on, man. Crown and Coke?" Glen said as Case sat down at the lone open seat at the bar.

"No Coke," he said sternly, staring seriously in Glen's direction, as he watched the bartender put ice in the glass in front of him.

"Alan gonna have beer or Jack when he get—"

"Alan's not coming."

"Oh. Just you tonight?" Glen questioned, pushing the glass full of Canadian bourbon to Case.

"Yep."

"Everything alright?"

"Yep."

"You sure?"

Putting the glass to his lips, Case seemed to stare through Glen as he responded the same way once again, before proceeding to drink the entire glass, slamming it down on the black bar top.

"Alright, then..." Glen paused. "Another?"

Not speaking, but rather putting his hand out above the glass awaiting it to be replenished, Case raised his eyebrows in disgust toward Glen for not refilling it without command and turned to the mid-forties-looking woman sitting to his right. She wore an outfit not suited for late-November, a lime green miniskirt and a white, strapless top. Her hair was dark red, and the make-up on her face appeared to have taken several hours to doctor up.

"So what's your name, sweetheart?" he interrupted her chat with a woman similar to her in age, but noticeably shorter, and with bright, blonde highlights streaking through her brunette hair.

"Lara. And you are?"

"Of course you are Lara. Who else would you be?" he said, pausing and knocking back another full glass of bourbon before continuing through his face, scrunched up from the taste.

"I'm Case, Lara. What brings you to The Hollar tonight?"

"We live in the development. This is my friend, Dianna. Her husband is out of town for the weekend and we figured we would come down for a few drinks. Why did you say *of course I'm Lara?*"

"Not important. Good to meet you, Lara. And Dianna," he babbled on, extending his damp hand from the condensation of the glass for a handshake.

"You said your name was Casey?" Dianna said, authentically awaiting his answer.

"Case. No. Why? Don't ask me why," he asserted, turning his entire body toward them on the bar stool. "Glen..." He knocked his knuckles on the bar to get his attention during a break in the sounds from the jukebox.

"Yeah?" said an unenthusiastic Glen as he approached the three, leaning his massive forearms on the edge of the bar.

"Don't act so excited, buddy." Case's head bobbled back and forth as he spoke of the bartender condescendingly toward his two new acquaintances. "What's with this guy?"

The two women withheld any reaction from the comment as they looked to see the bartender's face.

"I said 'Yeah?,' Case. What do you need?" Glen's voice bellowed.

"Another Crown on the rocks... and whatever these lovely ladies are drinkin' tonight."

"Case, you've been here ten minutes, don't you think you should pace yourself?"

"I appreciate your concern, Mr. Harley," mocked Case. "But what are you ladies drinking? Glen will make you whatever you want after he's finished pouring that there Crown in my glass."

Glen reluctantly filled the glass once again with the light brown whiskey, melting the ice almost immediately as it swirled into it.

"I'm sorry, you said your name was?" Case stammered, looking at the woman in green to his right.

"Lara."

"Oh yeah! How could I forget? What would you like, sweetheart? Anything. Anything in the world."

"I'll have another daiquiri," she said, watching Glen concoct it before them.

"What about you, Miss Husbandsouttatown?"

Both women laughed, somehow seeming charmed by Case's ignorance.

"I'll just have a beer."

"Beer?! Husband flies the coop for the weekend and you don't want the hard stuff?!" Case said, attempting a joke. "What about your Lare – Uh... where's your husband tonight?"

"Don't know. Don't care."

"Oh. Yeah? Whysat?" Case said, moving his attention back to his glass as he emptied it once again, feeling less and less control with each breath that he took.

"We've been split for about six months now."

"Oh that's a shame there, honey. That there daquiri should help you with that." He pointed toward the frozen mixture Glen had just set down on the napkin, then moved the same finger toward his glass and his eyes back at Glen.

Glen bit his bottom lip out of anger toward one of his regulars, knowing that this was not the Case he was accustomed to dealing with. He shook his head as he emptied the remainder of the bottle into the glass.

"I'll have to get another bottle from the back, Case. So don't chug this one."

"Ok, Ok," said Case, pushing his stool away from the bar as he leaned in on his arms to brace himself. Glen walked away around the corner as Case looked back toward the older women.

"So, you left your husband. That's interesting. What happened?" Case blurted out loudly over the loud Eric Church song booming through the speakers of the room.

"He left me. I didn't leave him."

"No wayyy," said Case, making an awkward face accompanied by a disturbing noise with his lips and tongue. "Look at you. No guy would leave something like that."

"That's sweet of you to say. But yeah, he did. But it is what it is. I get to have fun like this again."

"And this. Is. Fun.... Ain't it?" Case said, leaning toward her and placing his hand on her thigh where the bare skin of her leg met the skirt, finishing his drink with the other hand.

He washed the whiskey around in his mouth and closed his eyes as he swallowed, with his hand still on his neighbor's leg. He suddenly felt tired. He opened his eyes and looked to his right to see her smiling and laughing at him. He closed his eyes once again as he set the glass down. This time when he opened them, it was to red and blue lights behind him, and his own pale face in the rear-view mirror.

CHAPTER 23

Still here four a reason

• • •

"CASE."

"Case."

"Case."

"What, Dad?!"

Brett Metzger's voice was surprisingly calm, given the circumstances. Neither of them understood how the car was drivable. The mangled tire that lay upon the side of the road clanged as Case's father whipped it to the side from his knees. The unusual warm feeling that had overtaken the area had left overnight, and Case's hands shivered as he bent to pick up what was left of the metal and rubber and place it in his father's truck.

"Case," his father uttered again. He spoke softly yet his words cut through the wind clearer than if they stood in a silent room. The bed lining of the truck shook as Case hurled it over the tailgate. He was surprised that his father was talking to him, for the ride back to the scene included no conversation.

"Dad. I heard you. Why do you just keep saying my name? I said 'What?' like five times already. I get it. You're disappointed. Well, guess what?! I am, too. Do you think I am proud of what happened? Do you think it feels good that I have no idea what I did to my car? I messed up. I know that!" Case erupted as he slammed the tailgate shut.

When he walked around the side of the truck to see his father kneeling by the car, he saw what he should have heard in his father's voice. The rough, dark red skin of his dad's face shimmered with tears in the morning sun. As the wind dried his face with each gust, the gloss of a new tear slid down his face. Case immediately felt more regret than he already had for his actions.

"Disappointed? No, son. I don't think you get it."

"Look, Dad... I-I'm. I'm sorry I didn't mean–"

"You don't get it. You don't know what it's like to hear the phone ring at 3 in the morning. And seeing the look on your mother's face. I never felt so helpless in my life. I had no idea what she was going to say when she put the phone down. I couldn't move. She held that phone to her ear for what seemed to me like a week while I waited to find out what it was about."

Case had to remind himself to breathe. The cold air filled his lungs as he felt weaker than ever before. He had thought he was disappointed in himself before, but had found a new low as he fell deeper and deeper into a depressed feeling with each word that left his father's mouth.

"You're my oldest son. I was so scared. I've never prayed so hard as I did when your mother was holding that phone. For all three of my boys. It was a relief to hear you were at the police station. Not disappointment. You were alive. I can't imagine putting any of you boys in the ground. I love you, son. So goddamn much. You are smarter than this. My boy wouldn't have done this. And I don't know who you were last night. But I sure as hell pray to God that you know who you are now. You are lucky. You could easily be gone. You could easily be..."

Case watched as his father squeezed his eyes shut tightly and rubbed his face. His dad couldn't speak anymore, but he didn't need to. Case had been fearful of his father's reaction, but hadn't thought about the emotional burden he had placed on those who cared for him. He needed to learn his lesson. As his father had said, he could have easily not been feeling the cool sensation of air in and out of his lungs. The way the chill of the air felt as if he was chewing some mint gum as he concentrated on each wave of breath, realizing that each of his breaths was a privilege. He was still here.

His mind raced through all of the horror stories of people whom he had known who had died from drunk driving. Why hadn't he learned from them? He hated himself for allowing the alcohol to take him over. For letting himself lose control. For putting his family through this. The look on his dad's face hurt worse than any pain he had ever felt in his life.

'Why am I still here? And there are so many people who don't get to learn their lesson. What makes me special?' he thought to himself as he sat down in his car bearing a spare tire and bent sheet metal dangling inches from the ground. 'Why me?!' he screamed to himself through the tears, watching his father's truck yield onto the road behind him in the rear-view mirror.

"Tell me, God. Why am I more important than John!? Why do I get to live when he doesn't?! And Megan?!" he cried, referring to friends from high school and college who had seen a fate much different than his own while making the same mistake. "There has to be a reason!"

He sat in his car for several minutes after pulling into the driveway, leaning his head on the steering wheel, searching for any type of answer that would allow him to gain the courage and strength to exit his car and face his family again. The thoughts of the legal punishment that lay before him found their way into his thoughts, but they didn't bother him. He had done wrong. He deserved everything that was coming to him. He was much more concerned with making it up to those who cared about him. Making clear to them that he was sorry for what he had done. That they knew he wouldn't put them in that position again. Ever again.

"Gonna be expensive, that's for sure," said Lorrie Metzger, sitting next to her husband at the kitchen table.

"Yeah. I know." Case shook his head, still in disgust with himself.

"Did the cop say anything about what you need to do from here? Might as well be proactive," his mother continued optimistically.

"Not really. He just said there was a really good chance that I would get probation before judgment. Seeing as I don't have any other criminal record."

"What's a good chance?" his father interjected.

"He said 4 to 1."

"You don't remember anything between being at The Hollar and getting pulled over, but you can remember specific odds that the officer said to you..."

"Yes."

"Can't say I'm surprised. You remember everything, kid."

"That he does," added his mom with a smile.

"I remember it because of four two one, Dad."

"What?" his dad responded, puzzled by the remark.

"You know. The numbers from the clock. The ones I see all the time."

"Ohhhh. Four- TWO- One," his dad reacted, emphasizing that he understood that the word 'two' was a number this time. "You and those damn numbers. You and any numbers. I don't know how you remember half of the stuff you do. You are ten times smarter than I have ever been. But you make some of the most un-smart decisions."

Case bowed his head in disgust at himself and retired to his room. As he lay back, placing his hand behind his neck for support, he closed his eyes. The thoughts that raced through his mind hardly stopped to allow him to register each one, but one in particular caused him to open his eyes. He stared toward his dresser where photos of all of his friends and himself sat in dollar store frames that had been given to him as an office Christmas present weeks earlier. He didn't focus on the one of Alan, Ben and himself all holding their glasses in the air for a toast, or of Jason and Marie's wedding photo. He stared at the photo of him and Lacey. This was it. Enough was enough. Suddenly he felt loose. Like he had nothing to lose. Not like the night before when he had allowed his drunken self to lose control, but in a good way.

He had always been known as being somewhat eccentric, and he thought so himself as well. After all, he had convinced himself that random numbers seen from place to place weren't just numbers. "I might be crazy," he said aloud to himself. "But I'm not still alive to sit here and sulk. God has more of a plan. Something more for me to accomplish. I have work that couldn't be left undone."

Just then, he heard his mother yell down the steps.

"Case!"

"Yes, Mother!" he yelled back from his bed, peering over his shoulder toward the sound of his voice, still in his bed.

"Case!"

"I said what Mom?!"

Her light footsteps trickled down the steps quickly, and he knew that she had not heard him for a second time. As she turned the corner he spoke before she could.

"I said what twice, Mother?"

"Oh, you did?"

"Yep. What is it?"

"We're running over to your grandmother's for a while, they are making lunch if you want to go."

"I'm good. I have too much on my mind. Not really hungry," He replied, sitting up in his bed as she stood in the doorway. He glanced toward the picture of him and Lacey again while she tried to convince him to come along.

"THANKS, Mom, but I don't feel like going, and I'm not exactly proud of what happened last night," he emphasized. "I will go over and talk to them about it when I'm ready. I think I'm gonna go over to Alan's in a bit and tell him what happened. I'm sure nobody has any idea except Scott. He called me this morning."

"Eddie knows, and your brother knows."

"I know Cage knows, it's pretty fuzzy still... but I am pretty sure I saw him there last night. He didn't go with me, though, obviously."

"He was. He should be home soon from Amanda's. You should take him with you to Alan's."

"If he is home I might see if he wants to come."

"Alrighty, well, we will be back in a few hours, then. Love ya."

"Love ya, Mah," Case said, looking toward his phone, lying back in bed once again. Scrolling through the messages from the night before, he saw one from Cage. 'Call me if you need me to come get you later,' it read. He chuckled to himself, for it seemed that was all he could do. Last night's events were almost seemingly predetermined. Like no matter what course he had taken to get to that night, it was going to happen anyway.

His thoughts were surprisingly clear about the entire thing. He knew he was in for a long road ahead in being reprimanded by law enforcement and the state for his actions. But that was just what they were. His actions. He knew he was wrong, and it took him a very short period of time to realize that. Whatever was in store for him, even if it was jail time, he deserved. It wasn't even a tough pill to swallow. The clarity that rushed upon him actually made him feel thankful and brave. He was more thankful for each breath as he concentrated on them individually, closing his phone. And above all, breaking down and finally asking Lacey out for a 'real' date didn't seem far-fetched. He had been given the gift of a second chance, and there was no way he was wasting it this time. No response could equate to the feeling that has followed him throughout the night before into the morning. The feeling of helplessness his father's tears surrounded him with. The aimless purpose of his heavy drinking less than 24 hours ago. He couldn't fathom any reaction from Lacey making him feel like less of a person than the rock-bottom he had landed on. Nothing could. Nothing.

• • •

The jingle of the chain lock rattled in Case's cold ear as he awaited Alan opening his apartment door. As the latch turned, the two looked at each other respectively as if no altercation had ever happened weeks ago. They hadn't spoken much since then, but it was true friendship. The kind of friendship that doesn't know what a vacation is. No matter the amount of time elapsed between conversations or visits, it felt like they had been shooting the breeze together the day before.

"So at least it's not cold out," Alan said sarcastically as the two sat down across from each other in the matching recliners of Alan's single-bedroom apartment.

"Yeah, man. Makes no sense. It wasn't cold at all last night. It's what, like 20 degrees today?"

"Cold front, I guess," Alan remarked, "So what's goin' on?"

"Got myself in some trouble last night."

"Ha, like what? You forgot to pull out?" Alan laughed.

"Yeah, not exactly."

"Well, don't just sit there like a d-bag and make me guess. You gonna tell me what's up or what–?" Alan was cut off by Case's statement.

"I got a DUI."

"W-wait what?! Where? What happened?!"

"I was at The Hollar."

"Well, I could have told you that part of the story."

"Quit it, smart-ass, I'm trying to tell you what happened."

"So I guess you don't want a beer, then?"

"No. Do you want me to tell you or not?"

"I'm just messing with you, man. Where did they pull you over?"

"Like two miles from the house. I don't even remember getting in my truck. I remember getting out of it, though."

"Damn. What'd you drink? Crown?"

"Yep. Not sure how much."

Case went on to explain that he had shredded his tire, and walked him outside to show him the damage. Alan seemed much more serious about the entire situation once he found out that there was an accident involved.

"Wow, man. You don't know what you hit? You're lucky it isn't worse."

"I'm lucky I'm alive," Case said, tucking his hands into his pockets as the cold winter wind swirled around them in front of the apartment complex.

"That, too. I'm glad you're ok. Let's go back inside. I'm freezing my nuts off out here."

As the warm air hit them back inside the apartment, it brought an almost itchy sensation to both their skins. Case's pale white face had turned to a faint shade of pink from the cold, and he rubbed his hands together quickly for warmth before rubbing them upon his beard. Their conversation continued to one closer to Case's current frame of mind as they watched reruns of an old TV show in the living room. Even though he was hell-bent on pursuing Lacey once and for all, talking to Alan about it seemed necessary. He had to run it by him to see if he thought it wasn't a good idea.

"It's about time you grow a pair," was all Alan could reply with.

"Oh whatever, Alan. I'm actually going to ask her out. I'm gonna do it."

"As refreshing as it sounds to hear you say that you're finally going to man up, I don't believe you. You've said that before. So I'll believe it when I see it."

"I know I have. But I'm serious this time. I've got nothing to lose."

"What do you mean?"

"The way I felt last night sitting in the station waiting on Mom to come get me. The sound in her voice when I told her where I was. I've felt the feeling I always imagined would follow asking her out if she said no. Last night, I went to Hell and I bought the ticket."

"You're comparing going to Hell.... with asking Lacey out on a date.... Seems reasonable," Alan said, rolling his eyes. "You don't need to have an epiphany, you could have asked her a long time ago and you just never have."

"I just feel like I need to take advantage of everything I can. Do the things I was scared to do before. Maybe that's why I'm still here."

"Could be. But I still think you just ran out of excuses to be a pussy," Alan smirked, taking a swig of iced tea.

"Touché."

"So you realize that you have to take her on the best date of all time now, right? You built this up for years. You can't fall short now. Gotta pull out all the stops."

The awkward silence that followed was broken by Alan bringing to light a statement that couldn't be more true. The apartment walls were staring at both of them as Case pondered Alan's question, brainstorming how to make something unforgettable and effortless at the same time.

"She's gotta say yes first... but I'll think of something."

"Well, she doesn't HAVE to say yes," Alan said, raising his eyebrows toward Case.

"What do you mean?"

"Well..."

CHAPTER 24

Unfourgetwoble

● ● ●

"You did what?!" Lacey lashed toward Case as the two sat together on the bench. Its wood was old and splintering its spots, and the small metal beams that held them together had turned a dark orange with rust. Case rubbed his thumb across the aged metal and brought it to his face, observing it for just a moment, if only to avoid answering her for another split second.

She sneered at him now. "Case", she said firmly and abruptly, her eyebrows almost touching one another from the look of anger and disappointment in her face.

"Lace," he finally said in an eerily similar tone, mocking her voice and lowering his brow. It was a defense mechanism. He wasn't proud of what he had done, and she was the last person on earth he wanted to admit it to.

"It's not funny, Case."

"I know that. I'm not laughing."

"You know how I feel about drinking and driving. Why didn't you call me?"

"It's complicated."

"No, it isn't! It doesn't get much more simple than 'Hey! I'm drunk. I can't function a vehicle. I need to call someone,'" she uttered at the end of the bench sarcastically, in almost a robot-like voice.

"Alright, alright. I know. I didn't want to tell you it happened at all. I knew you would be the only person more disappointed in me than even myself..." he said above a whisper, resting his warm, beanie-covered forehead against his near-frozen hands. His hands stood still, but his head shook back and forth as she sat next to him, still in disbelief.

"You know." She paused. "This is the exact opposite of what—"

Case brought up his head from his palms and quickly looked toward her, confused as to why she had stopped talking so abruptly.

"Opposite of what?"

"Nothing, Case...Never mind. I'm sorry I said anything."

"Said what?!"

His intrigue grew larger with each beat of his heart, for nothing made it race harder than being around her, smelling her perfume, hearing her voice, feeling her smile. He suddenly felt nervous, just like he thought he would when he had left his parents' house earlier that day. More nervous than the time he waited between rings of the phone at the police station to hear the rattle of the phone before his mother's voice picked up. The butterflies that fill your stomach before a championship game. The chilling sensation that starts at your temples and spreads down your spine.

"Hey. It's ok...I know you're just concerned about me. And I know I was wrong. I know that," he said gently, placing his hand on her leg like he had never done before, at least not to her. Case could feel her smooth skin just beneath the tight, dark blue fabric, and he couldn't help but remember why he had met her in the first place.

"What were you gonna say, Lace?" he said again gently. Her head buried into her sweatshirt that covered clear past her bent knees as her interlocked fingers held her legs in place.

"Nothing," he heard, muffled through her sweatshirt.

"Don't say nothing, I know nothing means something."

"It isn't important. And it is freezing out here."

"Alright. It isn't that cold. I can barely see my breath," said Case, attempting to lighten the mood.

"Well, you never think it is cold. If you thought it was cold I'm sure I would be frozen solid," Lacey said, cracking a smile once again.

"Listen, Lace...."

She sat up, still cuddling herself in multiple sweatshirts, both of a different color. As she looked at him, waiting for him to continue his statement, he noticed how the cold beams of light shined off her face and the green sweatshirt beneath her gray Georgia Bulldog sweatshirt and multicolored scarf made her eyes seem brighter than ever. Something in them brought him comfort in what he was about to say. Something that he had never felt from looking in her eyes before.

Maybe it was how beautiful she looked sitting in the snow-dusted park on the bench next to him. Maybe it was the newfound courage that his life-changing experience brought to him. Maybe it was all of the short-lived relationships since Lara. Possibly a combination of a number of things, but Case had fAlan over the edge. There was no turning back. Life had changed for him only weeks before, but he knew as the words escaped his mouth that it was about to change again one way or another.

She didn't speak, only looked into his eyes as the hibernating words spilled from his heart into the crisp air of a Maryland February. He wasn't nervous. He didn't judge how to guide his dialogue on emotional intelligence or looks in her face. His words rolled on as if rehearsed, even though he hadn't really prepared for this moment as he always thought he would.

"I asked you to come here today, because we always used to. In high school. Breaks in college. Late nights or really early mornings after going to bowling or a softball game. We have had some long conversations on this bench. Sometimes even deeper conversations than I ever thought I could have with someone outside of my own mind. We have sat in silence and watched the leaves fall after my football games. We've hidden behind the trees when those sketchy-looking guys in the trench coats were over by the swings pushing each other in the dead of night."

She chuckled at the memory, and began to get lost in his words, amazed at how he remembered such specific times. Times that she had forgotten about until just then.

"I knew you forgot about that." He joined in her laughter before continuing.

"I pushed you on that same swing over there until past 4 in the morning when we were really just kids trying to figure out what life was. And every single time it felt like not a half-hour had passed. Time speeds up when I'm with you. I don't know where it goes. It seems like yesterday Scott and Marie and Ben and Alan... and you... and me... were caught by the cops building a fire on the edge of the park over there. I still don't know how the rangers got here so fast. But we ran like hell. That was years ago, Lace. But I remember it like it just happened. I remember you laughing and it sounded like you couldn't breathe lying on the hill, and I was so worried about you, but you were smiling so I knew everything was gonna be ok. I've sat here alone twice in my entire life on this bench. The first was before I met you, after the first day of middle school in 6th grade and I felt so alone like I didn't know anybody in the school. I sat here for hours on what was a brand new bench wondering if one day I would have someone who would sit here with me. Just to listen to how bad I thought my life was going. Someone who would tell me my journey was only just beginning and to stop complaining. I didn't care who it was going to be, but I felt like there wasn't a soul for miles and there were probably 30 other kids here that day."

"You never told me that."

"I never told anyone. I told Mom I went to a new friend's house after school and had dinner."

"Well, you have plenty of people now," she comforted him, rubbing her glove-covered hand on his shoulder softly.

"The second time. Was three weeks ago. I woke up after being driven home from the police station by my mother. It felt like a dream. No. A nightmare. I wanted to wake up again and it wouldn't have happened. Dad and I put the spare tire on my car and pulled the metal back so I could drive it home. Mom and Dad went over to Grandma Metzger's and they invited me, but I wanted to be alone. I ended up going to Alan's, but I came here first. It felt the same as it did the first time I sat here alone. Exactly the same. 15 years later, I felt like the kid in middle school who thought he had no friends. I hadn't felt that low since then. And as I sat here, I remembered everything that I was just talking about and so many other times I didn't mention. What was once the stomping ground, or the place that resembled how much there is to enjoy in my life, felt like it was all erased and I was back to my first afternoon here. I cried. I cried like a baby. Luckily this time there weren't 30 kids running around that would have inevitably pointed and laughed at the 26-year-old man crying on his own shoulder in the park."

This time she didn't laugh, but smiled gently in his direction, lost in his story.

"I clenched my eyes tight together so hard, trying to make it a dream like I had right when I woke up, but it just squeezed more tears out like I was a sponge. I opened my eyes to look up to the heavens and ask why God would let me make such a horrible mistake. Why I deserved to be here...and just when I did the wind picked up and it felt like it was negative 50 degrees. Then I saw the flurries. They were blowing all around out of nowhere. And then out of the blue I thought about how you and I have never sat here and talked while it was snowing. Or even when there was snow on the ground for that matter. We always used to go inside your house by the fire if it was snowing. Or Ben would bring the Jeep out and we'd go out to Tee's hill and ride the tubes until we were too tired to walk back up the hill. We never came here. Out of all of those conversations we have had in this very spot, there's never been snow."

Riffling through her memories, Lacey was at a loss to find one where they had done anything in the park in the cold of winter. He was right. They never had.

"It made no sense to me. I don't know why I all of sudden thought about that, but then I shivered. Not because of how cold it was, but because I started thinking about all of the things I had never done, all the things I've never said... And for some reason I don't think I will ever figure out I walked away from a grave mistake unscathed with a chance to do all of those things. Like sitting here with the most beautiful woman I've ever met in my life while the ground is covered in snow, I'm doing that right now. Because I was given a second chance and I'm not going to waste it. I'm not going to sit here and not tell you how much I care about you. How much I think about you. How when you're happy it makes me happy, and when you're sad I feel sad. How every single song on the radio reminds me of you. How the reason that I don't ever feel cold around you like you say....is because I get lost in the warmth of your smile. And I don't have a fiber of my soul that is thinking about how hot or cold it is at the time. I am never happier than during any time that I spend with you. Whether it's a minute. Or the entire day.... and what I really came here to talk to you about more than anything...was to tell you that I want to do more things that we have never done before...like me taking you out on a real date. One that you deserve. And if it doesn't go well, then at least I've done one more thing that I was given a second chance to do...."

Her lips felt cold against his as they both shut their eyes, leaning into one another. The breeze whistling through the trees of Jefferson Community Park might as well have been fireworks. The few stubborn leaves among the snow-covered limbs of the oak tree line rustled as if an audience was giving a standing ovation. She pulled away from him briefly and pushed his black beanie just above his hair with her right hand so she could see his entire face, which radiated jovially in her direction with a hint of shock.

"Case. Your second chance... is the best first date I've ever been on."

CHAPTER 25
One for the Money

• • •

TIME HAD SPED UP JUST as Case said it did whenever Lacey was around, and given their history it was no surprise. The months that had passed since their first kiss in the park were quickly an afterthought. It took little time for the entire group to adapt to Case and Lacey being an item; they had all expected it to eventually happen at some point. The only question for any of them was why it hadn't happened sooner.

There were few nights that the two didn't spend together from that day on. They would talk into the hours of the night, discovering things about one another that somehow they didn't already know. If something kept them away from each other, it was short-lived. Whether it be their work schedules, a snowstorm, or an evening meeting, they made time to spend with each other.

Case had found that his life had become everything that he ever imagined it would be and more. The numbers hadn't lied. It brought great satisfaction to him to find that his thoughts hadn't been crazy, and he thanked God every night before laying his head on the pillow for the long and rocky road that had led him to where he finally was.

Things were also much simpler than what he had imagined. He had envisioned that if he was ever given an opportunity for their relationship to evolve to what it had, it would have taken months before it would feel like a "normal" relationship. But the realization he had come to was that he had never truly fAlan in love with anybody but Lacey, and the sheer amount of love that encompassed his entire life was finally focused in a direction which he truly wanted it to be. Toward her.

Lacey had always daydreamed about the idea of falling into more than the love of friendship with Case, but had never imagined the level of perfection that had seemingly filled her life since that day. In the minutes that Case spoke to her through the piercing cold wind that surrounded the park, all of Case's emotions and feelings that he gathered over several years poured into her and filled her soul. She had found love in the most unlikely of places. A true love unlike any other.

As any newly blossomed love does, it acted as a buffer against any misunderstanding. In what could have been a combination of dear friendship that had fully developed, or an already established trustworthiness between them, came a profound and unconditional caring trait which they shared. To those who didn't know them, they appeared as if they had been a couple for years, and to those who did know them, they already were.

"Caaaase. Lacey is here!" yelled Cage down the stairwell to the basement.

"How are you today, Mrs. Metzger?" Lacey said to Lorrie, preparing a meal atop the island counter in the kitchen.

"I'm good! How are you, honey?"

"I'm fine. Thanks for asking," bellowed Brett Metzger's voice as he entered the kitchen, closing his water bottle and making loud booms across the tile with his work boots.

"I was talking to Lacey, dear," responded Lorrie, rolling her eyes at her husband while smiling and shaking her head. "He knew I was talking to you, he is just a smart-ass."

"It's ok, I know," Lacey said as she smiled. "How are you, Mr. Metzger?"

"Oh we're just dandy, girl. How about yourself?" Brett said, embracing her open arms for a welcoming hug.

"I'm good. Case getting ready?"

"Who knows? He hasn't been upstairs all day," said Brett.

"Where are you all going tonight? What ya getting into?" interjected Lorrie quickly, wiping her hands with a paper towel and turning off the tap water at the sink.

"He won't tell me."

"Sounds like your son, Brett." Lorrie rolled her eyes and continued, now leaning the small of her back against the sink. "His father loves to surprise people, too, can't ever let you make plans."

"Whatever, woman. Let the boy be," Brett said, returning the eye-roll before jerking his attention back in Lacey's direction. "You want me to take your jacket for you?"

"That's Ok, Mr. Metzger. I'm sure he will be ready soon."

"If it involves you I'm sure you're right, darlin'. Good seein' you again, I gotta get back here and get Call in the tub. I'm sure he is terrorizing Cage's room in the nude by now. Ya'll have fun at the racetrack."

"Racetrack?" Lacey said after chuckling at the remark, puzzled.

Brett smirked in her direction as his boots dragged on the hardwood floor past her before turning back and lipping the word "Whoops" and placing his hand over his mouth like a mime who had accidentally become audible.

"You're so bad, Brett Metzger," Case's mother said in a firm tone toward her husband, although looking toward her eldest son's significant other.

"It's ok, I will still act surprised," Lacey said with a smile, "I've never been to the racetrack. I've never even gambled at all really."

"Honey, you're dating a Metzger, there is no bigger gamble on this earth," Lorrie said jokingly. Before Lacey could respond in the brief silence, she continued. "But I'll tell you what. To talk to Case, you would think he won the lottery."

"Aww that's sweet, Mrs. Metzger."

"What's so sweet, Mah?" Case said, emerging quietly from the basement door.

"There you are!? Lacey has been patiently waiting on you, young man."

"Mah, Cage just yelled downstairs like three minutes ago. I'm sure you all didn't brainwash her in three minutes. Take ya'll at least four or five to do that."

Lorrie smirked at her oldest son in a similar facial expression to how she would look toward her husband, as if he was up to no good, but with warm acceptance and love.

"No, I think they got me, babe. You were gone for so long," joked Lacey mildly, playing along with Case's mother's comments.

"Well, guess I better get you out of here, then, gorgeous," he said, placing his hand on her hip outside of her spring jacket and kissing her forehead gently. "You ready?" he questioned as his mother left the kitchen, stating a general farewell that neither of them heard.

She shook her head subtly up and down, as if simultaneously and subliminally stating she was ready to go and asking for another kiss at the same time. Case kissed her forehead once more, then placed his forehead against hers and leaned his face in less than inches from hers.

"K.," he whispered.

The soft, romantic whisper and the silence that followed were broken quickly by an abrupt scream just outside of her ear, which jolted her quickly.

"Cage! Are you two comin' or what?!"

Lacey heard Case's brother's voice faintly echo through the hallway in unison with light footsteps. "Yes! Sheesh, we are coming!"

"Well, you're yelling at me downstairs to come up here and you're takin' your good old time getting out here." Case's words began before he could even see his brother's shadow begin its way around the corner, followed by yet another shadow.

"Hi, Amanda!" said Lacey overecstatically. Amanda wasn't what most would consider a type "A" personality. She had been dating Cage for over a year now, and never really seemed to talk much; however, since Lacey had begun spending much more time around the house, she had opened up much more.

"Hey, Lace! Look at you! Beautiful as always!" replied Amanda.

"Thank you, honey," Lacey said with a smile. "How have you been? It's been a few weeks since I've seen you."

"The girl chat can continue in the car, can't it?" interrupted Case.

"Case, why do you have to be such an ass?" said Cage, shaking his head at his older sibling.

"What? We are already late because of you. They can talk all they want, I'm just saying we need to get going."

"Whatever."

Case and Cage sat in the front of the Mustang as they whipped through the turns onto the highway toward West Virginia. The voices in the back of the vehicle were full of laughter and giggling as the two brothers sat silent in the front seat, both thinking simultaneously how great it was that the two got along so well. Cage smiled to himself as he watched the trees along the highway fly by, the moonlight leaking between each branch until it reflected off the cars as they passed. Amanda had always been herself around him, and even through all of his brother's smart aleck and slightly condescending remarks had become an accepted part of the family over the past year, but something was still missing when around more than a few people. Her shyness melted away when Lacey was around, and Cage loved it. The happiness that she brought to Case radiated to all those around him, and Case found himself thinking the same thing as he passed an old, rusty truck in the slow lane as the Mustang crossed the state line.

"Put it on a country station, babe, maybe they will play that new Blake Shelton song we like," Lacey said, pausing from her conversation with Amanda and placing her hand on his shoulder as he held the steering wheel. Case peered back in the rear-view mirror, and saw the exact opposite of what he had seen months before on the day his life changed. Smiling back at him was the most beautiful woman he had ever seen, and the love of his life, even if he hadn't used those exact words with her yet. He knew he loved her, like nobody else before. A real love, a love that could move a mountain, but he was afraid of uttering the three words that had eventually led him to sorrow so many times before, and he had held back.

"Ok," said Case as he winked at her, which she barely saw through the darkness of the inside of the vehicle. He turned the dial slowly toward his favorite country station, 92.1, "Cowboy Country."

The four sang out the hits in the passing minutes, until they pulled into the parking garage at the Casino in Charles Town, West Virginia. Lacey and Amanda had been singing together so loudly in the back they hadn't paid attention to where they were until the vehicle had stopped.

"Wait, where are we?" questioned Amanda as the vehicle came to a stop between two other vacant spaces.

"A parking garage," replied Case.

"Thanks, Case," Amanda said, rolling her eyes and unbuckling her seat belt."

"Babe, be nice. Now can we know where we are? Since we're here?" said Lacey, all the while knowing exactly where they were going.

"We're in Charles Town at the Casino," added Cage. "Case has to have everything be a surprise."

Just then, Cage felt an unexpected pain in his left arm as his brother's fist crashed into it with immense force.

"Ouch! Asshole!"

"Surprised?"

"Babe!" Lacey said in an escalated tone.

"Sorry. I just know you have never been here. I like to keep you all on your toes," Case said as he turned and leaned back across the console, looking at the two women in the back. "I thought Alan and them would be here by now, this is where we always park."

"Well, I think you hurt your brother."

Looking back over to the seat next to him his eyes met Cage's. Cage knew the look, and, although he yearned to put his older brother in his place, he played the younger brother role well.

"It's ok, Lace, I'm used to it. That's my brother."

His comment was sharper than any quip or derogatory comment he could have made, and Cage knew statements like that dug into his skin the most. Case began to boil inside, almost regretting inviting his brother to come along. It was as if he forgot how much he loved his brother for a moment, and that the woman of his dreams sat directly behind him.

"Alan is coming?" said Lacey to break the tension that had built in the seat in front of her.

"Yep, him and Ben, and Scott and Marie."

"Oh, yay!" she responded emphatically.

"I thought you said Lincoln and Winn were coming?" Cage questioned.

Hearing his brother's voice speak once again began to irritate him for no reason. An irritating sensation that only an oldest sibling could relate to.

"He said they called him into work. And then they are doing wedding planning stuff," Case said in a very monotone voice.

"Oh. That's a shame. I really would have liked to have met Winn. And I haven't seen Lincoln since high school," Lacey added. "What time are they supposed to be here?"

"7:30," said Case, looking down toward the clock on the dash, suddenly releasing all of the hostility that had been running through his veins in the moments before. "What the???" Case said in a surprised tone.

"What's wrong?" said Amanda, as all three of the passengers looked toward Case.

"The lights on the radio, guess one's out."

"Oh yeah, the line above the nine right there," Cage added, pointing to it with his index finger. "It's been like that the entire way here since you changed it. Figured you knew it was out."

"No. I didn't notice it," Case said calmly, the numbers staring back toward him burning into his eyes. He took the keys from the ignition and opened his door after pausing for a brief moment. The door being ajar cut the illumination from the radio, where his car had made his favorite station 42.1.

• • •

"Just bet one time, Cage," Case said, noticeably irritated by his brother's refusal to join in on the fun. "It makes it more exciting. I know you aren't just enjoying the horses run in a circle."

"Fine. Let's go get a ticket, babe," Cage said, finally submitting to his brother's constant requests. "But only so you will stop complaining."

"Yay!" said Lacey. "You guys can learn with me so I'm not alone!"

"I know how it works, I just don't like throwing my money away. I don't have much, I'm a college student, remember?"

"I'll pay for it," said Lacey, reaching into her black and white-patterned purse sitting at her side. "We can split it when we win and Case doesn't," she continued with a wink toward her partner.

"Beginners do always have the best luck," Case replied, leaning over to put his arm around her.

"Well, obviously I don't have any luck at all," Alan chimed in from the bench in front of them. "I'm gonna go see if they will let me take another round at the buffet, technically I never left."

"Good Lord, didn't you have like three plates al—" said Ben before being cut off.

"Shut your mouth, Ben. You know you are gonna stand up and follow me over there and soon as you see them let me get some more."

"Are they always like this?" asked the brunette girl Ben had brought along, who he had yet to introduce to everyone by name.

"No," replied Case, "sometimes it's worse."

The brunette girl laughed as she stood up, "Are we going to follow him, Benny?"

"Yeah, Benny," Alan mocked the nickname they all heard for the first time, adding a quip referring to an Elton John song. "Bring your jets and let's go. You know you're comin'."

"Jets?" the girl said puzzled.

"You're ridiculous," Case said, laughing through his smile as he shook his head.

"They really have always been like that," Lacey said as they walked away.

"Yep, but it's hilarious to watch, though."

"They are worse than you and Cage."

"That's saying something."

"So is the next race starting soon?" she questioned, interlocking her fingers with his, grasping the small square of paper with his hypothesis of the results.

Case looked up toward the extra-large monitor and scoreboard shimmering clear in front of the pitch-dark of the night beyond it to see the clock. "Yep, just another minute or so."

"So which one do we want to win, again?"

"Well, we want number 8 to win, but we need number 4 to come in second and number 2 to come in third."

"So, if number 8 wins, we win."

"Not exactly: the bet we did for this one is called a trifecta. You have to get first, second, and third right to win."

"Oh, well, wouldn't it be easier to just say number 8 is going to win and that's it?"

"It would be, yes. But it's more of a higher risk-higher reward thing. If you get the winner right it is going to pay you less than if you got all three right. We can just do the winner for the one after this if you want."

"No, it's ok. We will do it like you did. I trust you," she replied, squeezing the gaps between his fingers harder, and she planted a kiss on his warm cheek as the starting gun sounded alarmingly in the background.

"Ok, babe. Here we go!" Case said loudly, leaning forward into the slight wind that swept across the track so he could see them coming down the straightaway. His hand firmly in hers, they watched as the horseshoes stomped upon the freshly combed dirt directly in front of them.

"Is 8 winning?! I can't see them anymore. Is he close?!"

"I can't really see them either," Case said, straightening his back to peer toward the far end of the track where the field of horses had spread out.

"Do they finish over here again?"

"Yeah, they do, looks like 8 is near the front, babe! 4 and 2 are up there, too!"

"This is so exciting!" she said. "Thank you for teaching me."

Case took his eyes from the oval of dirt for a moment and looked at her in the eyes. "Ok, gorgeous, I'm gonna close my eyes. Maybe it will be good luck if I don't look. Tell me who first, second, and third are."

"Ok, I'll try! Here they come!"

"I can hear them down here, Lace! Who won?" Case said, his eyes squinted shut tightly with his face turned toward away from the track and toward hers.

"Um...."

"Did we win, babe?! Was it 8-4-2!?" Case spoke loudly with his eyes still shut.

"I don't think so... but we were kind of close!"

"What does kind of close mean?"

"We had number 4 in second and number 2 in third, and they came in first and second. Looks like number 1 came in third and number 8 came in fourth. So we were pretty close."

It took only a moment for the visions of the numbers to align in the darkness behind his eyelids before he opened them. *This is twice in two hours*, now he quickly thought. *4-2-1? Really?*

"I'm sorry we didn't win, handsome." Lacey spoke as he opened his eyes, rubbing her thumb back and forth slowly over the tiny blonde hairs standing up straight on his hand.

He looked down toward her hand in his for a brief second before locking eyes with her once again, and everything surrounding him was drowned out, both audibly and visually to the point where all he saw in front of him was her beautiful face, and her curly, dark blonde hair waving in the wind.

"Lacey..."

"I'm sorry." She frowned emphatically, sticking her bottom lip out to express her empathy that their horses had not won. "We just didn't get the right ones in the right place," she continued, turning her head slightly to the side and slightly shrugging her shoulders.

"Everything is in the right place when I'm with you. Even when something does turn out as planned, being with you makes it perfect."

"Aww, babe." She blushed.

"That's gotta be what real love feels like," he uttered, staring into her eyes as they opened a bit more in what could be described as both shock and anxiousness for what he would say next.

"In fact, I know that is what it feels like. Because I am so in love with you, Lacey Sewell. I know we have only been together for a few months now, but this feeling has engulfed me all day. Every day. Since that day in the park. And no matter what comes and goes, this feeling makes everything ok."

"Case Metzger." She paused, only slightly. "I love you, too."

CHAPTER 26
Worth two in the bush

• • •

"So this is the lovely young lady who's fAlan under the dreadful Metzger curse," Grandma Metzger said with a smile as Lacey and Case walked hand-in-hand up the ramp toward her.

"Ha – Grandma, don't scare her. I don't want her going anywhere. Grandma, this is Lacey. Lacey – Grandma."

"Pleasure to meet you, dear. You are even more beautiful than Case described. Please come on in, don't pay any attention to Harold, he's asleep in the chair," Grandma M said with a kind smile toward Lacey, holding open the screen door to the large, old, red-brick house.

"Thank you, Miss Metzger. Case talks about you all the time. It's great to finally meet you, too."

"That's a surprise, I assumed he just always talks about you. You've certainly got my grandson knocked out cold." She continued to smile behind them as they entered through the foyer into the living room, the screen door slamming into the old white frame behind them.

"Oh, come on, Grandma, don't embarrass me," Case said, turning a similar shade to the bricks of the structure in which they stood.

"Well, what fun is it if I can't, child?" she said as she winked at him, sitting down with them at the kitchen table.

"It's fine, Mrs. Metzger, please continue," Lacey said, pulling her chair in close to the table and smiling mischievously toward Case.

"Oh, trust me, dear, I wouldn't have it any other way. Would either of you care for coffee or tea, or I think we have some soda out on the front porch?"

"I'll take some sweet tea, but I will get it, Grandma."

"I will take some coffee, thank you," said Lacey.

"I said I will get it, Grandma. Don't worry about it."

"Oh child, sit down. I can do it."

"Alright, alright," Case responded, shaking his head and scooting his chair back in across the large oak table from Lacey.

"I really like that craft hanging by the window. It's beautiful: where did you get it?" Lacey said, looking toward a wooden carved frame with a picture of a majestic-looking black bird with a orange stomach and red lines below its eyes, sitting in the palm of a hand. "Worth two in the bush." Lacey read the craft's words aloud, a questioning and curious tone in her voice.

"Harold made that for me several years ago," Grandma M stated as she set an eggshell-white coffee cup atop a dish in front of Lacey. "He uses my love of birds against me when he's being ornery. I don't even remember what the tiff was when he made it," she said as she joined Lacey in looking toward it.

"Case said that you are a huge bird lover, but worth two in the bush? What does it mean?"

"You've never heard the saying 'A bird in your hand is worth two in the bush', babe?"

"Huh-uh."

"Mmhmm. Harold even said that in our wedding vows all those years ago. He is a sweet man and always has been. But don't tell him I said that if he wakes up," Grandma M said as she sat down with them at the table, handing Case a tall glass of iced tea.

"It means what you have already is worth more to you than things that you don't have, babe. What you already have is yours, and you don't have to go searching for it anymore. So it's worth so much more to you."

"Makes sense. That's so sweet he used it in your wedding vows Misses Metzger."

"It can mean other things besides that to certain people. But that's what it means to me, and to this family."

"I love it. I am sorry that I had never heard that saying before today."

"There are so many sayings to live your life by, but Case's grandfather knows that one means more to me than anything. Every time I look up and see if it reminds me of our wedding day. I don't notice it hanging there as much as I should."

"I don't know much about birds. Case says you know just about all there is to know."

"That's a bold statement, but I do love watching them and taking care of them. See all of my bird feeders at the window there? Sometimes when the window is open, there a few of them that will actually eat from my hand."

"That's unbelievable. They must know how much you love them."

"I like to think so. Maybe it's just that I'm the old woman who gives them food," Case's grandmother said, smiling at the two of them.

"Oh Grandma, you're not an old woman. You got that coffee and tea like you were a waitress in college," Case joked.

"Don't let him fool you, dear. He's full of quips, isn't he?"

"Ha, that he is, ma'am."

"Gets it from his father, and his father's father. And probably every Metzger before even my time. It must be in their blood." She winked again.

"It's all part of the Metzger charm," Case continued to joke.

"If that's what you want to call it. I suppose it worked on me," Grandma said, looking in Lacey's direction with heightened eyebrows and tightened lips. "More coffee, honey?"

"Oh, no thank you. I will probably be up all night from just this one cup. So what is your favorite bird?"

"Well, you don't see them around here much anymore. But—" Grandma Metzger was cut off by the ringing of the telephone. "Excuse me for a moment," she said to the two of them as she excused herself from the table to answer the cordless phone upon the marblestone countertops of the kitchen.

"Hello. Yes, Brett, he is in the chair asleep, I will get him for you.—No, it's no trouble at all, he has been out for a while now. Your oldest troublemaker is here at the table with me." Case and Lacey heard her voice trail off out into the living room where Case's grandfather's snores could be heard when they suddenly stopped.

"I'm not sure what her favorite bird is, babe. I didn't know that she had a favorite, I thought she just loved them all."

"Hmm. That one in the picture up there is beautiful."

"I don't remember the names of any of them anymore. I used to ask her all about them, sitting over there by the window in the corner... Guess I just grew out of it."

"Your grandma is so sweet."

"She is a special lady."

"I agree."

"What time do you need to be at your parents' house again?"

"7."

"Ok, sorry, I didn't expect to be here more than a few minutes. I hadn't stopped in to see them in a while."

"It's fine. It's only a little after 6."

"Ok. I'm glad we did get to stop, though. I've wanted you to meet her for a long time."

Case pushed his chair away from the table and collected the empty glasses and mugs in his arms like a busy bartender, pinning each of them between his forearm and chest. As he proceeded toward the kitchen sink, his grandmother entered the room once again through the wide archway leading to the living room.

"Now that is a site to see," she said, smiling toward Lacey. "That boy must really be in love," she said, as if Case wasn't in the same room.

Lacey chuckled, biting her bottom lip slightly while she looked toward Case who had the most puzzled look on his face. Although he was certain he knew what a comment meant, it was his natural reaction to act as if he didn't know.

"What is that supposed to mean, Grandma?"

"Oh, nothing, child. I'm just being an observant old woman," she said with a smile.

Lacey found herself wanting to stay and learn more about her counterpart, but knew that she could not. All of the stories about Grandma Metzger had been true, and then some. There was something about her, something about the table at which she sat, something about the house. Lacey felt as if she belonged there. Grandma Metzger could make a complete stranger be engulfed with the warmth of kindness and love. Her voice was soft and she spoke slowly, but the emotions her words brought to each person she spoke to stirred fast.

"Uh-huh. I'm sure you meant nothing, Grandma. Suggesting I don't help clean the table, I assume."

"Now nobody said that. You must have a guilty conscience, child," she said, turning toward Lacey and winking.

Lacey smiled brightly, much to the chagrin of her significant other. "Grandma Metzger, it was really great to finally meet you."

"You two need to run off so soon?"

"Yes, I'm sorry. I didn't realize what time it was, I am supposed to go to my parents' house. My aunts and uncles are coming over for dinner."

"No need to apologize, dear. Family comes first."

"Great to see you, Grandma, I will stop by later this week to see you again. I've been really busy lately," Case added, putting his arm around her. She stood about a foot below him, but was at the perfect height for him to rest his arm.

She patted his hand upon her shoulder a few times, and Lacey stood up from the table, pushing in the old chair behind her.

"You know you are always welcome, child. You, too, my dear. Feel free to stop in with Case whenever you'd like."

"I would love to. I love learning about new things like the birds and more about how ornery your grandson always has been. I probably don't know the half of it." She smiled toward the both of them.

"Would be my pleasure, dear. I didn't get a chance to tell you what my favorite bird was before the phone rang, but that will give you a reason to come back and see an old woman, I suppose."

"She will be back with me, Grandma. I gotta get her out of here so I don't make her late. Love you."

"Great to meet you, Mrs. Metzger." Lacey waved from the passenger side of the Mustang, as the wheels rolled back through the damp dirt and gravel of the farmhouse driveway.

"It's almost 7, guess I better punch it," said Case, pulling out onto the road.

"I can be a couple minutes late, it will be ok."

"Alright, alright…. Hey, Lace…."

"Hm?"

"I love you."

"I love you," she returned, "What are you getting into tonight when I'm at my parents?"

"Have to go into the office and get those last two reports I was telling you about done. Jenn has been harping me about them that they need to be done by next week. It won't take me long. I might even be able to do them from home."

"Oh, I forgot about you saying that the other day. I figured you finished them by now."

"No, I have been focusing on other things this week, there was a big meeting with senior managers from a bunch of sites here this week and they had me sit in on them and give my input."

"Oh, ok. My Case is so important," she snickered.

"Yeah, right," he laughed, "I just do what I'm told."

"You're going places, baby." Lacey placed her hand on his leg as he drove and she stared into his eyes for a few brief moments at a time when he could take them off the road long enough to look at her. When he looked out over the windshield she smiled toward him, and thought to herself how lucky she was and then placed her hand on his.

"They know how special you are, it is impossible not to. Trust me, I know."

"If you say so, gorgeous."

CHAPTER 27

Fourk in the road

• • •

CASE STRAIGHTENED THE RED TIE upon his neck after placing the manila folders on his boss's desk. Being sure not to interrupt her since she was talking on the phone, he knocked twice politely on the top of the desk to alert her that they were there. He was almost out of the doorway to the office when she stopped him.

"Case..."

"Yes, ma'am?"

"What are you working on today?"

"Kylie had the data from the Cannon account that she wanted me to help her analyze. And just the end-of-week reporting that needs coding. I have three or four reps out today, there must be some kind of bug going around."

"I see – well, can you let them know that they need to pick up each other's slack? I need to speak with you. What are you doing for lunch today?"

"I'm not sure... wasn't sure if I would even have time for lunch. Do you want me to take a seat now?" he said, motioning toward the two chairs at the foot of her large desk.

"No, no. I have another call I need to be on. Just go do what you need to do, I will come grab you when I get off this next call."

"Oh ok... something I need to be worried about??"

Jenn waved her hand toward the door for him to leave the room, not acknowledging his question as she placed a wireless headset on the top of her head once again.

Case suddenly felt a panic coursing through his body as he shut the door behind him. He desperately tried to think of something that he had done wrong. A deadline he may have missed, a complaint from one of his reps? He walked slowly toward his office which was significantly smaller than the one he had just left, with an almost ghostly blank stare upon his face.

"You ok, boss?" said Jaime, one of his more tenured direct reports.

"Yeah – yeah I am fine."

"You look like you might be under the weather, look a little pale."

"No – I'm fine. Thank you, though, Jaime."

He shut the door to his office behind him and exhaled deeply. He ran his fingers across the top of his short haircut when he was startled to see that Kylie was sitting at his desk.

"Forget something?"

"I didn't even see you there, Ky. Why are you in my office when I'm not here?"

Kylie spoke slowly and enunciated carefully, "Be-cause you told me to?"

"I did?"

"Yeah, I asked if you could help me with the Cannon file and you said to come over and meet you here at 10…"

"Oh… Yeah, I guess I did, didn't I….? Sorry," he said as he sat down.

"You alright?"

"Why does everyone keep asking me that?"

"The pale look on your face and the armpits of your shirts just scream 'I'm comfortable.'"

Case exhaled deeply as he held his tie in place and lifted his arm to see that he was sweating profusely.

"Yeah, Case, I'm not sure why anybody would think something is wrong…"

"Shut up, Ky. I will fire you for insubordination."

Kylie chuckled and tilted her head back to insinuate her laugh. "That's kind of hard to do when I don't report to you, isn't it? We have the same boss."

"Well…"

"Just tell me what's wrong, Case. This may be your office, but the door is shut. We're friends. What's up?"

"I've been fine all morning, I just..."

"You just what? You're never at a loss for words."

Case sat down in his chair and leaned back, gripping the rubber band ball from his desk and throwing it softly up and down in his hand. As he stared purposely toward the ball in his hand and not in the direction of his friend and colleague across the desktop, he once again was reminded of the embarrassing sweat rings which had developed on his powder blue shirt. Immediately catching the ball and placing it back on the desk, he crossed his arms to obstruct Kylie's line of sight toward them.

"Case. Are you kidding me right now?"

"What?!"

"Well, first of all... I know you. I really know you. I know when something is wrong with you or when something is bothering you." Kylie paused. "Secondly, don't treat me like I am your subordinate, I am your boss's analyst. We work on the same reports. This isn't news to you."

Case stared less than emphatically toward her and the positioning of his eyelids showed an extreme level of aggravation and annoyance with her words. Without even realizing he was doing so, he shook his head from side to side subtly.

"Thirdly, and most importantly," Kylie paused once again to compose herself from laughing, "I pointed out that you are sweating like you just got done a pick up game, so the crossing your arms deal isn't really helping you at this point."

Case bit his lip out of embarrassment, and he finally cracked a smile. "Jenn just dropped a bomb on me. She is on the phone: she said that she needs to have a chat. Was asking what I had planned at lunch. You remember what happened when she asked Steve that same question?! His desk was empty in a week!"

Kylie rolled her eyes. "You are such a drama queen. I don't know how you convinced Lacey to date you. I don't know how she puts up with you. Speaking of which, how are things?"

"Don't change the subject, Kylie! I don't know what I did wrong...What would I do without this job? I've worked so—"

"I know what she needs to talk to you about."

"Wait, what? How do you know?"

"Answer me a question: how are things with Lace?"

"No, no. You don't just say something like that and then make me wait to hear it."

"Ha, yes, I do."

"Things are fine! Tell me!"

"But it's so much fun seeing you get flustered. Doesn't happen often I have to enjoy this."

"Kylie!"

"Yes, Case?"

"Don't be smart! What is going on?"

After a long pause, Kylie straightened her body in the chair and leaned forward, placing the Cannon file on the desk, looking Case straight in the eye, loving every minute of the torture she was inflicting.

"Think about it, Case."

"Think about what?! The fact that things are going really well with Lacey? And that I am going to ask her if she wants to get a place together soon?!"

"Well... that is a much better answer. But not what I'm telling you to think about."

"You confuse the shit out of me sometimes, Kylie. Now being one of those times."

"You're ridiculous. What has Jennifer's main focus been for like the past year?"

"Better production, increasing staffing..."

"Whose team is performing the best in production?"

"Mine is."

"Ok... and increasing staffing... Do we have space to bring in more people here?"

"No, Kylie. We don't. That's why we haven't."

"So you have been involved in the same discussions I have over the past few months," Kylie continued, leaving the silence stand and hoping Case had begun to piece the puzzle together.

"What discussions?"

"Are you really this naive right now? I think you might actually be sick on top of worrying yourself that way."

"The new office discussions?"

"Yes! God. Thank you!" Kylie emphatically breathed a sigh of relief.

"But why would she want to talk to me abo—?"

The uncertain and nerve-racking feelings that engulfed Case's psyche and body remained, but suddenly shifted in another direction. The perspiration around his shirt felt cold now, and he couldn't believe that he hadn't seen it before. While part of his irrational version of the future about his desk being emptied remained, he now saw the prophecy clearly. Jenn had received approval for office space in North Carolina, and she was going to ask him to manage that team, which would require his relocation.

"Oh my God, Kylie." He placed his hand at his forehead and attempted to avoid the shuttering chill that accompanied the clarity of the situation, but to no avail. "She wants me to move, doesn't she?"

"Yep."

"Why do you look happy right now?!"

"Um, I'm happy for you... You're the best. Nobody else can get a new office up to speed like you will be able to."

"My life is here, Kylie. Mom, Dad, Cage, Call, Scott, Alan, Ben, you..... Lacey."

"You can't pass this up, Case. You'd be so stupid. Not that you already aren't."

"I-I – I can't. I can't just pick up and leave. H-H-How do you even know that is what she wants me to do?"

"I heard her tell someone on the phone."

"What did she say?"

"I'm going to ask Case to lead the new team, I'm working on relocation assistance..."

"She said those exact words?? Ky-I-I – Um."

"Breathe."

"I-I-I I'm not sure what a pa-pan-panic attack feels like… b-b-but I thi-thin-think this is one."

"Oh stop it. This is what you've worked for. You deserve this, Case. And you will be fine. Imagine what it will—"

"Imagine what?!" he gasped, "I'd be walking away from everything I know. Everything. Everyone I love."

"You aren't walking away from everything. You're walking toward everything."

"You don't understand. I really was about to ask Lacey to find an apartment or a house somewhere. I mean—it's only been nine months, but it's really been so much longer. We're perf—"

"Perfect for each other. I know. I've heard."

"This isn't funny, Kylie. I am going to ask her to marry me, too."

"Whoa."

"Yeah. See?"

"Well, she would be happy for you, and you can still ask her to move in. Just will be a bit further away," Kylie added with a wink.

"Yeah, it is that simple, Kylie… 'Hey, babe… I know we have been dating like nine months now, but I'm going 400 miles away and I want you to come with me and leave everything you love, too.'"

"You really think she would say no? Honestly?"

"I'm not going to find out what she would say. I'm not going to ask her. I'm not going to North Carolina. I can't."

"Case! Quit being stubborn. I know it's a lot to take in at once, but think about it. There is so much opportunity for you."

"There's nothing to think about, Kylie! I'm telling Jenn no. What is she going to do? Fire me for saying I won't go?"

"No. But I don't think you are going to stay happy if you don't go."

"How would I not stay happy?"

"Well, Jenn isn't going anywhere. You are kind of trapped out here… There would be nowhere to go but up if you took this on."

Clearly irritated further and further by each of her comments, Case abruptly attempted to change the subject back to the Cannon file. Kylie fought to change his mind, but she knew that her efforts were a waste of time. From her prior experiences with her oldest work friend, she knew that there was no changing his mind, especially when it involved Lacey in any way, shape, or form.

"We've wasted enough time already, Kylie. Do you have the Cannon file with you or not?"

"Fine. Fine. I'm done trying to convince you. But I still think you are making a grave mistake. Why not just talk to Lacey about it? Or your parents? You might be surprised what they say."

"The Cannon file…"

"Yeah," Kylie said, shaking her head. "Here it is right here."

• • •

"That was really nice of your parents to let us have this table," Case grunted, carrying the solid oak coffee table up the last flight of steps.

"Oh stop, Case, it isn't that heavy," said Lacey. She paced back and forth at the front door of the apartment, which sat on the third floor, maneuvering the different pieces of furniture to where they would fit perfect in her head. The weeks that had passed since Case had asked her to move in with him had gone even quicker than all those before. She had agreed to move in with him without hesitation, and was eager to have a place that they could call their own.

"Babe, can you please open the door more? There's no way this is going to fit."

Case watched her approach the door slowly, noticing her hair was up for the first time that day. The red and black bandana that held her hair up clashed with the green T-shirt she was wearing, but he didn't care, nor did she. In the moment he forgot what he was doing, mesmerized by her beauty as if he was seeing her for the first time. She held the door against the outdoor wall of the hallway and leaned against it, looking back at him.

"Well, are you going to take it in there, babe?"

Her words registered just as the wood started to slide through his damp fingertips. Gravity had taken its toll on the table and it moved in slow motion toward the brown carpet that was laid out throughout the complex. As it struck his foot, he simultaneously fell to the ground with it, yelping in pain.

"Goddamn it!"

"Babe! Are you ok?" Lacey said, quickly kneeling down at his side and trying desperately to push the wooden table from his legs.

"I don't know!"

"Did it land on you?"

"Did it land on me? Are you serious?"

"I'm just trying to help. Can you stand up? Does it hurt?"

"Hell, yes it hurts," he said as he stood. He inspected the short legs of the table and ran his fingers across the clear packing tape which held the swinging doors of the table shut. "Doesn't look like it got damaged anywhere."

"Are you sure you are ok, honey?"

"Yes, I'm fine. Can you get the door?"

"Case...?"

"Babe, I said I am fine!"

"Your leg... It's bleeding. Pretty bad."

"Of course it is," he said, peering down toward the gash right below his knee. Seeing the blood running slowly over the dark blonde hairs of his leg suddenly made the pain much worse than it had been before, but he would refuse to show it.

"Put that thing back down, let me clean your leg up."

"Babe! My leg will be just fine!"

"But our carpet won't be. Or anything else you walk on."

Case could hear the escalation in her voice. It wasn't a scream or even a slight yell. To a normal ear it would have sounded simply like a couple's normal conversation, but he heard the aggravation from his defiance to listen to her. He nodded toward her in agreement and placed the table on its side in front of the door. He ensured she had gotten out of his line of view before his face grimaced in pain.

"Son of a bitch that hurts," he said under his breath. He knelt down on one knee and touched the red gash with his fingers, feeling where the skin had separated. He breathed in a quick gasp of air through his clenched teeth as the pain from his touch caused him to quickly jerk his hand away.

"Babe, come in here and sit down so I can wrap it up! Is it still bleeding?!"

By the sound of her voice he could tell she was looking through the half-empty cabinet below the bathroom sink, and the words echoed through the apartment and out the open door.

"But what about the carpet?" He shook his head in mockery, and walked slowly into the apartment.

"What was that?!"

"Nothing. Coming."

He entered the bathroom to see that he had been correct, and all he could see was half of her body, the rest hidden in the cabin below the sink as she riffled through different liquids and creams. She had brought them all to the apartment, so there was no way he would be able to find what she was looking for any better. He leaned against the door jamb and held his leg in the air to keep the blood from dripping when she stood.

"Found it."

"Found wha–?"

"Come out here and sit down."

"Alrighty," he said, stopping her with his clean hand and pulling her in for a kiss. "I like it when you take care of me like this. Scratch that – I love it."

She simply smirked up at him and ran her fingers across the short, red hairs of his beard, motioning silently toward the couch on the living room. She placed a black towel on the floor at the center of the couch as he candidly walked toward her and sat down. He noticed that there was a small trail of blood that had followed him into the apartment that was barely noticeable. She had seen it and knew that they would likely become stains in their home, but was most concerned about fixing him. She propped his leg onto her bent knee and wiped his leg with a washcloth, causing him to flinch in pain. He thrust his head back on the couch and stared toward the ceiling, determined not to let her see him in pain.

"C'mon, babe. How long have we been together now? You know it is ok to let me know something hurts, right? I won't think less of you." She smiled.

He tightened his lips and didn't speak, staring down at her and eventually smiling, noticing that she had finished wrapping his leg up.

"All done," she said quickly as if it was one word. As she stood, she lightly smacked the bandage on his leg, and ran to the kitchen, laughing the entire way.

"Ouch!" he screamed before joining in her laughter, and began to chase her, even with a limp in his step, around the kitchen like kids chasing each other on the playground. Their love was still new after nearly a year, and they each found a new way to make the other happy every day since they had gotten together. Case often mentioned to her that he was always taught that when love was real, it felt new all the time. Lacey had told him on numerous occasions that their love felt old and new at the same time, and that's what made her the most happy in every moment they were together.

Lacey slowed around the corner on purpose, allowing Case to catch up to her and gather her body in his arms. He grabbed her around the waist and spun her body around toward him, staring into her eyes once more. In his gaze, he thought briefly about how much he didn't deserve to have her and about how perfect she was to him. He shook his head at the thought and smiled directly into her eyes.

"What, babe?" she whispered.

"I love you," he said, not giving her a chance to return the endearment before planting a kiss on her lips.

"Sweetheart, your phone is ringing," she said, struggling to get loose from his grasp.

"Let the voicemail get it."

"It might be the cable guy! Let me go!" she laughed. "We've already missed his call twice. I don't want to be around you if you can't watch football," she joked.

"Fine," he said, letting her go as she disappeared into the hallway and the master bedroom.

The silence that filled the air as she left his side felt familiar to Case, and he looked around the half-filled apartment slowly, fighting a thought that something bad was about to happen. He noticed to his right that he had left the front door hanging open the entire time they had been playing Wile. E Coyote and Road Runner in the living room and kitchen.

As he placed the wooden table down on the carpet of the living room, he yelled back the hallway as he hadn't heard Lacey say anything for few minutes.

"Babe, was it them?!" he said, closing the front door. He had to pick up on it and pull it with force to get it to shut. She hadn't said anything, causing his concern to raise further.

"Lace?!"

The light in the bedroom was not on, and she sat upon the edge of the bed, holding his phone in both hands. She didn't look up toward him when he walked in the room.

"Babe, are you ok?"

. . . .

"It wasn't the cable company?"

. . . .

"Then who was it?"

She finally looked him in the face as he sat down at her side on the sheet-less bed. She had a look of utmost disappointment on her face and her eyes were full of sorrow. They glistened in the light leaking through the blinds at the opposite end of the bed. Case saw her tears forming before they began to fall and slide down her cheeks.

"It was Jenn," she said, with a blank, emotionless face.

"What did she say?"

"I didn't get it in time. It was a number you didn't have saved, so I thought it was the cable company leaving a message."

"So what did she say, babe…?"

"She said that she got an extension on the North Carolina office and they wouldn't be staffing it for another six months…"

The only sound in the room was the ceiling fan spinning around and Case's throat as he swallowed slowly, fearing what Lacey would say next. She waited a few more seconds and continued, gathering her words slowly and carefully.

"So if you decide that you have changed your mind about moving and you talk about it with your girlfriend some more, she isn't going to open up a position for hire yet."

"Babe… I was—"

"Don't talk to me about it now. Apparently you already have and I just didn't know about it."

"But babe—"

"I don't want to talk right now. I'm going to get the last few boxes from my parents' house."

Case sat still on the edge of the bed and watched her leave the room, frozen in his seat with his arms at his sides. He heard her struggle to open the door and then finally get it open. When he had finally stood up and turned the corner toward the living room, the door was swinging slowly back open on its own.

CHAPTER 28

Fourging ahead

• • •

"What did I tell you?" said Kylie, leaning back in her seat at the lunch table. The cafeteria was near capacity that day, but the lunch buddies still had found time to meet. The closure that had come with giving Jenn her answer was short-lived, and Case had once again become a nervous wreck for different reasons.

"Things just haven't been the same, Ky, I screwed up. I screwed up bad."

"Well, while you eat your hat over there I am going to eat my yogurt if it is ok with you." Kylie laughed. "Did you talk to anyone else about it?"

"Alan and Scott. I'm afraid to tell anyone else."

"Why? Because they will tell you that you are an idiot, too?"

Case shook his head in disgust at himself, before it shifted toward disgust across the table.

"That is foul. Why do you eat your yogurt like that? Haven't I asked you to use a damn spoon when I am around? It gets all on your hands. Ugh," Case shrilled as though he had gotten a cold chill as he watched her scoop the yogurt up in the foil paper that had originally covered the dairy treat.

"What?" Kylie reacted, her mouth full of yogurt.

"You are like a dude sometimes. No wonder I listen to you."

She wiped her hands on the unused napkin beside the plastic bags in which their lunches sat and adjusted her shirt near her chest. "Yep," she proclaimed in a deeper voice than normal.

"Anyway…" Case continued. "I haven't apologized or anything. I haven't been able to find the right time. Or the right words to say. Where would I even start?"

"What did Alan say? Or Scott?"

"They said she would get over it and not to worry about it. Huge helps." Case rolled his eyes.

"Well, they aren't wrong. Doesn't mean you shouldn't apologize, though. You two are meant for each other and I'm sure you have been in worse predicaments or arguments with her before."

"That's just it. We really haven't."

"So what? You think she is going to pack up her stuff and move back to her parents now after your first 'fight'?" Kylie continued, physically putting 'fight' in quotations with her sticky hands.

"I don't know. We have been perfect together since day one. This just doesn't make me feel good at all."

"Perfect relationships have fights, Case."

"Coming from someone who doesn't believe in perfect relationships anymore…"

"Well, I might not. But I believe in destiny. A lot more than I used to, thanks to this guy Case and his girlfriend or soon-to-be fiancée at work. He taught me that things happen for a reason."

Case blushed at the comment, realizing for the first time that his belief that he and Lacey's journey toward each other affected all those he came into contact with in a positive way. The accomplished feeling that had overcome him left as quickly as it had come, when Case finally heard her refer to Lacey as his soon-to-be fiancée.

"Thanks, Kylie. I am having a hard enough time with this and then you remind me about the ring that I have waiting for me over at the mall. I certainly can't ask her anytime soon. I had it all set up so perfectly. Our first weekend in our own place together. I could see her saying yes. I could see the happiest look on her face. Now I can't even pretend to see it."

"Hey," Kylie interrupted him, placing her now empty cup of yogurt into the bag in front of her. "You going to stop being a drama queen now? I have to be like a dude in order to keep the equilibrium in our conversations."

Case didn't find her comment funny at all and did not join in on her one-woman laughing party in the booth of the cafeteria for even a second.

"You are hilarious," he said. "I don't see how any of this is funny."

"It is funny. It is funny because you always worried 'bout the ones who didn't matter. The girls in your life that you knew deep down weren't meant for you. Now deep down you have always known that Lacey was it, Case. You know that she is it. You know she would say yes, regardless. You could have asked her the day you started dating. I have seen her look at you and you know what? She looks at you the same way you look at her."

Case couldn't speak, he could only register Kylie's dialogue and pray to God that she was right, which, if his past was any indication, she probably was.

"Now are you going to eat or what? We need to get back upstairs soon. At least I do."

"Probably not. I'm not really hungry. And we always talked about her cooking us dinner on Thursday nights and me on Friday nights. Guess I will just wait and see if she still does… See if my apology can make her feel good about me again."

"She never stopped, Case."

"I wish I was as sure as you. Or sure at all for that matter."

Kylie winked at him as she stood from the table and gathered her trash, discarding it in the bin as she turned the corner and out of sight. Case watched her disappear and then followed suit, walking slowly back toward the steps, impatiently waiting for the clock to strike 5:30.

• • •

A week had passed since Lacey had found out about Case's decision to not move to North Carolina, but she still felt as if she just found out. The two of them had finished moving in and exchanged words when necessary, but the trouble in paradise had taken its toll on the both of them.

Case had tried on several occasions to explain himself, but he would always convince himself she didn't want to talk about it. He struggled to find the words that could make her understand why he hadn't consulted with her about the decision, and never anticipated that it would cause her such pain. He ran through all of the scenarios in his mind as to why she was so upset. Was it simply that he didn't talk to her about it? Did she feel like she was holding him back? Did she think that he used her as reasoning with her boss not to go? That had to be it. 'No,' he would think, 'she knows I wouldn't do that. Right?'

Thursday night when he got home from work, he found her in the kitchen preparing a salad. She placed the knife down next to the celery that she was cutting up and looked up at him as he forcefully pulled the door shut.

"I really need to fix this," he said placing his coat on the rack by the door. She shook her head up and down and picked the knife back up to continue. "So how was your day, gorgeous?"

"Good."

"That's good. Dinner smells awesome."

"Thanks."

Case finally had enough. He couldn't stand her not being herself. For the first time, regret filled his mind for not having listened to Kylie, for not letting it be their decision instead of his own.

"Babe. I'm sorry."

"Sorry for what?" She stopped cutting once again, but did not look up.

"For this," he said, outstretching his arms and motioning around the room. "This isn't us."

"Ha—Us, huh?"

"Yes, us. I should have talked to you about it."

"It's fine."

"No. It is not fine. I made a decision for the both of us instead of getting your input."

"I'm not kidding, Case. It. Is. Fine."

"Babe, don't be like this. I am trying to apologize."

"This isn't something you apologize for," Lacey said, turning and throwing away excess vegetables into the trash can to her left. Case continued to watch her, thinking about how much of enigma he was facing. Something inside him told him that she truly was over it, but his past wouldn't allow him to believe it. He blinked several times and took a few deep breaths while she still faced the other direction.

"What do you mean, this isn't something you apologize for? I was wrong. We probably would have made the same decision but I will never know that for sure because I was selfish."

Lacey didn't look the least bit bothered by the situation anymore. She appeared somewhat pale and had bags under her eyes from having gone to work earlier than normal since the move. She paused and shrugged her shoulders subtly while he spoke. She wiped the countertop where she had been cutting with a washcloth back and forth and patiently awaited her opportunity to speak, for she knew that once Case got rolling, there wasn't much room for her to interject. Without being rebutted, Case continued to defend himself on his own.

"Sweetheart, I know I was wrong. I really do. I'm not being facetious. I'm not trying to be condescending, I swear. We are in this together and that is how it will always be from this day forward. I love you too much to waste one day or even one second with us being mad at each other."

Lacey's lips broke to speak but he continued before she could.

"Baby, please. I'm begging you to forgive me. I haven't been able to function for a week now because things haven't been the same." As the words left his mouth he found himself daydreaming about how he had gotten to this day. He remembered over ten years of memories of waiting to be able to have this argument, and how he had given up that he ever would be in a situation like this with her.

"Case Metzger," she said abruptly, snapping him from his daydream.

"Y-Yes babe?"

"Are you done?" she smiled.

"Yeah. I am sorry I just—"

"I thought you just said you were done," she stabbed lightly, bringing a chuckle between both of them.

"I do forgive you. I forgave you the same day. We haven't seen each other much and I am exhausted every day because I am not used to this schedule yet. I don't need to hear you tell me all the reasons that what you did was wrong. We both know what they are, but I also know you. I know that you don't make the same mistake twice where others would. It takes one look into those big, beautiful blue eyes from across the room for me to know that you love me, and that you always have. I was upset about it for a day, but I also know why you thought at the time you were doing the right thing."

As Case watched her speak in the artificial light of the kitchen, she might as well have been standing in the middle of a meadow in a sundress, with beams of the sun shining through her hair waving in the wind. His dark and bitter view of himself was always met through his eyes by how he saw her. Although he heard her words loud and clear as she spoke, each word that softly glided into his ear was accompanied by his conscience whispering "I love her" in the other ear.

After a very slight pause to take a breath, Lacey continued softly. "I could have not heard a word you said to me just now. Or the day we kissed in the park, and I would have known everything you were saying. Your eyes have never lied to me and I know they never will. You and my family are the reason that I came back from Georgia and never moved away again. I loved it in the South, but there was something here for me. I knew that in my heart. Maybe one day we will go when our hearts know it is right. But obviously yours knew it wasn't right."

"So you are saying that I should keep apologizing?" Case interrupted, smirking from ear to ear.

She laughed lightly and her eyes looked toward the sky without her head moving, like she was looking to find her own eyebrows, pretending to be offended that he had interrupted her. She placed her hands on his hips above his black belt as she felt his soft lips touch hers and closed her eyes. As his hands made their way up her back, he gently stroked the ruffled shirt between her shoulder blades, continuing the compassionate kiss until she pulled away.

As she opened her eyes, she whispered to him, "Like I said, when I see those eyes, you never need to say a word."

His eyes opened slowly as if awakening from a slumber, and they both smiled once more. She stared deeper into his eyes and sighed out of utter relief and happiness. His smile matched hers when he closed them again and leaned into her, pulling her chin toward his lips. "I'm sorry."

CHAPTER 29

On One Knee

• • •

"Wait, what?" said Case, staring at his father across the table in disbelief.

"You heard me."

"Yeah. I did. I just expected a different reaction. I thought you were going to try to talk me out of it." Case paused. He nervously spun his glass with only ice remaining in front of him with his fingers. Next to the glass lay a black jewelry box that was closed. He had broken the news to his father that he was going to ask Lacey to marry him, after only ten months.

Brett Metzger stretched across the table and opened the box to look once again. He stared into it at the shiny diamonds for several seconds as if reading a book, concentrating on the intricacies of each one.

"You sure you can afford this, son?"

"It's here, isn't it?

"I remember what I paid for your mother's. And that was a different age. I can't imagine how mu–"

"Dad. It's already paid for. All my extra money has either gone toward paying for my probation, or into a savings account for that. I really hope she likes it."

"She is going to love it. You know that. Stop worrying yourself to death," Case's father's voice echoed through the hallway of the home. He still spoke to Case as he ventured to the back of the house to check on Call, who was putting a puzzle together and listening to music, laughing by himself.

"You better get out here and give your big brother a hug. His life is about to change," Case heard his father's deep voice boom. Just then, he heard his youngest brother, who was now near his own size stand and walk quickly through the hall. Call's footsteps were heavy, but just the pure mention of Case's presence excited him.

"Call! Buddy! I was wonderin' when you were going to come out see me! Where you been?!"

Call still did not speak clearly, but mumbled several sounds in place of speech. There was a specific noise that he would make resembling the word 'Case,' but it more closely resembled the hissing of a snake, with a 'c' sound before it. Call was always excited to see his oldest brother, and always greeted him with the tightest of hugs, and this day was no exception.

"Now that is a tight one, Call!" Case said, embracing his brother with both arms. "You see what I got for Lacey? I am going to ask her to be a Metzger. What do you think about that?" He continued, fetching the box holding the ring from the table. Call snatched the box and inspected it, turning his wrist in every direction for a few seconds before discarding it to his right on the floor.

"Call! Be careful, buddy. We can't throw that."

Call made a few audible sounds, and stared down to the floor by the box as Case picked it up, making sure that it was still in immaculate shape.

"Say you're sorry, Call," Brett Metzger said, approaching from around the corner.

"S-uh" was as close to sorry that Case would get, but it was sufficient to him. He knew his brother didn't understand how valuable the item in the box was, or even what marriage was. The one thing that he knew that Call did understand was love. Case was quickly reminded as Call's attention was brought back to the music sounding from his bedroom.

"Hey, boy. Did you tell your brother congrats?" Brett spoke to Call as if he understood every single word, and for all they knew, why didn't he? Call was irritated that his trip back the hallway toward the music had been interrupted, and slowly turned around. He stared toward Brett for a moment, and then covered his face with his hands, physically showing his impatience.

"Call," Brett said sternly. "Give your brother another hug, he is going somewhere really important tonight." Call uncovered his face and exhaled deeply like a bull ready to be released from the shoot, looking toward their father. Call stared toward Brett for another moment, as if subliminally saying 'Do I have to?' Brett didn't respond with words, instead crossing his arms and raising his eyebrows.

The mannerisms of Brett Metzger were enough for Call, and he approached Case just as he was placing the ring in his pocket. This hug, that had evidently been forced by his father, suddenly didn't feel that way to Case. He had felt this hug before on several occasions. Call's grasp was not too tight, but also snug at the same time. He gripped his older brother around the shoulders and patted his back as he had so many times before during the hardest of times. The repetitive pat on Case's back took him back to each of the individual times that his brother had made him feel that everything was going to be ok, even without understanding any of the issues that lay in front of him.

Case smiled and patted his brother on his back as well, thinking to himself how great life was in the moment. He thought about all of the lows in his life that had led him to this emotional high. An emotional high that continued for several moments even as his youngest brother disappeared into the bedroom and shut the door behind him.

"So did you tell your mother about all this?"

"Yeah, I called her outside when I got here. I didn't realize she wasn't going to be here."

"What's she think?"

"She seemed really excited. You seemed excited, too, when I told you, Pop," Case said, reaching for the front door.

"Why wouldn't I be, son? I've never been more happy for you."

"Thanks, Pop. I will let you know how it goes. I'm supposed to meet her dad in like 20 minutes. I'm sure he can tell what I am going to be asking him about," Case said as he opened the front door a crack.

"Oh, I'm sure."

Case opened the door the rest of the way and put one foot out the door when his father stopped him with a question.

"Case."

"Yeah, Pop?"

"I'm just curious…"

"Curious about what?"

"What reaction did you expect from me? Why didn't you think I would be happy for you?"

"It wasn't that. I knew you would be happy for me no matter what. I just thought that you would think I was rushing into this…. Since, you know… we haven't even been together quite a year yet."

"Sounds to me like you wanted me to tell you what you are thinking yourself." Brett's matching icy blue eyes met his son's, freezing them both.

"Maybe, Pop. Maybe that is it. I'm scared that maybe it is too soon. But the more I thought about it, when am I ever going to think it isn't too soon?"

"You wouldn't. Trust me son. I'm proud of you."

"Thanks, Pop," Case said. Embarrassed by the aura of the moment, he stared down toward the concrete steps at the front door, and away from his father's eyes which his emulated.

"What is to be, will be, son."

"You sound like Grandma," Case said, looking back up toward his father's face once again.

"Imagine that…"

Case looked toward the sky, and then toward his watch. "I gotta get going."

"I know you do. You will be fine, son. Go start the rest of your life, as soon as you can."

Case saw his dad wink toward him as he finished talking and shut the door. He climbed into the drive side of the Mustang and backed onto the road, headed toward Lacey's father's favorite restaurant, 'Grammy's.

• • •

Grammy's was a small diner on the outskirts of Jefferson, and rarely would the waitresses working there see a face that they hadn't seen before. This night was no exception. Lacey's father, Darryl, sat in the same corner booth that he always had whenever it was available. He had brought his entire family there for hundreds of meals. He looked up from his newspaper to check the door once again to see if Case had walked through, and this time he had.

Case saw him sitting in the corner, and suddenly felt nervous. The fool-proof plan of inviting Lacey's dad to dinner in the restaurant he was more comfortable in than his own recliner suddenly felt as if it was not a good idea. 'What if he says I can't ask her?' he thought. 'What if he doesn't approve? I will never be able to set foot in here again.'

The uneasiness fled the scene like a found-out bank robber when Case sat down and was greeted by Darryl Sewell.

Darryl Sewell was a sweet man, having raised two daughters almost all on his own. He had worked for the MARC train station his entire life, and Lacey's mother traveled with work almost three weeks of every month. He was a man's man, who enjoyed a black cup of coffee and the sports section every evening, and he was a regular Mr. Fix It like Case's father was. He wasn't quite as broad and muscular as Brett Metzger, but he was equally as tall. What his stature lacked, his deep, raspy, masculine voice made up for. Case had only ever imagined what it would be like to be on the wrong end of an argument with Darryl Sewell, but his imagination also told him that was somewhere that he never wanted to be. He hair was trimmed short in a military cut, and he always wore collared shirts, no matter how casual the encounter.

"Case! How are ya, son?"

"I'm good, Mr. Sewell. How have you been?"

"Oh, I'm just fine. Just ordered me a cup of coffee, reading the paper. Have more time for that these days with an empty nest," Darryl Sewell winked toward Case, folding his newspaper and placing it beside him in the booth. Case couldn't tell if Mr. Sewell was onto why he had asked to meet with him that evening, as he had never done so before without Lacey being with him.

"Catch the Orioles game last night, Mr. Sewell?"

"C'mon, Case, Lacey isn't here. You don't have to be all proper on me," he said, lightly punching Case's arm across the table. "Besides, I have told you time and time again to just call me Darryl. Mr. Sewell was my daddy."

Case chuckled and placed his fingers in his jeans pocket, checking the safety of the ring for the fifth time since entering the diner. "Ha – sorry."

"Yeah, I seen the game. Wish they woulda left the lefty in there. They prolly woulda won that won instead of blowing it again."

"You aren't kidding, Mr. Sew-, Darryl. Sorry."

"You're awful flustered. You alright over there?"

"Yeah, I guess I am just nervous."

"Nervous about what, son?"

"Why I asked you to have dinner with me tonight."

"I just figured you wanted to get away from Lace, she's a pistol. But you know that," Mr. Sewell said with another wink, taking a long sip of the coffee that had just been set in front of him. It was steaming hot, yet it didn't seem to faze him. It may have been the size of the moment that Case sat in, but seeing him take a swig of the hot liquid made him even more intimidated, causing his words to be stammered even more.

"I-uh. I-I."

"Spit it out, boy!" Darryl laughed out loud. Darryl was enjoying giving Case a hard time when he was interrupted by the waitress.

"What can I get ya'll seeve-nin? The usual, Darryl?" she said in a thick Southern accent, much too Southern for Maryland.

"Joy, give us a minute. Case and I are conversin'."

"No problem. Hollar at me when ya'll's ready."

"Thanks, darlin'." Darryl brought his attention back to across the booth. "So what's got your tongue tied tonight, Case? You and I sat in this same booth and talked a number of times: ain't ever seen you like this."

"Yeah, when Lacey and Mrs. Sewell were in the bathroom, or up getting us some more silverware. I've never been here with you without Lace."

"If I am anywhere near as sharp as I once was, I reckon you asked me to come and meet you here tonight because you got a question to ask me…" Darryl Sewell said, turning his head to the right and making a mischievous smirk toward Case, inferring that he knew what direction the conversation was about to turn.

Case just stared in an awkward silence toward his significant other's father. Not sure if he should feel relieved or scared, he didn't breathe. He only waited for further clarification of what he had just heard. The smirk on Darryl's face only grew wider as he let the silence of their booth fill the moment for a few more seconds before continuing.

"What do you keep reaching in your pocket for, son? Looked like you had a box in there or something when you walked in."

Case's plan was more apparent than he had even known, but the embarrassment of the moment was relieved by the smile on Darryl's face. A smile that made Case's intuition feel free once again, and allowed him to utter his next words.

"I guess there isn't much element of surprise going here, is there?"

"I figure you asked me here on your own and are callin' me Mr. Sewell left and right for some specific reason," Darryl winked toward Case yet again.

"Well, sir. I guess there is no point in beating around it…. I love your daughter. And I wanted to ask… If it would be alright if I asked her to marry me…"

"Which daughter?" Darryl exploded into laughter at his own attempt at humor and Case pretended to be amused by the joke, but couldn't truly laugh at anything until he was certain of Lacey's father's answer.

"Heh heh heh… Case… son… You know you have always been my daughter's heartbeat since almost outside my memory. She has always enjoyed your company, and her mother and I always wondered why you two never had gotten together. We had always kind of hoped for it. She is the daughter that we raised when she is around you, and unless there's something you ain't tellin' us, you seem to enjoy her company as well."

"I do. I really do, sir. I've been in love with her since the day I met her. She makes me the man I am supposed to be," Case said, in a very serious tone.

"You make her happy. So if she says yes, which we both know she will, you have my blessing."

"Thanks so much, sir."

"Watch the 'sir' stuff. You marryin' my daughter is already making me feel old," Darryl said, placing his hand on his hip in his seat and cracking his back to insinuate a more decrepit body than his own.

"Well, I really do appreciate it. I'm sorry that I was acting so weird. I was just so nervous."

"No need to be sorry, son. I'm glad you take me picking on you so well. Part of why I said yes." He smiled, waving for Joy to come back to the table to take the order.

"Ya'll ready?"

"Yes, ma'am, Miss Joy. I will take a grilled cheese tonight, and I am gonna go ahead and order that chicken sandwich for my wife. She will be here soon, I reckon."

"She will?" Case said aloud.

"Yeah, she flew back in this afternoon. She had called me right before you walked in. She is on her way here. But don't worry, I will deliver her the news."

"What news, Darryl?" interjected Joy, the waitress.

"Case here is gonna be my son-in-law."

"Well, congratchylations!" She smiled brightly at both of them. "What can I get you to eat, Case? Somethin' that goes good with butterflahs?" she laughed lightly.

"He's gotta get going. I'm sure he doesn't need to stay and eat."

"I was going to stay. I don't have to go yet."

"The way I see it you got one more question to ask tonight. Better go get ready."

"Are you sure, sir?"

"She text me and said she was headed back up the road from Baltimore from her meeting a few minutes ago."

"She must have gotten out early. I thought she was going to be down there a few more hours. She may have text me, too. I left my phone in the car."

"Get goin', son. I'm sure you have a big plan. I will talk to you both later this evening."

Case felt overwhelmed by the circumstances. Everything had come together. Even though it had fAlan into place in a less conventional way than he had hoped, he was ecstatic. Nonetheless, he couldn't overcome his desire to go back to the apartment and wait for her to get home to watch the rest unravel.

"Alright. Well, if you are sure that it's ok. I will go."

"Go do what you need to do," Darryl said with a smile, drinking another gulp of coffee.

"Thank you," Case said, extending his hand for a handshake with his future father-in-law. The firmest of grips went unnoticed by Case, who was so lost in the moment that seemingly nothing could faze him.

"Case."

"Yes, sir?"

"Before you go, do you mind if I see the ring?"

"Not at all!" he exclaimed, pulling the box from his pocket.

Darryl held the box in one hand and pulled his glasses from his chest pocket with the other. His eyes grew larger as he opened the box.

"That's some rock!" the waitress shouted.

"It sure is. She will love it. She will be even more beautiful with this on, which I'm sure neither of us ever fathomed possible, son," Lacey's father said in a calmer voice than before, gently closing the box and handing it back to Case.

"She gets more beautiful every day. I wanted to get her one that she deserved."

"You are what she deserves, Case. I couldn't be happier. I'll see you later."

Case felt the warm sun on his skin and he exited the diner and didn't even realize he had already made his way to the car, for the thoughts in his mind had engulfed him. He couldn't force the smile from his face if he wanted to the entire ride to the other end of Jefferson to their apartment, and if it weren't for the neighbors carrying groceries up to their own home reminding him his keys were still in the ignition, he would have left the car running in the parking lot until it ran out of gas.

He entered the apartment, and pulled the door shut easily behind him. He pulled the contents of his pockets out and placed them in the basket by the door and began to unbutton his shirt to change. His heart was still pounding. He wanted to call her to see how close she was. He wanted to know how much time he had. He dialed her number as he stared out the front window into the dark purple sky of the summer, where he saw a single star and a reflection of a full moon in the likeness of the window. The phone rang five times before going to her voicemail, and he ended the call.

Case felt something inside him that told him it was better that she hadn't answered: she would have known something was different in his voice. There was no way he could mask the excitement in his voice longer than a few seconds. He began back toward the bedroom to change into his three-piece suit to begin his plan when his phone began to ring in the basket behind him. He quickly turned back in a direct 180-degree turn and looked toward the light of the phone glimmering in the basket, remembering his thoughts from only moments before. "I can hide it. I have to," he said aloud as he crept toward the basket talking to himself and picked up the phone.

Case was disappointed to see that it was not Lacey calling him right back, but her father instead. Somewhat relieved that he wouldn't have to hide his excitement from someone who already knew his night's itinerary, he hit the answer button and raised the phone to his ear, unbuttoning the remaining tabs of his shirt with his free hand.

"Hello."

"Mr. Sewell?"

"Mr. Sewell?"

"Are you there?"

CHAPTER 30
Fourever

• • •

THE SUN HAD TURNED A dark orange as it began to set in the distance beyond the church. The parking lot seemed to fill in fast-forward. Case couldn't believe that this day had come. He stood in front of the large door entering the side of the church with a blank stare upon his face. Several people including some of his closest friends and family greeted him as they entered but it was as though he could barely hear them. The bells hanging at the steeple weren't ringing, but they were in Case's ears. He couldn't concentrate on anything.

The words were drowned out. For the first time in his life, Case felt without emotion, like nothing in his life could ever get better. His life had reached its plateau. He leaned forward on the rail and looked down into the bushes below the ramp, focusing on two birds who had just flown in from the tall oak tree to his right. The tree's shadow seemed to be cast the entire length of the pavement across the cars.

The two birds chirped at one another, moving their heads around quickly as if in conversation. Case continued to look at them, but not truly seeing them. He closed his eyes for long periods of time and took heavy breaths.

"You ok, son?" he heard Lacey's father say, approaching Case from behind and placing a hand on his shoulder.

"I don't know anymore, Mr. Sewell."

Darryl held his arm on Case's shoulder and nodded in respectful fashion toward the last of the well-dressed men and women entered the church directly behind them at the top of the ramp. He pulled back on Case's shoulder which was met with great resistance. A single tear fell from Darryl Sewell's eye as he tried to pull Case close to him once again. He removed his hand long enough to wipe the tear from his face. Determined to embrace the young man in front of him, he stepped forward next to him, this time placing his arm around the lower portion of Case's back.

Darryl watched slowly as Case attempted to stand up straight and no longer stare into the ground. His quick movement startled the chirping birds beneath him and they abruptly flew in opposite directions into the early evening. Case's face was pale except around his eyes. They were red and puffy as if he hadn't slept in days, and despite his attempts to hold back his tears, it was evident that they had marked their territory.

Case struggled to piece together anything to say to Lacey's father in this moment. A moment that he thought that would never come. Instead, he turned and looked Darryl in the eyes. Case squinted and planted his head into Darryl's shoulder.

"I know," said Darryl. "I know."

Case couldn't comprehend all of the emotions that had left him and came screaming back in Darryl's embrace. He still couldn't speak. He had been through the doors to the church on numerous occasions since he and Lacey had started dating, but for the first time was fearful of walking through them.

"Let's get inside, Case. You know Mrs. Sewell is a wreck. I need to get back to her."

Case walked slowly behind him, watching his own steps. Everything that he had imagined he would feel as his foot hit the red carpet had come to fruition. His hands and arms trembled more and more with each step. He stopped and peered through the cross-shaped window of the chapel, seeing a beautiful array of flowers arranged from end to end of the sanctuary. He closed his eyes for another extended period of time before opening them to see Lacey's father holding open the next door to the center of the room and motioning for him to join all of their friends and family through the next wall.

Case stared toward the highest ceiling he could ever remember seeing, and wiped the streams from his face. What could have been interpreted as a smile was forced upon Case's face when he walked in the room. Several of the people sitting in the pews began to whisper amongst themselves as he followed Mr. Sewell toward the front of the church slowly. Brett and Lorrie Metzger sat in the front row, next to Call and Cage.

As the preacher spoke, Case didn't hear the words. He knew his ears were drowning out every other sound in anticipation of hearing her take another breath. His eyes were fixated in Lacey's direction the entire time. He couldn't take them off of her, and, even though he was paying the littlest of attention to the preacher's words, he knew when he was almost done speaking. The time in the sanctuary had flown by and taken a lifetime to complete all in the same moment.

He reached into his pocket and pulled out the ring. It glimmered in the light of the blinding sun through the painted glass windows. The sun had saved its brightest beams for last, as it disappeared into the horizon outside of the church. Case stared at the ring in his fingertips, and tightened his lips together. He had gotten the attention of everyone in the first few rows as silence filled the room while they stared. The preacher closed the Bible and Case got as close to her as possible.

In that moment, Case thought about how she was just as beautiful as she had ever been. Her hair and her skin were perfect, but her hands were cold. He tried his best to withhold his emotions, but he burst into tears once again as he placed the ring on her left hand.

"I love you, Lace," he said through his sobbing.

He knew she would not reply. He knew she would not take the breath that his ears were waiting to hear. He knew she was gone, and that standing there in front of everyone was acceptance of that. He squeezed her fingers in between his and bowed his head.

"Forever," he said, squeezing his lips together to keep the tears from rolling into his mouth. He couldn't take it anymore. He let go of her hand for the last time and quickly walked down the aisle and out of the church. His father and Cage stood up and ran after him, apologizing to each person they weaved through on their way out of the chapel. The rest of the people who remained in the room all began to file a line to see Lacey, the majority of them joining in Case's emotion as he stormed out of the room.

"Case!" his father yelled across the parking lot.

"Case, where are you going?!" Cage screamed as he caught up with his father.

They were too late. As quickly as the Mustang door had opened it had shut again. The two of them watched as the car rolled with speed out onto the road and off into the distance.

"Go follow him, Cage. I will get Call and your mother. Call me when you get to him. He is in a dangerous place right now."

"Can you blame him, Dad?"

Brett Metzger breathed aloud a sigh of empathy for his oldest son. "No. I can't."

"He's not going to his house. And he's not going to go drink. He's not going to do anything dumb. I know him, Dad."

"He can't focus on the road if he is in the condition he is in right now."

"He's not going far, Dad."

"How do you know that?"

"He's going one of two places."

"Where?"

"Well…" Cage paused and shook his head. "He is either going to sit on the park bench where they always went to and where he kissed her for the first time. Or he is going to see Grandma."

"And you are sure about this…?" Brett questioned.

"Yeah. He always has when he gets upset."

"Well, go check both places, son. Make sure he is safe."

"Ok, Dad," said Cage, jogging in the direction of his parents' car once his father handed him the keys.

• • •

The driver of the truck had been in a much more dangerous condition than even Case was when his vehicle struck Lacey's. In a small city north of Baltimore, she had gotten off of the highway due to a detour. As she just placed her phone back in her purse from texting Case and her father, the stop light had turned green. She accelerated forward and was struck on the driver's side. The paramedics said that it was instantaneous, and that she hadn't felt any pain. The drunk driver of the truck was thrown from the vehicle and had passed away in the hospital later that same night, they were later advised.

Case blamed himself. His actions of a similar nature hadn't taken his life or another that cool January night, but instead took away what he had loved most in the world when he least expected it to. Her family begged and pleaded to him that they knew he had learned from his mistake and that it was nothing more than coincidence, but he would not be convinced. He cursed his own life. He cursed the numbers that had led him to nothing but eventual pain.

The apartment had been wrecked through his rage at first. He couldn't handle that she was gone and never coming back. The turned-over furniture and shattered glasses, and a large, broken mirror filled what was once their home together. The clock that had hung above their couch and had randomly stopped with the hands pointing toward the four, representing 4:21, was thrown hard into the wall and the drywall had broken. Everything representing a four, two, or one in the apartment had been destroyed. Case had become emotionless on the day of her viewing, because he had dispersed everything that he had. He had shut out the world. The entire world.

To Case, the only explanation that made sense was that it was God punishing him for all of the wrong roads he had taken. As far as he was concerned, he had finally gotten what he deserved: The world had become right by being so wrong.

He spoke aloud toward the heavens above him, first apologizing and then in anger before becoming apologetic once again. Cage watched Case flail and cry from a distance in his car until he finally collapsed to the park bench and buried his head in his own palms. Cage cried a few tears of his own for Lacey, and sympathetically for his brother.

"He's fine, Dad. He is in the park. And the saddest part of it is I don't think he realizes she is, too."

CHAPTER 31

Four Twenty-One

• • •

BRETT AND LORRIE METZGER HAD not heard from their oldest son in almost a week. As much as they were worried that he was ok, they knew that he was. They knew that he wouldn't do anything to hurt himself. They knew that he loved them. They knew that he didn't know how to handle what had just happened over the last few weeks. It was an unthinkable task for anyone to stand back up off of the ground and show life that it wouldn't supply the final blow. It truly was. But if there was one person who could defy that logic, Brett and Lorrie knew that Case was it.

Lorrie begged and pleaded for Brett to go with him to Case's apartment to ensure that he was ok, but Brett would not allow it.

"He knows where we are. He knows we love him."

"But Brett! Nobody has heard from him in a week. They haven't seen him at work. He hasn't called us. He has to know we are worried. He needs us," Lorrie cried. The tears streaking down her face drew a hug from her husband and soothing words that followed.

"He does need us. But he needs this time more. We did a good job with him. We made some mistakes as any parents do. But I'm so proud of what I see in him, in all of our boys. Case is stronger than I ever thought anyone ever could be."

Brett squeezed his wife in his arms even tighter and kissed her forehead. He grabbed her head by the ears and wiped her tears from her face with his thumbs as one of his own fell onto his shirt.

"He doesn't understand. He doesn't know. He has been searching for several years now. But he is going to find himself throughout all of this."

"I hope you're right, honey," Lorrie trembled. The phone on the counter began to ring almost instantaneously with the end of her sentence. She broke her husband's embrace toward the phone as she had for the last six days each time it would ring. Happiness and optimism would streak through her body in the steps toward the counter each time, that perhaps it would be Case saying that he was fine and that he would see them soon. Fear and pessimism accounted for her feelings with equality. It could be news that Case's car wasn't at his house. It could be worse than the stinging sound of the phone that shot through both of them the night Case was arrested. The emotions were too much to take.

Lorrie wasn't sure how, but she mustered up the vocals to say hello when she picked up the phone. A tight-lipped Brett Metzger stood feet from her, hearing the entire conversation through only his wife's words.

"Hello."

"No, we haven't heard from him at all. His friend Alan called yesterday and said that he was pretty sure he saw him driving in town yesterday."

"Oh…"

"He is….?"

"Well, that is great news. I am so glad he is ok. Thank you so much for calling."

"Ok."

"Thank you again."

"Alright. Bye-bye."

Lorrie's voice was enough to Brett. The relief in her caused relief in him. He smiled at her, knowing exactly what had just been said on the other end. It was his own mother after all. Brett knew it was her through the conversation. He knew by his wife's tone. He knew by the way the light came in through the kitchen window and reflected off of her face in a different way as the conversation concluded. Nobody could ever calm someone down more abruptly or with more efficiency. The wise calmness of her voice could deliver the worst news yet still sound full of love.

"He's over at Mom's, isn't he?"

"Yes. Thank God," Lorrie whispered. She dropped her chin to her chest and breathed a sigh of relief.

• • •

"Case Metzger," his grandma said from the kitchen table. She hung up the rotary phone and placed it back on a side table which hid the wastebasket.

"Case. Metzger."

He still didn't answer. He didn't know what to say. He wasn't sure he remembered how to keep his eyes open for longer than a few seconds. His eyes were tired, but not from his lack of sleep. That could have been the reason, but they had been churning out water for nearly a week straight. He felt sorry for himself. He felt sorry for Lacey. He felt angry. He felt sad. He didn't know where to even begin.

"Case. You know better than to let your mother and father and everyone else worry about you for a day, much less a week," Grandma M said.

He could tell that she wasn't mad. She didn't even seem disappointed, which didn't make sense to him. She looked as though she had no emotion. That really didn't make sense. But nothing did anymore.

"Child, I know that you are going through something tougher than maybe not even an old woman like me can imagine." She paused. "I'm so happy that you are here and that you are safe. I know that you probably didn't come here to talk. So I won't make you. Let me know if you need anything, ok?"

Grandma Metzger stood slowly from the table, grabbing a cane to help her walk across the kitchen. It was the first time that Case had ever seen her with a cane. At first he disregarded it, but soon after he found his mind having its first clear thought in some time.

"When did you start using that?" he uttered, stopping her just before the archway to the kitchen. She turned toward him slowly.

"Oh this?" She held up the cane.

He nodded.

"A couple weeks now. Your grandfather said he thought it was a good idea. I personally don't think I need it. Maybe it's because I'm stubborn." She winked.

"You seem to get along fine to me."

"Me, too... Let me go check on your grandfather and make sure he is still alive. He takes more naps than a cat nowadays."

When she returned to the kitchen and sat down near him, Case was staring up at the 'worth two in the bush' sign with tears welling up in his eyes, remembering the very seat in which Lacey sat when she saw it for the first time and they had explained what it meant.

"That young lady..." Grandma said, placing her wrinkled hand on top of his. He stifled his tears for a moment and looked toward his grandmother now, raising his eyelids in anticipation of her finishing her sentence.

"Do you think she would be happy that you are teary-eyed right now? Or do you think she would want you to smile and remember every moment you two spent together?"

Case didn't speak, he only listened.

"I think we both know the answer to that question, child. And you knew her much more than I ever did. I only had the honor of meeting her a few times. I think she would want you to remember each one of the times that you had with her, like I do right now."

"It is so hard for me to think that way. It wasn't supposed to be like this, Grandma. Nothing ever pointed to this. It's all my fault. If I wouldn't have desperately needed her company like I did, if I wouldn't have bought into all of the signs that I thought meant she and I were destined to each other. If I just would have ignored them in the first place, she would still be here. She would probably still be in Georgia, happy as could be." Case broke down.

"Nonsense, child. Everything happens for a reason. You know this."

"I used to think that. I truly did."

"You still do. You are just a bit lost right now, child. She is still right here with you. With everyone."

"Everybody says that."

A long pause filled the room, and Case laid his head upon the mat on the table with his eyes wide open, staring toward the wall.

"I remember her sitting right there," his grandmother nodded. "It was a few weeks or months ago, but I still remember you two sitting there like it was only moments. She asked me what my favorite bird was. Do you remember that, Case?"

"Of course I do," he said, not lifting his head or moving a muscle.

"Did you ever tell her what it was, child?"

"No. How could I? I don't even know what your favorite bird is."

"Yes, you do."

"Grandma. No I don't," he said, lifting his head from the table. He stared at his grandmother in a peculiar fashion.

"Well, what is the bird in that craft there?"

"Grandma. I don't know the birds like you do. I can't tell blue from a jay. That looks like an oriole, but I know it isn't."

"You're right it's not. That bird that your grandfather painted there was my favorite bird. Although I haven't seen one in a long time. You just don't see them around here much anymore."

"What is it?"

"With your memory, Case... you don't know what kind of bird that is?"

"No. I really don't." Case had become irritated that she wouldn't just tell him.

"That surprises me. You don't remember the bird that you are named after," she chuckled to herself.

Case was struck by what she had said. *What was she talking about? I wasn't named after a bird, Cage was. So was Call.*

The bird theme of their names was with his younger brothers. His mom loved C names, names with one syllable. He could remember vividly that Cage had been mutually chosen by his parents. Cage began with a C, and several birds lived in cages. That was what was explained to him. He never gave it a second thought. The same went for Call. It began with a C, and birds chirped and called to each other. That was how they communicated. Case's name was different. His name had nothing to do with that, and he had never thought otherwise.

"You mean to tell me you don't ever remember your old grandma talking to you for hours upon hours about the caseca?"

"Caseca?" he said aloud. "What on earth is a caseca? I've never heard you talk about that."

"That's right, there is a caseca." She pointed toward the 'two in the bush' sign on the wall. Your father named you after my favorite bird."

"No he didn't. He would have told me that."

Grandma Metzger chuckled to herself once again. "You are my oldest grandchild, Case. I was there the day you were born. I remember him telling me that he and your mother were naming you Case. I had never felt so honored in my life."

Case felt stunned. He didn't know how he could have gotten this far into life and not known the actual origin of his name. His name did fit in with his brothers. He had to know more.

"W-w-well, why is it your favorite?" he stuttered. "What makes the caseca so special?"

"Look at it. It's beautiful. It's the most majestic bird that I personally ever saw. There used to be several of them that would gather at the window before you were born. They would flock to my window. So many of them that I couldn't even count them all. I would put ears of corn out there for them. Your father loved them, too, but I think it was more because I loved them," she smiled.

"What do you mean, 'saw', Grandma? They aren't around anymore?"

"I saw one a couple years ago, but only one. It brought me back to those days. Sitting there with your father watching them. In fact, every time I hear your name or see you, I go back. You and your brothers are the casecas of my life now."

"Wow," Case said. "I honestly never knew."

The few brief minutes had taken him away from his thoughts of guilt and tragedy that had filled his life for the last week, but they came crashing back to him. As exciting as it was to hear the story of how he got his name, he was right back to where he was before.

"The male casecas were always known as being very strong, very protective. The looked out for the entire flock," his grandmother continued. "They were somewhat strange. Different than the rest of the species, very particular."

Case continued to feel bad for himself, yet was fully engaged in the conversation. Grandma Metzger could tell by his eyes that he was intrigued by what she had said.

"You don't think a bird can be particular?" she looked at him. "Ask anyone who remembers them. They always migrated back north to Maryland and the surrounding states on the same day every year, like clockwork. The male casecas would all come back on the first day of spring, or at least close to it. The first time every year I would see one would always be March 21st, which was sometimes way too early, I always thought, based on how cold it would still be."

"Grandma. The first day of spring is March 20th," Case spoke up.

"Usually," she said. "But sometimes it is March 21st. And I never saw them one time in my entire life on March 20th. But surely enough on the 21st, there they would be. It was as if they were coming up early to check the area for safety before the rest of flock would join them. They were 'casing' the area." She laughed.

Case found this all very hard to believe, but given his circumstances, he thought anything was possible. "So they honestly always were back on the same day every year and never a day before?"

"Never."

"What about the rest of the flock? Was that the same way?"

"You bet. Exactly one month later they would all be together. The males that would be at my window on the first day of spring, and every year, would be joined by the females and their young, and we could barely see into the field out the window. They were all so beautiful. You didn't care that you couldn't see beyond them. They were all that I wanted to see."

"So on April 20th every year you knew that they were all going to be there. It was like a holiday then, I guess?" Case smiled for the first time since he could remember. The look on his grandmother's face as she spoke about them was enough to make him forget everything, if only for a second.

"No, child. I told you. To them the first day of spring was March 21st every year. I'm not sure why or how a bird could tell time and date. And it's funny that you say that, because it always did feel like a holiday to me. April 21st. Every year. Four Twenty-One. It was always the greatest day of the year."

"Four Twenty-One?"

"Yes, child. Every year to this day I sit at the window to see if they will be there. Hoping that they will bring that joy to me at least one more time. Your grandfather is my reason to keep moving on into the mystic, but the inescapable sensation that surrounded me the first time I would see those beautiful creatures every year makes life worth the battle."

Time froze around Case as he heard his grandmother's words. He couldn't believe what he had heard. There they were. Again. The numbers would never go away. They had outlived Lacey. They would outlive him. They were a symbol of greatness. Greatness that had come and gone. Greatness that was to come. Greatness that was in the moment. The overwhelming combination of the words that his grandmother had spoken along with the whirlwind of emotions that had joined him for not only the past week, but also his entire life, were too much. He had to go. He had to be alone once again. He had found a moment of clarity, and he couldn't waste it.

"Grandma, I gotta go."

"Now, child?"

"Yes, I'm sorry. I love you. Thank you for everything."

• • •

The sun was rising in the north and the brisk breeze that passed through Maryland that April morning held with it a hint of warmth that could have come directly from the sun. It twirled through the apartment complex and swam between the open windows of the Mustang and into the back of the U-Haul truck. Case's sweatshirt ruffled in the wind and he stared toward the sky. He heard his father starting up the truck and latching the bed tight with a zip tie. "I love you, Lacey. I'll miss you every day," he whispered toward the heavens.

Lorrie Metzger pulled the door of Case's apartment shut with a box in her hands. "I think this is the last one!"

"Thanks, Mom. I appreciate you all helping me with this," he said, looking toward her, and she walked down the steps.

"No problem, son. We love you."

"Love you, too, Mah."

"We gonna get this show on the road or what?!" yelled Brett Metzger from the U-Haul truck.

"Yes, Dad! North Carolina is still going to be there regardless of when I leave."

Brett Metzger rolled his eyes and the window back up and waited for his wife to join him in the passenger seat. Case sat down in the Mustang and buckled his seat belt. Staring out into the open skies in front of him, his attention was drawn to the hood of his car, where an orange, red, and black bird that he had never seen before stopped to rest, only for a second.

He took a deep breath and thought to himself how his journey had only just begun. He put the Mustang in gear and looked toward the GPS that would guide him to his new life in Charlotte: 421 miles to destination.

About the author

• • •

CRAIG ZECHER IS EXCITED ABOUT his debut novel, Four Two One. He currently resides in Knoxville, Maryland with his wife, Jessi, and their two daughters, Abigail and Aurora. He is from Frederick County, Maryland and attended college at Shenandoah University in Winchester, Virginia where he majored in Business Administration with a concentration in Finance. Craig also works in the banking industry where he is able to utilize his eccentric love for numbers. He enjoys writing in his free time, as well as spending time with family and friends, sports, and card games. He is a diehard Green Bay Packers fan and has been since the age of five and attends the United Church of Christ.

Made in the USA
Middletown, DE
09 April 2016